The Gun in the Golf Bag

Bob Bennett

Clink
Street

Published by Clink Street Publishing 2021

Copyright © 2021

First edition.

The author asserts the moral right under the Copyright, Designs and Patents Act 1988 to be identified as the author of this work.

ISBN:
978-1-914498-49-7 - paperback
978-1-914498-50-3 - ebook

This is the concluding novel in the trilogy

Easier Than It Seems
Retribution
&
The Gun in the Golf Bag

by Bob Bennett

This is an entirely fictional work. Whilst certain historical facts and events have been 'borrowed', a few liberties have been taken with the chronological context. The places and locations are real, but the characters are personations of my imagination. Any similarity or resemblance to actual persons living or dead is purely coincidental.

The Gun in the Golf Bag is a novel in its own right although it is sequential to Easier Than It Seems and Retribution.

For as thou urgest justice, be assured
Thou shalt have justice, more than thou desir'st.

Shakespeare

Chapter One

Helen Blake wanted a new identity when she left prison so she became Hazel Black. The assassination plan had been simple and straightforward enough, but it had required her to revert to her original name. Now with the plan and the mark duly executed just minutes earlier she was dazed and deranged to such an extent that she was traumatised and on the verge of collapse, a mental breakdown. Had she lost the plot? Who was she? Where was she? She stood shivering on the jetty and drew the hood of her blue anorak tightly over the woollen hat she was wearing as in an attempt to conceal herself from an elderly couple, also on the jetty, not that she had noticed them. They were all waiting for the last ferry of the day at four o'clock to take them back to Orford Quay from Havergate Island. The island, an inhospitable area of salt marsh, mudflats and vegetated shingle was a sanctuary to countless species of birds and a mecca for ornithologists. Helen – or was she Hazel? – had not been bird-spotting. Her visit to the island had been for an altogether different reason; a nemesis, the fulfilment of a plan. Her presence on the island had been quintessential to the means by which she would be rid of the iniquitous blight on her life. Now she had witnessed the final full stop. He was dead. The plan had been successful. She was free from that perilous existence and vulnerability to both her mental and physical wellbeing. The threat had been posed by a spectre from her previous life in the persona of a diminutive yet extremely dangerous Glaswegian. Duncan 'Jock' McClean. Not only had he been pursuing her with what she could only imagine was evil intent, but he was wanted by the police in connection with the murder of her husband and the suspicious deaths of at least three other people. Furthermore, not only was the notorious McClean a fugitive from the police but it was now known that he was an enemy of the Irish Republican Army. In fact, it would not be stretching a point to say that Jock McClean was at the top of the IRA's hit parade on any number of counts. Both the police and the IRA had come close to him in recent weeks but as always, in a style straight from the Scarlet Pimpernel's handbook, the elusive Jock had successfully avoided and evaded them. But now, he had been eradicated. He was the late Mr Duncan McClean.

January Storm, the Havergate ferry boat eased alongside the jetty. The elderly man was about to help his wife step aboard.

'Are you alright my dear?' The elderly woman was most concerned. The ferryman had also noticed that the slightly younger woman was, to say the least, not quite herself.

'Is she with you?' the ferryman, Reg White asked the elderly folks.

'No she's not. I'm not sure what's wrong wi' 'er but she don't look right do she?' responded the elderly woman in her almost poetic, lyrical Suffolk dialect.

'Let's get her aboard.' The ferryman took control. 'C'mon now, let's get you on the boot. Can you 'ear me? C'mon love.' He almost recoiled as he took her by the arm. 'Crikey – she's bloody freezin', all shiverin' an' tremblin' like.' Between them, Reg the ferryman and the elderly couple helped the slightly younger woman into the boat. The passengers sat together huddled in the shelter of the wheelhouse. The ferryman produced a blanket from a locker and the elderly woman wrapped it around the slightly younger woman's shoulders.

'Soon 'ave you warmed up dear. What's your name love?' The slightly younger woman managed to shiver a barely audible response.

'Hazel, except I think I'm Helen again now.' She was pointing and looking back at the island. The elderly woman's concern was redoubled.

'What is it? Have we left someone behind?'

'N-n-no. It's OK now. I'll be alright thank you.' The rest of the short journey across the River Ore was made in silence. *January Storm* coasted alongside the pontoon at Orford Quay and the ferryman made the boat fast.

'Here we are then,' he announced with concern in his voice 'Do you think you can manage?' He addressed his question to Hazel.

'It's OK! I'll come and get her.' A shout came down from the quayside. 'It's my mother. I'll take care of her.' The ferryman was visibly relieved that he wouldn't have to assume responsibility for his last passenger of the day. Hazel also seemed to have made something of a recovery at the sound of her son's voice. Her son, in his mid-twenties, wearing a parka and a worried expression, with his jeans tucked into his boots, came down the gangway. As the woman, his mother, stepped onto the pontoon he took her into his arms in an all-enveloping embrace. The warmth of this familiar contact appeared to give her strength. The couple looked on and the elderly woman smiled and spoke to the man.

'She's pleased to see you I reckon. I don't think she was feelin' quite herself. Oh yes, an' I think she might have left something on the island,' she said. The man smiled. 'Thanks for your concern, your help. She'll be OK now, don't worry. We're local – only just up the road.'

From the quay it was just a short walk to Lobster Pot Cottage. Tina, Hazel's daughter-in-law was waiting by the door. The sitting-room was cosily warm with the wood-burning stove glowing reassuringly. The kettle was on. Tina helped Hazel off with her anorak. After a few minutes silence the young man spoke.

'How'd it go mum?'

'Oh Ben, it was awful. Thank goodness it's over.' Silently she wept.

Chapter Two

It was Wednesday 31ˢᵗ January 1973. There were two men in a small rowing boat. It was far from an easy pull. Danny McFaddon was on the oars, a forty-something, strong and fit man. Perhaps it was his technique that was lacking? Also in the boat was Brian O'Connor, the ace IRA hitman with his incongruous choice of luggage, the golf bag. They were making good their departure from the scene of the shooting. With the last ferry from Havergate Island now returned to Orford, it would be the next day at the earliest before the body was discovered. Danny had picked Brian up from Stoneyditch Point and then between them, they'd dragged the dinghy across Orford Beach's shingle which in itself had been tiring enough.

'C'mon Dan, put your back into it,' Brian urged. The ebbtide was beginning to run hard now and the dinghy was barely making way against it as Danny tried to reach the *Samson*, riding to the tide at anchor some one hundred yards or so off the beach at Orford Ness. Sam Reynolds, the skipper of the *Samson*, together with his son Joe were on deck leaning on the starboard side gunnel watching (with some amusement it should be mentioned), the manner in which the tide was getting the better of the rower. Sam had previously received his instructions and a generous payment anonymously. He suspected that there might have been some connection with the delivery he'd made just weeks earlier and he was aware that he might be aiding and abetting in some form of criminal activity. But a charter was a charter as far as he was concerned. *Samson* was available for hire and these guys had hired him and his boat to take them to Lowestoft and that was what he was waiting to do although he was now getting just slightly concerned. Neither of the men seemed to have much idea of how to handle a dinghy and it would soon be dark. The weather forecast wasn't brilliant either. What's more Sam suspected that they had been up to no good and he needed to get some sea-miles under the keel before the balloon went up. Subconsciously becoming aware of Sam's concern Dan moved over on the dinghy's centre thwart and at risk of capsizing, Brian precariously moved to sit beside him. They took an oar each and immediately progress towards the *Samson* improved. As they got to within hailing distance, Joe skilfully deployed the heaving-line which Dan caught and once made fast the power of *Samson*'s capstan winch hauled the small boat alongside. Brian's golf bag was handed up to Joe's outstretched arms and the two men clambered aboard. With the dinghy streamed astern, Sam fired up the Cummins 475hp engine and engaged the hydraulic anchor winch. With the big anchor and its chain stowed in the well on the foredeck *Samson* headed north up the coast with the tide aiding their progress by some three knots the twelve knots capability from the mighty Cummins.

Danny and Brian were below in the saloon and reviving themselves with the aid of a bottle of scotch after their exertions. The mission had been accomplished. Brian, as always the quietly spoken, unassuming character had no qualms about the 'hit' he had made just an hour earlier. He was proud of his prowess, of his skill as a sniper. He was invisible. He was invincible even. It was rumoured in Nationalist pubs in Northern Ireland that Brian O'Connor could take the knob off a gnat at 500 yards. In truth, if gnats had knobs, he probably could! Only a very few of the IRA's top brass knew of him. Even fewer actually knew him personally although many knew of an anonymous individual and his reputation as an assassin. Danny, on the other hand was a worrier. He was a thinker, a planner, a motivator. Danny came up with the schemes and the logistics and it had been in response to Michael Doyle's request that Duncan McClean had now been dispatched courtesy of a long-range shot from Brian.

'You had better get rid of that golf bag. If anything's going to give you away, it'll be the golf bag.' It had been for that very reason that years ago Brian had adopted the golf bag to carry the preferred tool of his trade, the Remington M21A sniper rifle with the Zeiss ZF42 telescopic sight. A rifle case, slip or scabbard would have been a dead giveaway. The only downsides to the golf bag were the stupid questions people sometimes posed – 'Did you make par on the fifteenth?' or the fatuous 'Off to play golf are we?' There were those few occasions when carrying the bag did make him feel a little conspicuous, even on this particular mission – his last, or so he had professed to Gerry Doyle on his hospital bed. What was a man doing on the foot-ferry from Orford Quay to Havergate island carrying a golf bag? But then would people have been so distracted by the golf bag as to notice the man carrying it? Brian was fairly confident that no one would ever identify him without it.

'You're right, for sure. I won't be needing it again anyway – unless I take up golf!' Brian conceded.

'What d'you mean?' Danny could hardly believe the implication in what his colleague had said.

'I'll say to you what I said to Gerry. You've known me a long time. You know I'm a Republican, that I always will be. But this war – this war we're in – we'll never win. People are now referring to it as the Troubles. Feck me Dan, the troubles began even before the Great Famine of the 1840s. Protestants and Catholics have forever been at each other's throats. Partition has only exacerbated the situation and it's now Republicans and bloody Unionists. We are such a minority in Northern Ireland. We can never win and I have no appetite for any more bloodshed; any more killing. I'm through with it. Jock McClean was my last mark and even then only as a favour to my old mate Gerry Doyle.' The pathos of Brian's words hung in the air underscored by the rumble of the Cummins. Danny didn't know how to respond, so he didn't. He picked up the scotch bottle and poured them both another good measure. After a while Brian stuck his head into the wheelhouse.

'Let me know when we're in deep water would you Sam?'

'Sure thing.' Sam knew better than to enquire why. He was contracted to collect and deliver cargos or people or both from here to there, A to B, and while the money was right, he would work for anyone – no questions asked. On this occasion the payment had been too good to turn down. Even if he had known of the dramatic irony in this latest commission, it would have made no difference. Neither Brian nor Danny was aware that it had been the *Samson* which had been chartered by McClean to deliver the IRA's weapons cache to a remote location for collection by Black September. That particular cargo had been collected from St Katherine's Dock on the Thames and dropped off about a week earlier to a deserted spot on the River Deben, just down the coast.

'OK Brian, I'm now outside the Aldeburgh Ridge and we'll be off Dunwich afore long. This'll be about as deep as it gets at this distance off the coast unless I steam offshore another four or five miles.'

Brian appeared in the wheelhouse with the golf bag containing the Remington suspended from his shoulder. He moved on to the afterdeck. He stood there for a several minutes before hurling the bag containing both the spare magazines and the gun into the North Sea. The bag slowly filled with water and began to sink beneath the waves. *Samson* ploughed on and about ten boat-lengths further in the fading light the golf bag was no longer visible. Brian returned to the saloon. Danny had witnessed what had just taken place and understood. 'The end of an era,' he said. Brian responded, 'End of an era.' He spelt it out. 'E-R-A, and for me, the end of the I-R-A.'

The wind and been north-easterly all day and it had begun to freshen. The clouds that had threatened rain since breakfast time were now delivering and although it was barely six o'clock it was already dark. The red light from the wheelhouse gave an eerie glow and the reflection of the navigation lights in the sea merely gave a hint of colour to the swell as it surged against the hull. Looking to the south the sweep of the beam from the Orford Ness lighthouse every five seconds was still visible but then such was the intensity of the light it could be seen up to fifteen miles away on a good day. Now it was hardly penetrating the rain and the blackness of the early evening darkness.

'I reckon we're in for a gale,' pronounced Sam. 'We're all stowed and battened down dad.' The reassurance from Joe did little to comfort the passengers. Danny was already feeling queasy.

'How long 'til we make Lowestoft? He enquired anxiously.

'I reckon mebe two hours, p'raps a bit longer.' Danny retreated below and lay on the saloon berth hoping that the next two hours would be the quickest he'd ever known to pass.

'Here,' gestured Brian, proffering the scotch bottle. 'Another belt or three from the bottle will either kill or cure.' Danny, feeling distinctly unwell, eased himself up on his elbow and accepted the bottle. He felt the fiery quality of the spirit burn his throat.

'So where do we go from here – what happens when we get to Lowestoft?' asked Brian although the tone of his voice somehow hinted at a total lack of enthusiasm for whatever the answer might be.

'We're booked into the Victoria Hotel for the night and then tomorrow,' Danny hesitated, 'well tomorrow you're a free man. You can do what you want, go where you want. My orders were to assist you after the job and…' Before he could add anything further *Samson* rose on a steep swell and as the bow dipped into the trough Danny was thrown forward into a bulkhead. 'Bejesus, get me off this feckin ship.' Brian smiled and began to laugh. 'Pass me the bottle before you tip what's left onto the floor.' His laughter was infectious and soon Danny was laughing although neither of them knew what they were laughing at or why. Perhaps their frivolity had something to do with being thrown this way then the other as they danced involuntarily to the motion of the boat. But more likely it was the scotch and their slightly inebriated state; the nervous relief for an escape made good.

Up in the wheelhouse Sam wasn't laughing. The north-easterly wind had freshened now to a near gale force seven. With the counteraction of wind howling against tide the sea was building to the state which the Met Office would describe as 'rough'. The height of the waves was increasing and attempting to keep the boat on an even keel and prevent excessive rolling Sam was steering into the four and five metre breakers. *Samson* would then surf down into the troughs burying the bow in the next wave. The passage was becoming distinctly uncomfortable.

'Switch the radio on lad, long wave Radio 4. I reckon there'll be a gale warning.' Joe complied and, just as Sam was expecting, as the news bulletin ended a few minutes after 7.00 there followed the all too familiar announcement. *Attention all shipping! There are warnings of gales in sea areas Humber, Thames, Dover, Wight. The Meteorological Office has issued the following gale warning to shipping…* and so on, confirming exactly that which Sam had predicted. Then to the strains of *Barwick Green*, the signature tune to *The Archers* Joe took his cue to turn the radio off. With the experience of an old seadog on Joe's young shoulders, the gale warning was merely cautionary and no cause for alarm. Father and son looked at each other in that knowing sort of way and both shrugged their shoulders. No words were spoken. At least the fare-paying passengers didn't seem to be bothered now. From the wheelhouse it sounded as though there was a party going on below in the saloon. Sam was sure he could hear the empty whisky bottle rolling about on the cabin sole.

With the spume and spray stinging the windscreen and the crests of the enormous swells breaking over the bow, the wipers were barely able to cope. Even so, the loom of the Southwold light could just about be made out. Brian staggered up the companionway. 'How's it going Skipper?' As if by way of an answer gallons of foaming water crashed over the wheelhouse as the boat was tossed first one way and then another in the confused sea.

'Shouldn't be long now,' replied Sam. 'Sorry it's hardly a pleasure cruise. You should plan your next trip for a barmy summer's night. There's nowt better than sitting out in your shirtsleeves on the foredeck watching the sunset whilst necking a beer or two.'

The rate of the ebbtide had noticeably eased during the last hour and the effect of the conflicting directions of wind against tide had also assisted in the reduction of the severity and confusion of the sea state. The motion of the boat had stabilised and as a bonus, the rain had stopped as well.

'I think I see it Dad.' Joe was peering ahead through binoculars. 'Yeah, that's it – East Barnard buoy, a couple of degrees off your port bow. Sam strained his gaze in the direction his son had indicated and, sure enough, there was the reassuring quick three flashes every ten seconds, the characteristic of the East Barnard buoy. From there the well-buoyed Stanford Channel, to the East of the Newcome Sand would lead to the pier heads on the outer harbour wall.

'Call 'em up Joe – Channel 14.' Joe turned up the gain on the Sailor RT144 VHF marine band radio.

'Lowestoft Harbour Control, Lowestoft Harbour Control, this is *Samson*, *Samson* over.' Just a couple of seconds later came a hiss and crackle preceding the response. '*Samson* this is Lowestoft, over.'

'Lowestoft, this is *Samson* approaching from the south. Request permission to enter the Trawl Dock, over.'

'*Samson*, is that you young Joe?' *Samson* was a regular visitor at all the East Coast ports and the duty harbourmaster at Lowestoft, Dave Robertson was a good friend. '*Samson*, I think I see you, yes, come straight in there's no outbound traffic. You'll find space on the wall in the Trawl Dock. Bring your dad for a pint the Harbour Inn when you're tied up?'

'Lowestoft, this is *Samson*. Thank you sir. Will do. *Samson* out.' Sam was smiling at his son's strict observance of VHF protocol. Too often there was too much familiar chat cluttering up the marine band.

The passengers had heard the conversation and both had now come up from the saloon into the wheelhouse to observe the approach.

The occulting red light on the south mole of the outer harbour could be made out quite clearly now. Beyond it, the green. Sam had eased the throttle as *Samson* shaped up for entry between the pierheads. In the lee of the harbour wall the sea was all but flat. By comparison with the gale-surfing they had experienced during the previous three hours, this was millpond stuff. Sam made the sharp right turn into the Trawl Dock and the boat glided through the entrance. Joe went out on deck to prepare the mooring warps as *Samson* was gracefully brought to rest alongside the harbour wall. There was very little activity on the dockside and, with the boat secured, the Skipper, mate and passengers climbed the ladder set into the harbour wall and said their goodbyes standing on the quay. The four walked together and crossed the bascule bridge. Sam and Joe disappeared into the Harbour Inn, Danny and Brian walked the short distance further to the Victoria Hotel and using the false names adopted when the reservation was made, they checked in.

So, that was it, as good as done. Wednesday 31st January 1973. It had been one hell of a day for both the Irishmen, particularly so for Brian. His lifelong friend, Gerry Doyle had been avenged. Notwithstanding the Limehouse Basin fiasco which had resulted in Gerry's brother Michael and several of his Republican compatriots getting banged-up on remand awaiting trial on a lengthy agenda of murder and terrorism charges, Brian took some comfort in the knowledge that the assassination of the scourge of the IRA would provide some consolation. Danny's plan had been executed to the letter. Brian didn't know the identity of Danny's co-conspirators, neither the detail nor the background to how his target had been set up. This was how he worked; how he had always worked. He didn't want to know either. Ask no questions, just make the hit. The only difference this time was that he knew why he had to take out McClean. Here they were, safe and sound. Although it was now quite late, the hotel agreed to prepare something for them to eat, after which, and a couple of nightcaps, they were both sound asleep in their respective rooms.

Chapter Three

After a Victoria Hotel breakfast Danny and Brian sat in the lounge. Brian was looking through a regional tourist guide magazine. Danny was reading the *Daily Express*. Of particular interest was a report on yet further disturbances in Northern Ireland following a parade commemorating the anniversary of 'Bloody Sunday'. Danny sat and reflected on that dreadful day, Sunday 30th January 1972. He had been a part of it. He had marched in that civil rights and anti-interment rally that had taken place in the Catholic ghetto areas of Derry. He had assisted in negotiating the IRA's agreement to their not carrying weapons and made it clear that there was no intention of confronting the British Army. This was to be a commemorative and peaceful march and rally. What the IRA couldn't have known was that the infamous parachute regiment of the British Army had been brought in especially to deal with the march. OK, there had been some minor skirmishes and stone throwing, but in general the protestors were peacefully listening to speeches in the Bogside. The stone-throwing was used by the army as an excuse. Some of the soldiers marched into the Bogside ostensibly to stop the stone-throwing. Then, claiming they had been shot at they opened fire on the crowds and thirteen people were shot dead. Some twelve others sustained gunshot wounds, and a fourteenth person died later. Danny was all but overcome with emotion as he remembered the scenes. He shook his head as if trying to shake the visions from his memory. He returned to the article in the *Express*.

British Troops firing plastic bullets shot and killed 14
civilians taking part in a march organised by Sinn Fein

> *through the Bogside, Brandywell and Creggan areas of*
> *Londonderry to commemorate the first anniversary of*
> *'Bloody Sunday'. The march was successfully dispersed.*

That was all. Part of him was outraged. But then he thought 'What the hell?' He was going to mention it to Brian but decided against it. Brian had retired. His eyes were drawn to a photograph of the beaming smile of Edward Heath beneath which was a summary of the first month of Britain's membership of the Common Market and Prime Minister Heath's hopes for greater prosperity with no loss of sovereignty.

> *From the point of view of our everyday lives we will*
> *find that there is a great cross-fertilisation of knowledge*
> *and information, not only in business but in every other*
> *sphere. This will enable us to be more efficient and more*
> *competitive in gaining more markets not only in Europe*
> *but the rest of the world.*

What about dealing with the shite closer to home first? Danny wondered. He threw the paper on to the table. He looked at his watch.

'Time to go Brian.'

'I guess so. Shame though, I reckon I could get used to it here in East Anglia.' Brian returned the regional holiday-guide magazine to the display rack. They collected their respective belongings, settled their account with a stolen credit card and walked to the railway station.

Chapter Four

At about that same time a group of ten over-hormonal students from the coeducational high school in Woodbridge together with their soon to retire geography master had just arrived by minibus on the quay at Orford in readiness to board the first ferry to Havergate Island for an 'O'-level field trip. Weatherwise, it was a much better day. The gale of the previous night had passed, and the sun was shining in a clear blue sky. There was a bit of breeze from the southwest, chilly, but when compared to how the weather had been it was positively mild. *January Storm* came alongside the pontoon and the passengers eagerly clambered aboard and the boat took off for the island. Mr Ross, the master in charge had seen it all before. As important a part of the curriculum as it was, he was no longer the young dynamic teacher who imparted knowledge with an infectious enthusiasm. He was past caring, disillusioned even. Whether his students completed their assignments or merely went wandering off to find isolated spots to indulge in whatever it was that kids at their ages and stages of development did, he wasn't over-bothered. No doubt they would be drinking and smoking. Even heavy petting wouldn't have surprised him given the manner in which couples seemed to be pairing up. Whilst he should have been concerned, he wasn't. He smiled to himself as he filled his pipe, perhaps remembering his own youth, or it was more likely the prospect of a day out of the classroom he was looking forward to? The escape was as much a treat for him as for his delinquent and pubescent fifteen-year-olds. Provided they were all back on board for the last ferry back to Orford it would have been a day well spent.

The ferry drew alongside the jetty and Reg White the ferryman intoned his well-rehearsed announcement regarding the rules and protocols of the island and the timetable of the return trips. The students disembarked and dispersed this way and that with their geography project files and packed lunches. Reg had been about to cast off and head back to Orford when a piercing ear-splitting scream sent a flight of Brent geese into the air creating their own cacophony. He'd ferried more than enough school trips to the island to recognise the sounds of kids larking about or even the distress call of a youngster stung by a wasp. This scream was in neither of those categories. This scream was a reaction to something frightening or even sinister. This was a cry for help if ever he'd heard one. With his reverie shattered Mr Ross set off with a gait somewhere between a rapid amble and a jog in the direction of the agonising outcry. With the boat secured the ferryman also took off in the direction of the drama and soon overtook Mr Ross along the well-worn path heading across the vegetated shingle towards the source of the lamentable howling. Reg the ferryman, Mr Ross and most of the kids who had responded to the clamour were gathering around the lifeless figure of a man, prostrate on the shingle wearing a red yachting jacket with a pair of binoculars slung around his neck. His staring eyes were wide open but seeing nothing. There was a small black hole in the centre of his forehead.

'Stand back, stand back!' Reg ordered. 'C'mon, make way please.' Not only was Reg the skipper of the ferry he was one of the island's wardens. There was no doubt in his mind who should take charge of the situation, whatever it was. 'Sir, take your party back to the jetty.' Mr Ross began to usher his students back along the path. There was much speculation in hushed tones as the group was slowly herded back towards the river. One girl remained by the corpse sobbing as she struggled to return her camera to her rucksack.

'C'mon Gail, you'll be left behind,' urged Mr Ross. Often accused of being teacher's pet, Gail and Mr Ross had a familiar relationship in that they got on together very well. Mr Ross was very fond of Gail and didn't like to see her upset. He gently put his arm around her shoulders in an avuncular gesture of comfort and walked her back to the group which was now gathering on the jetty.

'I've never seen a dead body before,' she sobbed.

'I don't s'pose you have my dear,' acknowledged Mr Ross. He then went on to assess the situation with the ferryman and without hesitation they readily agreed that a return to Orford should be expedited forthwith. He tapped his pipe out on one of the jetty's fenceposts to summon order and he addressed his class. 'Now, it would appear that we have stumbled across the unfortunate victim of a shooting.'

'You reckon it was murder sir?' queried one of the boys with a ghoulish grin.

'That's not for me to say, but it could be by the look of it,' answered Mr Ross, who was now disappointed if not annoyed that his day out had been compromised. Furthermore, he was wondering what the blazes he would do with this group of kids for the rest of the day. Maybe Orford Castle he was thinking. 'Anyway, look, be quiet please, we have to return to Orford. The island is obviously a crime scene and the police when they get here, won't thank us for having trampled all over any evidence there might be. Mr White here, the ferryman says he'll be suspending any further visits until he gets clearance to resume. Now, are we all here?' The students, some of them complaining, others discussing what they had witnessed, climbed back onto *January Storm* and Mr Ross did a head count.

To the casual observer Ben and his mum could have been taking a morning constitutional stroll around the village but they fully expected the alarm to be raised when the first ferry returned from the island. They were standing in the queue of intending passengers when the *January Storm* arrived at the waterfront. With the boat rafted alongside the ferryman was first up on to the quayside followed by the geography field-trippers and Mr

Ross. Reg was clearly agitated and pushed his way through the few people waiting for the next crossing.

'Sorry folks, no more trips today. There's been a' incident on the island and I've got to call the police. We've found a body, see.' Ben took hold of his arm. Reg turned to face him.

'Excuse me but I think I know who the body might have been. When you speak to the police tell them you've had an anonymous tip-off. Tell them to contact a Detective Inspector Cartwright at Thames Valley Constabulary.'

'How come you seem to know so much about it? How come Thames Valley?'

'That's not important right now. Tell the local police to call DI Cartwright and to mention the name Jock.' Ben thought he'd said enough – probably too much. He found Helen trying to console a group of girls some of whom were crying.

'Time we weren't here mum. Let's go.'

Chapter Five

Despite the bright start to the day the skies had darkened and there was a feeling of rain in the air. In his 'official' capacity, Reg White had instructed Mr Ross and his students to await the arrival of the police and some of the group disappeared into the Riverside Café. After Reg had made his telephone call it was almost an hour before a police car arrived from Ipswich. A detective constable spoke to Mr Ross who was now feeling very important. Once the men from the coroner's office turned up, they and the police boarded the ferry and Reg took them over to the island. By the time they returned with the corpse in a body bag, DI Cartwright and DC Davies had arrived from Kidlington. It was highly likely that the unmarked Ford Capri, driven by PC Andy Lewis had passed Ben and Hazel travelling in the opposite direction on their way along the A45 towards the Midlands. They had considered it prudent to distance themselves from the proximity of the crime and were heading for the village of Burton Overy and Hazel's cottage. Ben's wife Tina and his best mate Jamie were following in Ben's MGB. Whilst on the one hand they were all mightily relieved in the knowledge that they would never have to worry about Duncan McClean ever again, they fully understood that inevitably there would be serious repercussions. After all, they were at the very least guilty of a conspiracy to murder and quite likely accessories to the crime as well. DI Cartwright would get to them soon enough.

The men from the morgue, assisted by Reg White carried the body bag and its occupant from the ferry and loaded it into the coroner's ambulance. The policemen stood in a huddle discussing what they knew and what they didn't know.

'OK Ray, let's have a look.' The two detectives from Kidlington walked over to the ambulance and flashed their warrant cards to the mortuary men. The phone call that Cartwright had received, and especially mention of the name 'Jock' had been sufficient to convince him that the body in the bag would be that of McClean. But, since neither Davies nor himself had ever seen McClean, either in the flesh or even in a photograph, they would be unable to make a positive identification. However, the contents of the dead man's pockets were enough; a letter from Helen Blake, addressed to D McClean, c/o The Anchor, Woodbridge, a bottle of Moët & Chandon, a packet of condoms, a keyring with a couple of yale-type keys, and a motorbike ignition key. In the man's wallet were his identity card and a significant amount of money.

'Looks like our man Jock was hoping to get lucky!' observed Cartwright.

'Yeah, dead lucky,' responded Davies with a rueful smile.

'Now, has Andy done talking to the ferryman over there?' With the deceased's few belongings placed in an evidence bag, the body bag was rezipped and the private ambulance departed.

'I don't think an inquest will be needed. The cause of death is a bullet to the brain. A remarkably similar shot to the one which killed our Colin Harvey.' Cartwright recalled that day just after Christmas when police motorcyclist Colin Harvey was leading the convoy taking Ahmed abu Mousa to Gartree Prison when both he, two prison officers and the Palestinian all lost their lives.

'Same sniper, by the look of it. Bloody good whoever he is!' Davies commented.

'Don't suppose we'll ever find out,' conceded Cartwright. 'Now, let's see what Andy's got.'

'This is Reg White, the ferryman, sir.'

'What can you tell us Reg?'

'Well, I remembers taking him over yes'dy afternoon. Quite 'stinctive in his red waterproof, and wi' 'noculars an' all. That's his mo'bike over there, the Yam'ha. I thought it strange when I never brought him back yes'dy and specially when I sees 'is bike still there' smornin'.' Davies was making notes.

'Did he meet anyone here or on the island maybe?' Cartwright asked.

'I reckon 'e might. There were a woman, see?'

'Go on.'

'Well, this woman, she went on the ferry afore 'im and she were still waitin' on the jetty on the next run. Strange but the same woman, she were 'ere 'smornin' as well. I's sure I seen 'er on the quay with a young bloke. 'E were 'er son 'e said. It were 'im what said I should tell the local coppers to call you.'

'Can you describe her? This woman?'

'Sort o' fiftyish I reckon, very attractive woman. The bloke wi' 'er were 'er son.'

'Yes you said already. OK thanks very much Reg. You've been very helpful. Give me a call if you think of anything else.' Cartwright handed him his card. Andy Lewis then made two further introductions.

'This is Gail Read – she discovered the body, and this is Gail's teacher, Mr Ross.' PC Lewis introduced the schoolgirl and her geography master. They both made a brief statement and DC Davies had his notebook out again.

'I took his photo.' Gail announced quite proudly.

'Sorry?'

'I took his photo – on my camera like,' she repeated.

'Well done Gail. Could you send me a copy of the snap when you've had them printed please?' Cartwright handed her one of his cards. 'Let me know how much you have to pay and I'll send you a postal order.'

'Have you made a note of the motorbike's registration number?'

'Of course guv.'

'OK – I think you know where we're going next.' Cartwright was summarising.

'OK, judging by what I've read of this letter, Helen Blake and Jock were having a tryst on the island – travelled there independently. Jock then gets himself assassinated, possibly by an IRA sniper, before he gets to…' he paused remembering the condoms '… drink the champagne. Helen Blake, can't be any doubt it was her, comes back on her own but says nothing to anyone. Then she's here this morning to see the body brought back. Seems to me she was being used as bait. So, we'd better go and have a word, yes? Doesn't the son Ben have a place here? Coincidence? I think not. I don't like coincidences.'

Lewis asked for directions from an old woman walking her dog and given the short distance from the quay, the policemen walked to Lobster Pot Cottage. Cartwright knocked on the door. Davies walked around the property. There were no vehicles on the drive.

'Appears there's no one at home.'

'What do you think Andy?' Cartwright knew that his driver would be ahead of the game.

'Burton Overy?'

'You've got it exactly! Burton Overy please Andy.'

'Guv'!'

Chapter Six

Back in her cottage in Leicestershire, Helen was reflecting on the way her life had become such a disaster.

'I've already spent five years at Her Majesty's pleasure in East Sutton Park women's prison as a result of my previous association with Jock McClean. And where was he? Jock? Done a runner; managed one of his disappearing acts. I know I couldn't cope with the guilty conscience, more than enough guilt for both of us. But had it been wise, confessing to the police to being an accomplice in a black-market enterprise and to harbouring a suspected murderer? Still, it was the best present ever when I was released from prison. To be reunited with my baby son Ben, now a man. What a chance encounter that was. Before that I don't think either of us were expecting to see each other ever again. Why hadn't I left him a note? Was it fair that Ben knew nothing of his mother's imprisonment? Me, his mother just disappearing without a word. Chances are that I'll be back inside before too long. Doesn't bear thinking about.'

Helen's eyes were brimming with tears. The very soul of her subjectivity was brimming with self-pity.

'Me and Ben are now extremely close. Why did McClean have to turn up yet again, plaguing our lives? Why had he become such a menace? What was he after? What did he want? Did he really love me? Why was he stalking the family and our close friends? Did he love me? Really? No, I don't think so. I think he was trying to get at the money which was no more legally his than it was mine. Trying to bribe me with his will. Still, it had been Jamie, Ben's closest friend since primary school who was coerced into the plot to rid us of McClean forever – not me, not Ben! I didn't know Danny McFaddon. He didn't know me. He was only using me in the IRA's plan. It was always for the IRA. Not for me. How stupid was I? I was the bloody bait in the trap. I know Ben had always wanted to involve the police in the plan but Jamie and McFaddon had advised against it. Didn't McFaddon tell Ben that he knew from first-hand experience that the police didn't look favourably on assassination or any other form of execution or capital punishment? But me and Ben, vigilantes? It might have got McClean off our backs but…? What'll the price be? Anyway, if the stupid police had caught him… we wouldn't be in this mess. Incompetence! It's their fault. The facts remain that the police have singularly failed in apprehending Mr Duncan Murderer McClean. What must it be? Must be over some seven years, he's got away with murder including that of Ben's dad. Ken! Ken Blake I still miss you sometimes. Poor Ben, brought up by his grandparents. Him and Tina, discovering his dad's body floating in a lock on the Grand Union Canal. Why? Oh why did I allow myself to be talked into this? What next? And now McClean is dead.'

Chapter Seven

It had been shortly after his first mysterious disappearance that McClean reappeared in Belfast and managed to get himself inducted into the IRA. As far as Jock was concerned, the Troubles were nothing more than a distraction. He had an entrepreneurial knack for turning an illegal profit from such inflammably agitated and riotous situations, just as he had when he had been a conscript during WWII. Whilst the Protestants and the Catholics were squabbling Jock had the ideal opportunity to get on with his pillaging and looting and thereby provide the stock for his latest black-market activities. However, and better still, he had infiltrated his way into becoming a trusted paramilitary and had been appointed as the Republicans' gunrunner and arms dealer, collecting and delivering illegal consignments of weaponry imported from America brokered by a dissident weirdo, Tom Wenzl. What the IRA didn't realise at the time was that many of the guns intended for the IRA to advance the Nationalist cause were being pilfered by McClean and sold from under their noses to the highest bidder. When this betrayal was discovered a car chase had resulted in Gerry, the brother of an IRA general, Michael Doyle, being seriously injured in a road accident. There were also two fatalities in the accident caused by McClean. The IRA's outrage demanded satisfaction by execution.

Gerry Doyle had previously known McClean who he always assumed to be in a relationship with Helen Blake. That was back in the day when the two of them were plying their black-market trade up and down the Grand Union. Gerry had been buying guns from McClean; guns stolen from the British Army during and shortly after the war. Since the accident Gerry had been in intensive care from where he plotted his and the IRA's revenge. The Doyle brothers by this time had become aware that, Wenzl, the IRA's sympathetic American 'friend', was also a traitor to the Republican cause. Not only had he co-conspired with McClean to rip-off the IRA but he wasn't a friend, neither was he American. He was Ahmed abu Mousa, a Palestinian and member of the Black September terrorist organisation. He had been amongst those responsible for the assassination of Israeli athletes at the Munich Olympic Games in 1972. There were no two ways about it. These two men were enemies of the Northern Irish Republican movement. It was all extremely heavy stuff. Vengeance would be wrought.

Michael Doyle had hoped to dispatch both of these perfidious infiltrators back to their respective makers at the same time as recovering the arsenal they had intercepted with intent to supply Black September. However, as always seemed to be the way, McClean was one step ahead. The police had been tipped off as well and Doyle's original plan was scuppered. In fact, the Irishmen only just managed to avoid capture. It was only the Palestinian who was arrested but police custody couldn't protect him from the wrath of the IRA. He was eliminated when a cell of the IRA ambushed a police convoy escorting their prisoner to a maximum-security facility near Market Harborough close to Foxton. It was only a matter of time before Michael Doyle and his men and officers of the Thames Counter Terrorism Unit independently initiated the identical contingency plan when they both discovered that the arms shipment would be conveyed by narrowboat to Limehouse Basin in London. But McClean, more artful than the Dickensian original dodged them all yet again. The police operation was not entirely botched as they did manage to arrest Michael Doyle by way of consolation. It was IRA strategist Danny McFaddon that finally contrived the bold move which would lead to McClean's last farewell. Helen Blake had been an integral part of the plan. She was coerced into being the lure; the bait which, even with all his Machiavellian stealth and his nose for a trap, McClean could not resist.

Chapter Eight

In the minds of the investigating detectives there was absolutely no doubt that the body was that of Duncan 'Jock' McClean. They were equally certain that the cause of death was a gunshot to the head, in an IRA-style execution. There was also little doubt that Helen Blake alias Hazel Black had been complicit by allowing herself to be the IRA's Greek gift to McClean in the sophisticated ruse to entice him to Havergate Island, the place of execution.

As Lewis drove into Great Glen, the lights were just coming on in the Old Greyhound.

'You guys hungry?' Cartwright asked.

The landlady had indeed just unlocked the door and the three policemen went in and were greeted by Diane Webster, Jamie's very pretty and voluptuous wife.

'Good evening gentlemen. What're you having?' Ray Davies' eyes lit up and his pulse rate increased by several notches.

'You buying, guvnor?' They ordered and sat at a table in the corner. Di carried their drinks to the table. She had instantly recognised the fact that her first customers of the day were policemen. But then she had met DC Davies once before.

'Sorry officers, my Jamie's not here but I'm expecting him any time soon. He's been to his friend's house in Suffolk for a couple of days.' And there without any prompting required was further evidence of a conspiracy. The detectives knew of the close friendship between Ben Blake and Jamie Webster. Cartwright gave his DC a sideways glance as he recalled Ray Davies' comments about the landlady. Ray had made no secret of his fascination or was it infatuation with the lovely Diane. Now he could certainly see what the attraction was.

'What're you thinking guv?' Cartwright nodded in the direction towards the bar.

'I see what you mean Ray!' Ray blushed with embarrassment. Cartwright tried to refocus on the case. He knew that if what they suspected was true, Helen Blake and others had a case to answer. But, like his colleague Armstrong, back in Oxford, Cartwright also had a great deal of sympathy for Helen. Jock McClean had blighted her life for something like thirty years. She'd spent five years inside for what to all intents and purposes had been his crimes. He was a multiple murder suspect and now his guilt would be taken to his grave. Cartwright had been reassessing the situation in the light of what they suspected.

'I don't propose to take any action against the Blakes as long as they're up front and honest with me. They've put up with McClean for long enough and, in my book, don't deserve any recriminations even if they were somehow involved with getting rid of him. After all, we've bloody well failed to nab old Jock for several years. But I will expect some cooperation with regard to the IRA's involvement. Those responsible for the ambush of Ahmed abu Mousa caused the death of Colin Harvey and a couple of prison officers. The IRA has been perpetrating all manner of their brand of terrorism and I reckon it won't be long before their bloody bombing campaign crosses the Irish Sea. We owe it to our colleagues to bring these bloody warmongers to justice. I'm hoping the Blakes should be able to provide us with some leads.'

'I hear what you say guv, but don't you think the Catholics in Northern Ireland have had a rough time of it – you know, like cowboys and Indians, the Republicans and Loyalists.' Was Davies expressing some sympathy for the IRA wondered Cartwright?

'Now is not the time for that debate Ray! And even if the IRA are representing the repressed, violence, bombing, killing, and maiming innocent people is not the way to redress the situation. So, enough!'

'Sorry guv.' Ray knew that he'd just been castigated and sought to make amends. 'Shall I get a round in?' Without waiting for a reaction he went to the bar and ordered two more pints, a lemonade for Lewis and three portions of cod, chips and peas.

After they'd eaten they drove the short distance to Burton Overy and Marsh Cottage, the country home of Helen Blake, or was she Hazel Black again now?

Ben answered the door. There was a certain resignation and inevitability about the way he invited the detectives in.

'Come in Inspector, we were expecting you.' Introductions were made all round including the long-time family friends Kate and Stuart Cross who were the full-time residents at the cottage since Helen had moved to Pin Mill. Kate had known Ben from birth and was like an aunt to him. Both she and Stuart had been involved on the periphery of the menace which had been McClean and listened intently to what the Inspector had to say. Ben was the first to respond.

'I had wanted to tell you what we were planning right from the word go but Danny persuaded me that to do so would not be such a good idea. I must say that in hindsight, I'm not sure whether I agree with him or not, although the fewer the number of people who knew...' His attempts to mitigate his own position were fairly flimsy and tailed off.

'Danny – who's Danny?' Cartwright asked. Jamie picked up the narrative.

'This fellow, Danny McFaddon, came into my pub, the Old Greyhound just after Christmas I think it was. I was just about to close after the lunchtime session. Ben was there, he had been helping me out. This bloke Danny, looked like a proper gent, suit and tie and everything, well, he put forward a proposal by which we could be rid of McClean for ever. For Helen's, sorry Hazel's sake, we had to go along with it, a no-brainer. It made so much sense, really simple. We knew that McClean fancied Hazel and it was Ben and me, me and Ben that convinced

Hazel that she could easily attract McClean to the island. It never occurred to us at the time that we we're getting involved with the IRA. I mean, as a plan it could have worked if we had told you what was going down. You could have ambushed Jock when he stepped onto the island. We don't know any more than that really. It wasn't until later that we we're told about the IRA. Seems the IRA was pissed off – 'scuse me Kate, Hazel – pissed off with McClean 'cause apparently he'd nicked a load of weapons from them, caused an accident that put one of the IRA's top blokes in hospital – he's likely to be in a wheelchair the rest of his life we were told. They wanted revenge and they saw Ben's mum, Hazel, as an easy way to set him up as a target. We don't know who the hitman was. We didn't even know there was going to be a hitman like that.'

'Thanks Jamie – thanks Ben. I don't think you've told us anything we don't already know, but thanks all the same. Now, as far as you lot are concerned, that's it! Case closed! There'll be no further action. But, in return, if you get even the slightest whisper on what Danny McFaddon or any members of the IRA are up to, I want to know straight away. Do I have your word on this?' The implied threat made by Cartwright was crystal clear to all. Everyone in the room was nodding away, their heads seemingly on springs.

'What if anyone asks?' enquired Hazel. Cartwright looked directly at her. He'd avoided doing so thus far and now he was feeling distinctly uncomfortable.

'You were staying with your son at Orford. You'd gone to the island just out of curiosity and for a walk. A bloke who was also visiting the island got shot dead. Coincidence!'

'You don't like coincidences guvnor!' reminded Davies. Everyone laughed and the tension that had pervaded the atmosphere dissipated as if some giant fan had just been switched on and blown it away. The detectives prepared to leave.

'Jamie, shouldn't you be at work! Your lovely Diane will be struggling to cope on her own,' Davies jokingly suggested. Jamie took him seriously.

'Yes, I know. Friday nights are generally busy.'

'Tonight will be!' suggested Ben. 'Come on we'll all go to the pub. There's something to celebrate.'

'Right, we'll stay and have one with you if you don't mind – is that OK Andy?'

'You're the guv, guvnor!'

Chapter Nine

During the next few weeks, life in the respective Blake, Cross and Webster households returned to normal. Hazel had gone back to Pin Mill where she took up her watercolour riverscape painting once again. Kate had her choir, dog, and daily crossword to keep her occupied, Stuart pottered about in the garden and was teaching himself woodturning on a lathe he'd requested as a farewell gift when he took early retirement from the civil service. Ben had resumed his work at the Academy, he was practising the piano again and Tina was back at the fine art gallery. Normality had never been so blissful. The winter was almost over and with spring just around the corner there was so much to look forward to.

Hazel had been in touch with her erstwhile employers, Meadows, Coleman and Pettegrew the firm of solicitors in Ely where she had worked as a legal secretary after she had been discharged from prison. McClean's outpouring in the letter to the woman he'd only ever known as Helen in the weeks before his death had attached a copy of his last Will & Testament. He was leaving everything to Helen. Hazel had given the bequest a great deal of thought. She didn't need his money nor his worldly goods but on the other hand she could redress some of his evil with the material wealth he had derived from it. Hazel was just a little concerned that her name change would cause a problem. She felt sure that one of the partners at MCP would advise her. In the event MCP could not have been more helpful. Despite the fact that she had left the firm without so much as a 'by your leave' or working a period of notice, she was the prodigal daughter welcomed back with open arms. MCP invited Hazel to make an appointment in Ely to discuss the implications, the potential pitfalls, legal challenges, and probable impediments. Although it was a few weeks before she received any information, when it did eventually arrive, the letter from old man Meadows, the senior partner explained how he had managed to validate the Will and get the beneficiary anomaly sorted in a fraction of the time it might have ordinarily taken. Hazel Black's Deed Poll application had been duly executed and she would henceforth be Helen Blake again. The Will's executors, Crean & Berry, a firm local to Woodbridge who had drawn up the will authorised the administration of the deceased's estate. With probate granted every last one of McClean's assets were transferred to Helen. What she wasn't expecting was title to the houseboat *Ironside* permanently berthed in Woodbridge Quay nor an almost brand-new Yamaha SS50 motorcycle.

It was shortly after one of her weekend trips to see Ben and Tina in Orford, that quite out of the blue, Helen received a telephone call from Maisie. Maisie Clarke had been Helen's cellmate at East Sutton Park Prison. She was doing ten years for causing grievous bodily harm to her husband who had regularly inflicted physical violence upon his wife. It was after she had sustained severe bruising and lacerations in a particularly malicious and alcohol-fuelled, unprovoked attack that Maisie was intent on revenge. The sodium hydroxide crystals were kept in the house for cleaning the drains. She mixed up a strong solution and poured the caustic soda over her husband whilst he was comatose in a drunken stupor. That she had suffered at his hand for a considerable length of time was deemed by the jury to be a mitigating circumstance and thus her sentence was shorter than it otherwise might have been. Ordinarily Maisie was a nice, average, quiet woman. She was never going to win any beauty competitions, extremely attractive nevertheless and perhaps a few years younger than Helen but with similar interests. To a casual, uninformed observer they might have been sisters. Theirs were certainly kindred spirits. Maisie explained that the principal reason for her call was her desperate need for a permanent address to satisfy one of her parole conditions. She was about to be released. Could Hazel help? Knowing only too well what it was like to be physically abused, Hazel had sympathised with Maisie. In prison they'd been almost inseparable. They would quite often sit in their cell and listen to each other's tales of woe and even though Helen's experiences of physical abuse at the hands of her husband Ken, Ben's father, had been twenty-five years ago the memories were still vivid. When Helen was paroled, she had promised to keep in touch with Maisie. Now she felt a sense of guilt for not having done so. She had to help. All of this was explained to Ben and Tina and their concordant understanding was complete.

***

Helen, Ben and Tina arranged a trip to Woodbridge to inspect Helen's recently inherited houseboat. They arrived at Woodbridge railway station, having travelled from their respective homes and walked the short distance from the station to the quay. On the quayside were various small traditional marine industries and facilities for hauling boats out of the river for maintenance and the like. *Ironside*, a former Thames sailing barge was sitting proudly on the mud in a small basin reserved for houseboats.

'This is magnificent – what a location – and look at the view – and a pub just across the road.' Ben was almost beside himself with excitement. Tina was taking photographs. Helen was chatting to an old salt in one of the open-fronted shipwrights' workshops.

'I can't wait to see on board!' exclaimed Tina.

The tide was out so the descent down the gangplank was just a little disconcerting although something that anyone would get used to over a short period of time. The next-door neighbour aboard his boat *Mary Gloster* gave them a wave.

'Mornin'. I'm Colin Smith. If you need any help just give me a shout.' He disappeared down below. *Ironside*'s new owner and guests also went below and were all mightily impressed with the high standard of the conversion. It had absolutely everything anyone could need from a fully fitted kitchen, bathroom, a large double bedroom to a light and airy sitting room. At the same time, many of the original nautical fittings had been retained.

'I could get a piano in here.' Ben could see himself moving in.

'The man I was talking to, Frank Knightly, is a shipwright and he did the conversion to a houseboat. It's wonderful don't you think? I reckon we could offer this to Maisie, what do you say?'

'I realise we haven't met her, but from the way you describe her Helen, I reckon she'd love it. I would!' Tina's positive response was sufficient for Helen.

'Right, then it's agreed. And, Ben, since you're not far away in Orford perhaps you could keep an eye on things for me?'

'Do you mean Maisie or the boat?'

'Well both, might be nice I would hope.'

'Mother! I'm a happily married man!'

They left *Ironside* and after a brief stroll around the immediate surroundings they went to the Anchor for lunch.

'Did your man Frank say anything about the previous owner?' enquired Ben.

'Not much really. Apparently he was a private person and kept himself to himself except when he was here in this pub, very chatty with the locals, apparently. He rode about on a little motorbike – I've inherited that as well – which reminds me, I must get the change of ownership registered. Do you think Maisie would want to use it?'

'What?' Ben hadn't been listening.

'The motorbike.'

'What about it?'

'Oh, never mind.' Their lunches were brought to the table and as Helen toyed with the seafood salad on her plate her mind had clearly wandered off. She was thinking about those days prior to her meeting with Jock, the day of his murder. The Anchor had been the 'care-of' address that she had written to him at.

'C'mon mum, food not so good? Eat up!' Helen was brought back from her reflective moment and tucked in.

'That Colin seems like a nice chap. Perhaps we can talk to him about the previous owner not that I particularly want to be reminded of him.'

Maisie was invited to stay for the weekend at Helen's home in Pin Mill. Helen met her from the train at Ipswich station and they drove home in Helen's Mercedes. Maisie was extremely impressed.

'This your car? Crikey! What'd you do, rob a bank?'

'Something like that.'

The next several hours were spent catching up, although reminiscences about life 'inside' had held little appeal for either of them as a topic of conversation. The following day, Saturday, they drove over to Woodbridge. Maisie was introduced to *Ironside* and it was love at first sight. Frank Knightly came aboard and pointed out the several various features of onboard living for which there were no bricks-and-mortar equivalents. A tenancy agreement was drawn up to satisfy Maisie's probation officer and so it was that on the 1st March she would move in and her future was thus assured.

Chapter Ten

It was mid-February. Danny telephoned the John Radcliffe hospital to enquire on Gerry Doyle's progress. After much fizzing and clicking on the line as his call was diverted from one department to another Danny got to speak to someone who was familiar with the patient.

'Good morning. I'm Ian Christie, the Registrar in the Intensive Care Unit. May I ask who's calling? Are you a relative sir? We've been trying to make contact with Mr Doyle's next of kin but without success since we don't know who it might be. We do have a letter he wrote just before... a letter intended for a Mr D McFaddon, but no address.' As soon as the Registrar paused to draw breath, Danny responded.

'Gerry's next of kin is unfortunately unavailable, he's on remand in prison awaiting trial. I am Danny McFaddon, I am a lifelong family friend and I've been looking after Gerry's affairs whilst he's in hospital and his brother's in prison.'

'Ah, good. I see. Yes. OK. Well, Mr McFaddon,' the Registrar paused, 'I regret to have to inform you that Gerry died two days ago on Wednesday 14th February. After further surgery on his leg – you'll know that we were attempting to mend the various fractures – he developed an infection which in turn led to pneumonia. He died quite suddenly. In fact he had already told me that he couldn't cope with the prospect of the rest of his life in a wheelchair, and now you've told me about his brother I rather feel that he gave up on life. The will to live, the fight had gone. There was nothing we could do. I'm so sorry.' Silence! After a moment or two the Registrar spoke again.

'Mr McFaddon, are you still there?

'Yes I'm here.'

'I realise this is a terrible shock. Please accept my deepest condolences.'

Silence again!

'Mr McFaddon, will you be responsible for the funeral arrangements? Mr McFaddon?'

'Yes.' Danny replaced the receiver, sat down and wept. After a while and when he had regained his composure, Danny redialled the number of the hospital. He explained the purpose of his call to the receptionist who answered the phone and dictated his address in Kilburn. He requested it be passed on to Dr Christie in ICU.

'I'll make sure Mr Christie gets it,' she corrected. Then he rang Brian. Brian O'Connor had travelled back to Northern Ireland and the small cottage he rented in County Antrim, between Glenarm and Carnlough, isolated and on the coast. No one knew the exact location. No one had ever known because that's how Brian wanted it. Danny did have a phone number though. He passed on the sad news. Brian was mortified. He and Gerry had been friends since their childhood in Belfast at the Christian Brothers' School. They'd enlisted in the IRA together and had moved to London together to form the Kilburn Battalion to which several atrocities had been attributed. That was back in the day when angry young Catholics really believed they could do something to further the Republican cause. And now one of his best friends was dead as a result of the cause.

The following day, the letter from Gerry, forwarded from the hospital, arrived at Danny's apartment in Kilburn. Having read it and re-read it, Danny phoned Brian again. In his letter Gerry clearly implied that he'd lost the will to live. He had also outlined the way he wanted his funeral to be conducted. Between the awkward moments of silence and the mutual attempts which the two friends made to console each other, they discussed the logistics of the arrangements which Gerry had specified. Brian agreed to drive across from Antrim to Belfast to see Ciara, Gerry's niece. Danny agreed to ring the Governor at HMP Brixton.

In the Northern Irish edition of the *Daily Mirror* an announcement of the death of Gerry Doyle was published a few days later. The news spread across the province like a rash.

Gerry had been in intensive care in the John Radcliffe hospital in Oxford since the accident. Some said he was lucky to be alive. He had been chasing a van, stolen by McClean and full of weapons illegally imported from America. It had been a filthy November night when Gerry was about to intercept the van. McClean made an outrageously reckless, almost suicidal right turn off the A34 right across the path of an oncoming articulated Atkinson lorry carrying a full load of ammonium nitrate – not that he knew what the cargo was at the time. Gerry, driving a Ford Cortina tried to follow. The van made it, the Cortina didn't. When the ammonium nitrate exploded as a result of the collision Gerry was thrown clear of the burning wreckage on to a verge some significant distance ahead of the carnage. It wasn't until the next morning that he was discovered by a farmer out exercising his border collies. He was barely alive, soaked to the skin, and hypothermic. He had sustained a comminuted fracture of the right femur, a femoral neck fracture of the left leg and a ruptured spleen. There were also multiple cuts and bruises. The prognosis was that if he survived, Gerry would certainly never walk again. The prospect of the rest of his life being disabled in a wheelchair and dependent upon others was not something he relished. Some may have said he was lucky to be alive. Gerry hadn't been so sure. He'd wished he was dead. And now he was.

A simple cremation took place on Monday 19th February and was very sympathetically organised by Homewood Funeral Directors in Kidlington. There were three mourners in the chapel. Brian had travelled from Belfast with Ciara. The resident Anglican chaplain had offered to officiate but, whilst he was present in the crematorium, his services and meaningless platitudes were not required. After all, to the chaplain, Gerry was just another deceased person. A hearse delivered a plain wooden coffin which Homewood's pallbearers carried into the chapel. The three mourners stood holding hands, with their heads held high. No words were spoken and after just a few moments of quiet reflection, that was it. Gerry Doyle was committed to the fiery furnace. The funeral car then took them to the Killingworth Castle Hotel in Wootton near Woodstock where they had pre-booked three rooms in false names. It was a sombre occasion but not a particularly sober one as Gerry's life was toasted over and over. Two days later, the urn containing Gerry's ashes was delivered by the funeral director to the hotel. With the urn safely stowed in Ciara's luggage, the three then took the first available flight from Luton, the nearest airport, back to Belfast.

The IRA Council had organised a memorial service for Gerry who had been one of the organisation's most loyal foot-soldiers. Mourners gathered inside and outside the Blackstaff Bar, the Republican stronghold in Springfield Road. Conspicuous by his absence was the pub's landlord, Gerry's brother, Michael, on remand in HMP Brixton. He had been arrested during yet another incident involving McClean which had since been referred to by police and IRA alike as the Limehouse Basin fiasco. The Blackstaff was now run by Michael's daughter, Ciara, and her partner Tom O'Rourke. Tom's mother Maggie had been McClean's landlady and his lover of convenience. Not only had she been involved in the same road accident in a third vehicle, but Maggie O'Rourke had also been carrying McClean's unborn baby. Both had died at the scene. A large gathering of several hundred people processed slowly from the pub to St Mary's Church in the Falls Road. Leading the procession were Ciara Doyle, Tom O'Rourke, Danny McFaddon, Father Francis McCann, and Brian O'Connor. The church was absolutely packed for a full Requiem Mass. Although Michael Doyle had made a compassionate application to the Governor of Brixton prison for permission to attend his brother's memorial, Detective Chief Superintendent Alex Simons of the

Thames Counter Terrorism Unit had vehemently rejected the application given that the pending charges upon which Doyle was awaiting trial included the murder of a police officer.

Had the lines of communication between police departments been rather more open and forthcoming DCS Simons might have thought to refer Michael Doyle's request to DI Cartwright. But since the abortive Limehouse Basin stakeout the DCS didn't hold the DI in particularly high regard. There again, had Alex Simons and his elite Counter Terrorism Unit had their collective finger a little more firmly on the pulse of things, they might have made the connection between Gerry Doyle's funeral, Michael Doyle, on remand, and the Limehouse Basin fiasco. Then, if they had managed to join the dots, the link to the assassination of Ahmed abu Mousa, two prison officers and the shooting of PC Colin Harvey might have emerged. Had Cartwright been made aware of a high-profile IRA memorial service taking place in Belfast he would surely have attended himself given the possibility that the perpetrators of the killings in the Foxton ambush might have been there and every chance that Danny McFaddon would have been amongst the mourners as well. McFaddon knew the identity of McClean's executioner. That was certain in Cartwright's mind. It was more than likely that a sniper with that level of expertise was also the killer of police motorcyclist Harvey. The service passed off with due reverence and without incident. Had the RUC staked out the Blackstock Bar they would probably have made several arrests for drunk and disorderly. But they hadn't been inclined to do so and so they didn't. For once it seemed that there was a mutual respect; and an understanding of just how futile the Troubles were with the interests of neither the Republicans nor the Unionists being served. The mutual respect? It didn't last.

It wasn't many days after the memorial service that hostilities recommenced. The Troubles had become troublesome again. Brian wanted no part of it and when Danny announced that he had a project to finalise in London, Brian decided that he too would return to England. He'd had more than enough of Northern Ireland and the death of his friend had been the final straw. Brian was now intent on enjoying his retirement somewhere where he was unknown and could maintain his anonymity. On the Aer Lingus flight back to London Danny made a concerted effort to involve Brian in his latest 'project' but Brian's final decision had been made and no amount of pleading by Danny was going to change his mind. Brian could still visualise those images of East Anglia he had seen in the tourist guide in Lowestoft. The more he thought about it the more he was convinced that the rest of his life would be spent in Suffolk or Norfolk. He would learn to sail, to play golf perhaps. He would take up gardening, coarse fishing or sea fishing, walking, bird-spotting, sketching, any number of activities. Brian was looking forward to a life of leisure in a climate of untroubled peace and tranquillity, a new lifestyle and even a new identity.

They had taken the Heathrow Express to Paddington together which is where they parted the best of friends.

'Now you be sure to keep in touch,' urged Danny. 'You can always get to me through the Kilburn connection. I'm often in the Alliance as are so many of your friends and acquaintances in the pub too, so they are.'

'Of course. For sure.' Brian responded trying to sound genuine but he had no intention whatsoever of maintaining any contact with old friends or colleagues connected to his former existence as an IRA sniper. He certainly would not be going anywhere near the Alliance, the pub in West Hampstead frequented by expatriate Northern Irishmen. OK, he had been a staunch Republican and supporter of the Nationalist cause but from now on he was disassociating himself from it all in its entirety. He was single-mindedly bent on a completely new lifestyle, a fresh start where peace and quiet were the order of the day. He even considered taking a wife, but then were peace and quiet and a wife mutually compatible?

Chapter Eleven

Brian studied the map of the underground and took an eastbound Hammersmith and City Line train to Liverpool Street. Everything he owned he carried with him in a medium-sized holdall. Gone was the golf bag. Temporarily he was of no fixed abode and the immediate intention was to get out of London and to East Anglia. He wasn't short of money. His account on deposit with the Allied Bank of Ireland was very healthy and he had other sources of funds available to him which he had stashed away. Such specialist services as he had provided were not acquired cheaply. He bought a one-way ticket to Norwich and made his way to the platform only to be surprised by the numbers of passengers waiting to board the train. He walked the entire length of two carriages and every seat was taken. In the next carriage there were a few single empty seats, but none of them by a window which he'd been hoping for.

'Excuse me sir, is this seat taken?' he enquired of a man, younger than himself; a respectable looking professional, judging by his attire.

'No, please, help yourself.'

Brian stowed his holdall in the luggage rack and sat down.

'Always busy this train, but a lot of people only travel as far as Colchester. Pity they don't catch the local stopping train. Oh sorry, maybe I shouldn't have said that – you're not just going to Colchester are you? I didn't mean to…' Brian interrupted him before he could finish his sentence.

'No, no, don't worry. I'm going all the way to Norwich. Even so, I guess it is a nuisance if you have to make the journey every day.' Brian was not naturally a gregarious person and he surprised himself by entering into conversation with a complete stranger. Maybe this was the 'new' him.

'Do you make this trip often? Brian asked.

'Every day I'm afraid. How about you?

'First time ever for me. I've had enough of London and city living. I'm going to look for somewhere to live in East Anglia.'

'Well done you. You certainly won't regret it. It's a beautiful part of the world. Sorry, the name's Ben, Ben Blake.' He offered his hand which Brian took in a firm handshake.

'Brian O'Connor. Pleased to make your acquaintance Ben.' For all that he had a musical ear, it seemed that Ben had not noticed Brian's Northern Irish accent.

The train pulled out of the station as last-minute passengers made their way down the carriage looking for seats.

'So, what has prompted you to move to East Anglia?' Ben was curious.

'I was there on business a couple of weeks ago.'

'What business are you in, if you don't mind my asking?'

Brian hesitated. 'I was a freelance consultant and used to undertake specialist work for the military – all very hush-hush.' Not a million miles away from the truth, he thought to himself.

'Sounds interesting,' Ben said in a disinterested tone of voice.

'Still, I'm retired now and glad to be out of it.'

'How about you?'

'I'm a music librarian at the Royal Academy of Music.'

'I rather wish I'd taken up music or something similar instead of...' He didn't finish the sentence. 'And you commute to London every day?' Such a prospect didn't appeal to Brian in the slightest and the note of incredulity in his question seemed to imply 'sod that for a game of soldiers'.

'Yes, I know. Madness isn't it? But then the inconvenience of the travelling is more than compensated for by the place where we live.'

'Well, it must be or you wouldn't do it would you?'

The train pulled into Chelmsford station and several commuters stirred themselves, collected their briefcases, shopping or whatever and got off. Brian watched with obvious interest.

'I guess you get used to the routine,' he surmised.

'Oh yes, it's not so bad until it all goes wrong, like when a train is cancelled or runs late, or there are delays due to signalling problems or a broken-down locomotive.'

'Mm I can imagine.'

'So Brian, why Norwich?'

'Train doesn't go any further!' he jested. 'I was in Suffolk a week or so ago and I thought I'd take a look at Norfolk before I made my mind up about where I might want to settle.'

'Where abouts in Suffolk were you?'

'Small place near Woodbridge, then on a boat up to Lowestoft.'

'What a coincidence. I know Woodbridge very well. We live near there – Orford. I doubt you've heard of it.'

There was an uncomfortable silence that followed. Brian excused himself to go to the toilet. When he returned Ben continued.

'Norfolk is a beautiful county. The Broads especially, but for my money, Suffolk has the edge. I think it's the rivers. Yes it's the rivers that do it for me. The Orwell, the Deben, the Alde the Ore, the Blythe. Then there is the sand and shingle coastline with miles of deserted beaches, the moods of the sea. The skies are, well it's hard to put into words, enormous, there's a feeling of limitless space – it's all so stunning. And then inland, acres and acres of unspoilt countryside and farmland. Quite near Woodbridge there are something like 4000 acres of forestry commission woodland. You come across pretty villages with chocolate box cottages, country pubs, we love it! Sorry Brian, going on a bit there! Didn't mean to sound like a travelogue.'

'No, don't apologise, you're telling me just what I want to hear. Sounds almost like the tourist guide I was reading last week.'

The train arrived in Colchester, and as Ben had predicted, the carriage was all but empty when the journey continued.

'Not long now.' Ben looked at his watch. 'I have to change trains at Ipswich, the next stop. Then there's a fairly short local train ride to Woodbridge. My car's in the carpark there.'

'Well, it's been really enjoyable trip, thanks Ben, great to talk to you.'

'Likewise Brian. I hope you find what you're looking for in Norfolk but be mindful of the tourists and holidaymakers attracted to the Broads and seaside holidays in the summer months. Great Yarmouth is like the Blackpool of the east! Anyway, you enjoy your retirement...' Ben had a sudden thought. He liked this man. He took an old envelope from his pocket. His address quite clearly typed on it, he scribbled down his phone number.   'Look, Brian, if you can't find what you want in Norfolk, I'd be happy to show you the sights of Suffolk. Give me a ring!' He handed the piece of paper to Brian.

'Thanks Ben, that extremely kind of you. I might just do that.' They shook hands as the train pulled into Ipswich. Brian spent the remainder of his journey considering his options.

Chapter Twelve

An unexpected letter had arrived for Helen at her Pin Mill address. She studied the postmark and noticed the franking, 'Crean & Berry, Solicitors'. 'What can they possibly want?' she thought to herself. Then she remembered the name. It was the firm who had authorised the administration of McClean's will. She hesitatingly slit open the envelope with the African wood paperknife her long-deceased husband Ken had given to her all those years ago. She withdrew the single sheet of paper from the envelope and read the letter.

Dear Mrs Blake,

We would wish to inform you that the Coroner has now released the body of the late Duncan McClean. Despite our extensive investigations it has not been possible to trace any family members. In consequence we are informed that no funeral arrangements have been made.

As the sole beneficiary of the estate of Duncan McClean you should be aware that his body will be cremated in accordance with the Local Authority's procedures in such circumstances unless you inform us that you wish to instruct Funeral Directors personally.

We invite your response as a matter of some urgency.

Yours Sincerely
pp Crean & Berry

It was almost a month since Jock's murder and Helen realised that apart from assisting with the ongoing investigations being carried out by DI Cartwright and his team, she had barely given him a second thought. She re-read the letter and considered the dilemma which it conveyed. There had been a time when she had been quite fond of Jock. They'd had some good times and lots of laughs up and down the Grand Union on the *Emily Rose*. She picked up the paperknife again and felt the smoothness of the black wood between her fingers. It was quite likely given that they were in the same regiment posted to West Africa that Jock had been with Ken when he bought it. A multitude of memories came flooding back.

She put on her coat and went for a walk along the path at the edge of the river as the tide flooded towards Ipswich. The weak sunshine was barely making its presence felt through the hazy clouds, but Helen's thought processes were keeping the chill at bay. It wasn't long before the grandeur of the Palladian architecture of Woolverstone Hall came into view. Helen had made her decision and turned about to retrace her steps home. Upon arrival she put the kettle on and made a telephone call to a family firm of undertakers. She then took a sheet of writing paper and an envelope from the bureau, made a pot of tea, and sat down to compose her reply to Crean & Berry.

She'd decided she couldn't allow Jock a 'pauper's funeral' and wrote to let the solicitors know of the arrangements she'd made with Grimes & Son for a proper send off.

It was days later that the plain coffin arrived at the crematorium. Helen was the only person in the chapel. She placed a single thistle on the casket, whispered 'Goodbye Jock', and left.

In accordance with the instruction she'd left with the younger Mr Grimes, Jock's ashes were scattered in the cemetery's garden of remembrance.

Chapter Thirteen

For five or six years the Troubles had become a way of life (and death) in Northern Ireland. To a slightly lesser extent the unrest had spilled over the border into the Republic as well. Loyalist paramilitaries and the Ulster Defence Force had begun bombing targets in Dublin. Sectarianism was heightened as a result and recruitment into the IRA increased. Rioting, bombings, gun battles, protest marches, sniper attacks were all rife in the poorer working-class areas of Belfast and Derry and the security forces, the Royal Ulster Constabulary assisted by the British Army were merely exacerbating the situation in their attempts to keep the peace. It had been the Loyalist bombings in Dublin in late 1972 and January 1973 and the subsequent media attention these bombings received which prompted the IRA to take its campaign to England. For the armed struggle in Ireland to succeed the Council of the IRA felt it was necessary to bring the struggle to the 'British Establishment' that it could be witnessed at first hand. When several top IRA leaders were arrested in late 1972, no further convincing to bomb England was required. Detective Chief Superintendent Alex Simons of the Counter Terrorism Unit was in for a busy year.

***

After saying goodbye to Brian O'Connor at Paddington the previous week, Danny McFaddon had made his way to the Alliance where he was expected to meet up with the volunteers from Belfast who had been chosen to form the eleven-man 'active service unit'. Four targets had been selected, the Old Bailey, the Ministry of Agriculture, an army recruitment office in Whitehall and New Scotland Yard. Cars packed with explosives had crossed to England by ferry and were driven to their various targets in the early hours of the morning of Thursday 8th March. Quintessential to the tactics for these hostilities was the timing. All four bombs were set to explode at 3 pm by which time the members of the active service unit would be on their way back to Belfast on prebooked flights from Heathrow. However, Scotland yard had been tipped off by the RUC. In turn the City of London police had been informed and were able to discover and defuse two of the car bombs before the scheduled detonation time. The bombs at the Old Bailey and the Ministry of Agriculture did explode and almost 250 people were injured mostly from flying glass which sliced through crowds which had appeared almost out of the blue to spectate the attacks. The active service unit's planned escape was thwarted however. The police and security services at the airport were on high alert. Surveillance was maximised with all passengers travelling to Dublin or Belfast being thoroughly checked. The bombers were arrested when the names they gave didn't correspond with their travel documents. Danny couldn't believe the ASU's stupidity.

Chapter Fourteen

Brian O'Connor had checked into the Alton House Hotel in Sheringham. He sat on the bed, wrapped in total silence. The realisation that he had cried at some point every day since Gerry's death merely compounded his inconsolability. Was there nothing to ameliorate his grief? In the forlorn hope that reading something might provide his mind with some wandering material he picked up the complimentary *News of The World* the Sunday paper that had arrived with his room-service breakfast. He was expecting celebrity gossip and titillating photos of young women in provocative poses but what he got was an exaggerated headline that almost jumped from the page.

London Devastated by IRA Bombing

*The IRA brought its bombing campaign to the heart
of London yesterday when cars parked outside two key
establishments exploded, killing one man and injuring
244. Most injuries were caused by flying glass which sliced
through busy streets. There would have been more casualties
if the police had not acted on a telephoned warning and
defused two other carbombs. It is thought that the bombs
were planted to mark the referendum being held in
Northern Ireland to determine whether the people want
to remain part of the United Kingdom. Most Catholics
are boycotting the poll but the IRA's actions leave no doubt
about its intention not only to continue its campaign of
violence in Ireland but also to spread it to the mainland.*

Brian threw the paper on to the floor in disgust, his emotions in turmoil. 'What's the feckin' point?' he asked himself. 'And why are the bloody Catholics not voting? Don't they understand we're more likely to change things using the ballot box instead of bloody car bombs?' He grabbed his jacket and slamming the door behind him he stomped angrily out of the hotel and went for a walk in an attempt to get the IRA and Northern Ireland in general out of his head. Most of the shops in the main street were closed, it being a Sunday and out of season. A newsagent's shop was open. He went in and bought pack of Players Navy Cut cigarettes although he'd given up smoking three years previously. He walked slowly onto the promenade. 'Mare Ditat Pinusque Decorat' announced the town's plaque and coat of arms bolted to a lamp-post – 'The Sea Enriches and the Pine Adorns'.

'That's as bloody maybe' he thought to himself. 'So feckin' what?' He lit a cigarette and almost immediately stubbed it out, cursing himself at his stupidity for running the risk of resuming the habit. He really was in the very depths of despair, deeply introspective and battling with the impulse to end his own life somehow, if only he had the courage. Self-pity had smeared black across his art of reasoning.

He was brought back from the brink by the sound of an explosion, but this wasn't a bomb it was a maroon, not that he knew that at the time. Then there came the excited shouts of men running, orders were being given, an engine being started, Sunday morning strollers and dog-walkers turned spectators gathering in groups by a concrete ramp a short distance to the north. Brian walked swiftly in the direction of the clamour and there was a tractor hauling the lifeboat *The Manchester Unity of Oddfellows* on to the beach and towards the breaking line of surf. A team of men in oilskins and lifejackets were about to launch the Oakley Class boat, obviously in response to an SOS. This scene of commitment, of dedication and the urgency with which these men went about their mission completely lifted Brian from his slough of despond and restored his power of rational thought and behaviour. Any notion of suicide was blown away on the freshening north-easterly wind. Brian had been saved by the Sheringham Lifeboat even as it set forth to aid the sinking ship or whatever other disaster it may have been that was unfolding out at sea. Here was a force of men and women intent on saving lives, not ending them.

He and the anxious onlookers stood seemingly mesmerised by the receding sight of the boat until it was barely visible. The tractor had driven back up the beach to the high-water line where it would wait for the lifeboat to return. The crowd gradually drifted away, Brian amongst them. He was mindful of the many similar groups of volunteers all around the coast for whom saving life was their *raison d'etre*. The aims of the RNLI could not have been any more disparate to those of the IRA. He looked at his watch. Mass. He would go to Mass. He asked for directions to the Catholic church and was directed to the somewhat austere-looking building that was St Joseph's. The congregation was fairly sparsely assembled around the church and Brian joined the queue to accept the liturgy of the Eucharist. He returned to his pew, prayed, and left. At least he'd got rid of the black dog he'd been carrying on his shoulders. The sun had made an appearance and the breeze had dropped. This interlude of early spring weather prompted optimism and reasons to be cheerful. This was the beginning of his new life.

Walking back to the hotel he stopped and perused a couple of estate agency windows. There were a few attractive looking properties that his eyes were drawn to but the asking prices at around £18,000 were more than he had been anticipating. Even so he decided he would call in at Watson's the next day and get the details on a small cottage in Somerton, on the coast to the north of Great Yarmouth. From the photograph in Watson's window it looked like the sort of property he had in mind and the location was a bonus, so close to the Norfolk Broads. 'No doubt that why it's expensive,' Brian thought to himself.

Back in his hotel he enjoyed a late lunch, a few drinks and returned to his room. He'd picked up a copy of an East Anglian Tourist Guide from reception, the same one he'd looked at when he was in the Victoria Hotel in Lowestoft. He lay on the bed and thought back over the events that had taken him to Lowestoft in the first place and those which had happened since. They now seemed like an age ago and he consigned them to the deepest recesses of his memory. He re-read the Guide, but it was as though he was seeing it for the first time. It wasn't long before he fell into a dreamless sleep. When he awoke he switched on the television. *Dad's Army* was just beginning. He found himself laughing at the pompous antics of Captain Mainwaring and his platoon but more from a perspective of the British Army making a fool of itself rather than the silliness of the home-guard. Private Walker, the comedic 'spiv' was particularly amusing and put him vaguely in mind of Jock McClean but in a much less sinister way. He freshened up and went down to dinner.

Chapter Fifteen

Maisie Clarke had moved on to *Ironside* and was settling in and becoming familiar with life on board a boat. For all that it didn't go anywhere, it was still a boat and twice a day it floated. When the tide was up the motion and the accompanying sounds and sensations of her home being on the move were gradually becoming more familiar but she didn't think she'd ever get used to the whistling of the wind in the rigging of nearby sailing vessels and yachts. And, when there was anything stronger than a gentle breeze the rattle of halyards on masts was something of an irritation as well. Even so, *Ironside* was now her home and she was very happy in it. Her neighbour Colin Smith on *Mary Gloster* was a great help to her. She took comfort in the knowledge that he was there, a real gentleman and very much 'hands-on' when it came to anything that needing fixing. It was also reassuring that he knew about the idiosyncrasies of houseboats and his presence certainly took a weight off Maisie's mind knowing that she could call upon him whenever she needed assistance, guidance, or just someone to talk to. Only some fifty or sixty yards away from the quay was the railway station which was handy and across the road was the Anchor, the pub where she could eat whenever she was disinclined to cook for herself. Life was good for Maisie, but it wouldn't be long before her situation took a turn for the worse.

It was Saturday morning. Maisie was up early and the day looked promising with hardly a cloud in the sky. The sunshine was pleasantly warm and sufficiently so to allow breakfast to be taken quite comfortably sitting in *Ironside*'s cockpit. As always, Colin was up and about and tinkering with something or other on

Mary Gloster. After breakfast Masie decided to take a walk down the river wall. The tide was out and there were several species of wading birds on the expanse of mud revealed by the low water. Her gentle stroll took her towards the creek at Kirton where she stood and watched some children rigging a dinghy and making ready to go sailing when the tide turned. After a while of idly enjoying her new surroundings her attention was drawn to the distant chime of the bells from the imposing tower of the church of St Mary the Virgin. She checked her watch. Ten o'clock – time to walk back and as she did so, at more of a purposeful pace, Maisie resolved to find herself a job. When she arrived back at the quay it was Colin who announced, 'You've had a visitor!'

'Who?' Maisie was so curious that it was abundantly clear from the spontaneity of her question that it hadn't occurred to her that her neighbour would have no idea who.

'He didn't say – I think he left you note.' 'He?' wondered Maisie. 'Who could it have been?' She hurried aboard *Ironside* and sure enough, there was an envelope wedged between the companionway doors. She took it below and put the kettle on. She opened the envelope and withdrew the single sheet of paper upon which was a scrawled handwritten message.

"I got your address from your probation officer. Meet me in the Anchor at mid-day. We need to talk."

The note was signed 'Graham'. Maisie's buoyant mood was suddenly deflated. Graham was her ex-husband. As far as Maisie was concerned he was most definitely her ex-husband although technically she supposed, they were still married. She hadn't seen him since going to prison. He hadn't made contact or visited during her imprisonment so what could he possibly want now? She went to the telephone box at the railway station and called Hazel for her advice.'

'You'd better go and meet him or he'll keep bothering or threatening you until you do. Look, I'll come with you if you like. I can be there in an hour.'

At 11.45 Helen arrived on the quay. She'd parked her Mercedes in the station carpark, and together they went to the pub. There were a few early drinkers in the bar, picking out the winners from the racing pages of their morning papers. Standing at the bar was a figure which Maisie thought she recognised. Together, Maisie and Helen went and stood beside him. As the man turned to face them Helen saw the full horror of his disfigurement, the scarred tissue of his badly burned face. She tried not to stare. He spoke.

'Hello Mais', how you bin? Yo' lookin' well.'

'Hello Graham. This is my friend Helen. We were inside together – cellmates.'

Helen offered to shake his hand but was repulsed by the deformity and mutilation of the hand he offered in return. Helen was embarrassed by her inability to look at him.

'Pretty ain't I? This is what my darlin' wife did to me.'

'What do you want Graham? What is it after all this time?' Maisie spat the questions out.

'Compersation. I want compersation.'

'Well, you're not getting any from me.' Maisie responded through gritted teeth. And turned away. Helen noticed the barman and a few locals distracted from the *Sporting Life* taking an interest in this situation in real life.

'Look, let's not make a scene here in public.' Helen suggested. 'There's a table over there. Let's discuss this quietly and calmly.' They took their drinks over to the table and sat down.

'I bin' an' seen a s'licita. 'Cos I reckons I'm 'titled to compensation for pain, sufferin' an' distress an' all 'cos o' my inj'ries.' Helen responded on Maisie's behalf.

'Well, Mr Clarke, go to your solicitor and tell him to file a claim in the County Court.' Her experience from having worked in a solicitors' office albeit limited would be, she hoped, sufficiently intimidating to put him off. 'If you are asserting a right to a remedy for your injuries, for trauma or distress or anything else, file a claim in court. Should you do so, Maisie will defend it most vigorously with a counterclaim for damages against you for the controlling, coercive, threatening, degrading and violent behaviour you inflicted upon her during your marriage. We'll see you in court.' Helen's forthright statement was awe-inspiringly vehement. Graham was visibly taken aback and he made no verbal response. He picked up his pint and downed it in one. Angrily he pushed back on his chair and stood up knocking the chair over in the process. As he made for the door, he turned and stabbed the forefinger of his withered hand directly at Helen. He was clearly rattled having previously reckoned that Maisie would have been a pushover.

'Should a knowed they cages bitches together. Youse'll be 'earin' from my s'licita.' It was a threat issued with venom. Full of vindictive spite he barged out of the pub slamming the door behind him prompting a smattering of applause from the other end of the bar.

'Crikey Helen, that was bloody marvellous. Where'd you learn all that? I am well impressed.' With a decelerating heart rate, Helen sipped her gin and tonic and smiled at her friend.

Chapter Sixteen

Detective Inspector Cartwright sat in his office in the Thames Valley Police Force's headquarters in Kidlington. He was agitatedly twiddling a pencil between his fingers.

'What's eating you guv?' It was Ray Davies, Cartwright's DC who had just entered the office carrying a file with him. He dropped it onto Cartwright's desk. Davies had worked with Cartwright for long enough now to know when something was bothering his boss. The DI looked up at the DC and with an expression that asked, 'Did I miss anything?'

Davies said, 'I've been through everything we've got guv – I've studied it all again twice, cross-referenced times, dates, places, the statements everything. If we have missed anything I'm buggered if I can spot it.' Cartwright always knew that if there were further clues they would inevitably lead back to what they already knew – or thought they knew. Interrogating Helen or Ben Blake was going too far and he was reluctant to follow that particular course. He sank back into his chair in an attitude of submission.

'So, Jock McClean, the bloody bane of our existence for so long, is on the slab with a bullet in his head except the pathologist has since removed it by now,' he smiled before continuing. 'Forensics have confirmed that the bullet is the same calibre as the one that killed Colin Harvey in the Foxton ambush, and there's little if any doubt it was fired from the same weapon. The Deputy Commissioner is now on my back as well as DCS Simons wanting to know why we're not doing anything to find the killer. We don't care who killed McClean. Good bloody riddance. But stirring up the IRA – be like stirring up a hornets' nest, a real can of bloody worms except these worms are vipers. I know that, you know that, and DS Armstrong knows that. Even then I doubt we'll find the sniper. It's as close to a bloody lost cause we're ever likely to encounter. What's more I've given my word and feel morally obliged to trying to protect Helen Blake. Why are we doing that?' He'd intended the question to be rhetorical but Ray Davies answered.

'Because she's an attractive wealthy woman, single and available, and you fancy her.' The minute he'd said it, he realised that perhaps he was being too familiar and should have been less vocal with what he had been thinking. He mentally prepared himself for a rebuke. But rebuke came there none.

'You're not wrong Ray. But there's more to it than that. Helen Blake is one of McClean's victims and she has done the time for his crime. She might have been complicit in some way with the black-market rackets years ago but she's no murderer and had nothing to do with the Colin Harvey shooting. I think we all know that was an IRA killing. I'll bet my pension Colin Harvey was murdered by the same gunman who executed McClean. Whoever he is he's clearly an expert marksman, ex-military sniper I shouldn't wonder given the accuracy of the shots from one hell-of-a-distance in both cases. We start digging about and Pandora's Box is a picnic basket by comparison. When we start lifting members of the IRA there'll be more bombings, more reprisals, and more injuries, even fatalities amongst civilians, members of the general public, innocent bystanders. You only have to look at what happened last Thursday. I'm telling you; we're buggered if we do, and we buggered if we don't.'

Notwithstanding the time of day, 11 am, Cartwright reached for the filing cabinet drawer, the one where he kept the scotch. Ever since he'd joined CID he'd kept a bottle stashed away, maintaining that a 'snifter' helped his thought processes in tricky moments. He poured two measures and passed one to his junior. After a respectable period of savouring his favourite single malt Cartwright noticed that Davies sat nursing his glass and merely taking an occasional sniff of its content.

'C'mon Ray, drink up. Nectar from the highlands this, taste that aroma of peat and burnt oak!'

'What's it called?'

'This is Laphroaig, distilled using water from the Kilbride Stream on the Isle of Islay,' he answered proudly.

'Aye, well so it might be,' responded the DC imitating a Scots accent, 'but it smells like Robbie Burns' underpants!' The two colleagues burst into fits of laughter only to be interrupted by the telephone ringing.

'Cartwright.'

'Sorry to bother you guv…'

'No bother Doug.' Cartwright had instantly recognised DS Armstrong's voice. 'What's up?'

'We have to follow this up you know. OK, so the murder of McClean might have saved the taxpayer and us a lot of time and money, and it was nothing more or less than he deserved. But collaring the murderer, in all probability the same guy responsible for shooting PC Harvey in the Foxton ambush, well that's a different matter. It's been worrying me sick, and I've had Simons chewing my ear off. I know it'll involve the Blakes which we said we wouldn't and I realise that if we start pulling members of the IRA we could well provoke unrest, even more terrorism…' Armstrong paused for breath.

'You're absolutely right Doug. Don't go beating yourself up over this. Ray and I have just been going over the situation and on reflection we agree with you. You're absolutely right. We have to do what we have to do.' Armstrong knew his DI too well and saw an opportunity for kidding his boss. In his West Country drawl he enquired, 'You been at the bottle again guv?'

'Well, you know what Oscar Wilde said?'

'I expect I will in a minute.'

'"We're all in the gutter, but some of us are looking at the stars." Bit like this case isn't it? We're in the bloody gutter right enough at the moment but after a wee dram of the Laphroaig, we'll be looking at the stars all right. We'll find him.' The DI's positivity was motivational. Cartwright drained his glass, and his DC's.

'OK, Ray, tell Andy Lewis seven o'clock Sunday morning, in civvies. We're all going to East Anglia. Did you get all that Doug?'

'OK guv, at least it'll get me out of having to visit the mother-in-law.'

The telephone call was terminated.

Chapter Seventeen

So it was that at 6.45 am on Sunday 18th March PC Andy Lewis had the unmarked Capri waiting outside the main entrance at Kidlington police station, the headquarters of Thames Constabulary. There was a hint of spring in the air and the daffodils in the ornamental tubs were just about to flower. The three detectives were prompt and by seven o'clock the car was on its way. In 1973 routes between the north and south were fairly well developed but those between west and east were very much the poor relation and the trip to Suffolk was far from straightforward. Even so, PC Lewis, the consummate police traffic officer and advanced driver was familiar with the itinerary having driven to Orford only a few weeks earlier. Cartwright had purposefully chosen to make the trip on a Sunday in the belief that there would be a far better chance of those he wanted to interview being at home. Pin Mill, just outside Ipswich was the first intended stop, the home of Helen Blake.

It was getting on for lunchtime by the time they arrived, the journey having been hampered by 'bloody Sunday drivers' enjoying the sunshine. Cartwright was thinking that they'd have made better time in a marked car. Lewis stood by the car as the others went off to find Helen Blake's rented cottage, which they soon located. Even Cartwright had to admit that the setting was idyllic. Davies knocked on the cottage door. No reply. Then, after barely thirty seconds, Helen appeared from around the back. For all that she was casually dressed for a Sunday, in jeans, red flat shoes with a pink sweater over a white blouse, Cartwright's heart skipped a beat before it began to race.

'Why, it's Inspector Cartwright. What a pleasant surprise – at least I hope it is.'

'Morning Miss Blake,'

'That should be Mrs but never mind. Helen, please,' she requested. 'What brings you all the way here on a Sunday?'

'I think you might know. We're investigating a fatal shooting on Havergate Island on Wednesday 31st January. We have reason to believe you were the last person to see the victim alive.'

'Oh come on Inspector!' Helen found the formality somewhat offensive. 'You know only too well that I was. Anyway, I thought I was off the hook, or so you implied.'

'Yes I know, and I sincerely apologise, but I'm under pressure from my superiors. A man was murdered and we believe the murderer was also responsible for the death of one of our colleagues at the beginning of this year. Now is there somewhere we can talk or do we have to stand here...? Helen interrupted the question.

'Yes of course. Excuse my lack of...' This time it was Cartwright's turn to interrupt.

'Of course, of course... no need to...' The conversation was taking on an air of embarrassment as was all too apparent from the manner in which Armstrong and Davies were attempting to distance themselves from the dialogue.

'Please come in. I'll put the kettle on. It'll be a bit cramped, but we can squeeze...'

'If only!' Cartwright was thinking, his cheeks reddening.

The cottage's sitting room was 'bijou' and furnished in that chintzy cottage sort of style. The three detectives sat on a two-seater sofa, the embarrassment becoming awkward as Helen busied herself in the kitchen. She delivered a tray with mugs of coffee, a bottle of milk and sugar bowl and placed it on the occasional table.

'It's only instant, I'm afraid, do help yourselves – are you sure you're comfortable there?' Armstrong took the lead.

'We know about the Christmas card. We know you felt McClean was a menace with evil intentions. What we can't work out is why you then took it upon yourself to arrange a secret liaison in an isolated place with the man you considered to be a threat. How did you make contact with him? Why did you make contact with him? What was it all about?'

Helen sat in her armchair nervously fiddling with her handkerchief. 'Look Sergeant, Inspector, I'll be absolutely and entirely honest with you. You know Jock McClean got involved with the IRA when he turned up in Belfast. He lived with a woman Maggie O'Rourke – I think she died in that accident he caused. Anyway, Maggie's son Tom sent a letter from Jock to my in-law's Ben's grandparents' address in Leicestershire. How he got the address, well, you'll have to ask him. The letter was written in 1965 – it must have been after I saw him for the last time – well I thought it was the last time. In the letter, he confessed to several murders and asked me to marry him.' She was about to mention the will but instantly changed her mind. Whatever she had inherited had no bearing on the murder. 'I was going to give it to you, the letter,' she continued, 'but Albert, my father-in-law suggested I should hang on to it as a "weapon and a shield" I think he called it. After all it did contain a signed confession.'

'Have you still got it, the letter?'

'Yes, I think so, but it's not here, it's at the cottage in Burton Overy.'

'We'll need to see this – critical piece of evidence this is.'

'Yes of course.'

Cartwright resumed the interrogation but very gently and with impeccable manners.

'So, you sent a reply did you? How'd you know where to send it?'

'Well, this Irish bloke, turned up at the in-laws' house asking for me. Mabel, my mother-in-law, bless her, told him about my cottage in Burton. It's only a small village as you know, but when he got there he called at Jamie's pub, the Old Greyhound to ask for directions. Coincidentally, Jamie, my son's best friend, and Ben, my son, were both there. Ben, bless him, tried to protect me and wouldn't let on where my cottage was. I think it must have been then that the Irishman came up with a proposition which he said would be to our mutual advantage.'

'Who was this Irishman?' I think you know. Jamie told you when you were here last month.

'Yes so he did! McFaddon, Danny McFaddon – that was it wasn't it? But how did you know how to contact him, Jock, McClean?'

'Ben got in touch with Fred – you know Fred Webb, the lockkeeper at Foxton?'

'Oh yes we know all about Fred – wily old bugger that he is.'

She continued the tale.

'Well, it seems Jock had written to Fred about his car, his Porsche. It was parked at Foxton but you, the police that is, were watching it so he transferred the ownership to some bargee or other, Wally somebody. That's how we discovered where he was, Jock. So, Ben and Jamie got me to write to him and suggest we meet up – you know the rest, you've probably got my letter.'

'Yes we have. Now Helen, think very very carefully before you reply to my next question. The IRA is involved in all of this and you will be well aware of the atrocities of which they are capable. Did you know the detail of the plan, what lay in store for McClean when he got to the island?'

'The detail...?' There was a drawn-out silence before Helen responded.

'No I did not! Not the detail.' The response was emphatic. As if by copper's instinct Armstrong waded in deploying the 'bad cop, good cop' routine. In a tone more aggressive than avuncular he demanded to know. 'So, if you are telling us that you had no idea that he was going to be shot, assassinated, I don't believe you.' Helen began to cry.

'No. I promise I didn't know,' she sobbed.

'What were you expecting to happen? A bloody tea-party? A picnic with members of the IRA perhaps?'

'No, I don't know. I said, I don't know!' The weeping intensified.

'Steady on Doug, there's no need for that. Ray, go and get Helen a glass of water.' Helen's sobbing subsided and she wiped her eyes with her handkerchief.

'Who shot Jock, Helen? Was it McFaddon?' Cartwright smiled as he attempted to coax an answer.

'I really, really don't know. When the shot came I was as surprised as Jock was.'

'OK, OK, it's all right, we're done here. Now, Helen, we're going to need that letter the one from Jock from 1965.'

Davies and Armstrong got up to go.

'You carry on guys; I'll be right there.' He turned to Helen again. 'Helen,' he asked as gently as he knew how, 'will Ben be at home? We need to take an official statement.'

Cartwright, put an arm around Helen's shoulders. She turned to face him and what he had intended to be a gesture of friendship and understanding became a much closer physical contact and her lips brushed against his cheek.

Chapter Eighteen

The drive from Pin Mill to Orford was no less tortuous than the one from Oxfordshire to Suffolk. Cartwright suggested that the others attempt to get some lunch in the Jolly Sailor whilst he called on Ben and Tina at Lobster Pot Cottage. Cartwright didn't ask questions. He merely requested a detailed statement which, from Ben's perspective described the series of events which lead to the assassination of McClean. No more or less than the Inspector had expected, Ben confirmed every detail of what his mother had said a few hours earlier without any prompting. There was no doubt in Cartwright's mind that what Ben had told him was the truth and the whole truth at that.

'Are you certain you've left nothing out, you've remembered every detail?' Ben scratched his head as Tina whispered something in his ear.

'There's one thing but I don't know that it will help.'

'Try me!'

'For the few weeks before he died – before he was murdered – McClean was living on a houseboat in Woodbridge.'

'Woodbridge? The Woodbridge just down the road from here?'

'Yes sir, that's right. A boat called *Ironside*. There might be some clues there, but I doubt it. Coincidentally, it's let to a friend of my mother's now, Maisie someone. Don't remember her surname, but she and mum were in prison together.

'Mmm, interesting, but I guess you're right.' Cartwright smiled as he thought about this piece of information. 'I agree. It's hardly likely that we'll find any clues there. Still, we'll go and take a look.'

DI Cartwright didn't like or believe in coincidences. He apologised for interrupting the Blakes' Sunday and left to join his colleagues in the Jolly Sailor. If only he had known that not so many miles to the north in the next county the assassin they were under so much pressure to apprehend was sitting where he had been for the last week in his room at the Alton House Hotel in Sheringham, Norfolk.

***

Cartwright caught up with his colleagues in the pub and after a swift pint for himself they left Orford Quay and proceeded to Woodbridge Quay and the houseboat *Ironside*. The DI explained why they were making the detour.

'It was McClean's last known abode before he was lured to his death. You never know, there might be something. Apparently, according to Ben Blake, the houseboat has a new tenant, Maisie somebody or other. Now here's an enigma for those who like puzzles. This Maisie somebody was in prison with Helen Blake. Coincidence or what? And you know how I feel about bloody coincidences!'

Sitting beside his DI in the back of the Capri, the colour had drained from DS Armstrong's face.

'You OK Doug?'

'Yeah, it's nothing guv. All the travelling, the early start and no breakfast. You know.'

It was dark by the time they got to Woodbridge. Andy Lewis parked the car in the railway station car park. This time he joined the detectives as they went for a walk around the quay in search of *Ironside*. A cheery voice hailed them from another houseboat.

'You blokes lost? Can I help you?'

'We're looking for Maisie.' The minute he'd said it Ray Davies wished he'd kept his mouth shut. It gave the impression that they were looking for a woman of easy virtue.

'On the houseboat *Ironside*,' clarified Lewis.

'Well, you've found the boat, right here next door to me. But I reckon you're out of luck. I saw Maisie go out a little while ago. I think she goes to church on Sundays. I'm Colin Smith by the way. You could wait.' Smith suggested. 'The Anchor should be open. Nice pint in there. I'm popping over myself.'

'Maybe we will, thanks Colin.'

DS Armstrong was looking distinctly uncomfortable.

'Must we guv? If it's who I think it might be, I know her, Maisie, and I'd rather not have anything to do with her.'

Cartwright was somewhat taken aback. This was not the attitude he'd come to expect from his DS. Armstrong was a committed and dedicated detective who'd leave no stone unturned in a quest for clues. The pub sign lit up and the front door opened as they crossed the road. They sat at a table at the far end of the saloon and Lewis went to the bar to order the drinks. A few minutes later Colin Smith came in.

'Usual Colin?'

'Yes please Sid.' Looking around and seeing the group of four, Colin walked over to their table.

'Mind if I join you?

'No, please.' Cartwright introduced himself and his colleagues. 'We're policemen investigating a murder on Havergate Island at the end of January.'

'Oh really? I read about it. I guess that must be why you're looking for *Ironside*. That's where he lived for a time – you know, Jock, the murdered bloke? Do you want me to make a statement? I was his neighbour.' For Colin, this was obviously one of the most, if not the most exciting thing that had ever happened.

'No, I don't think we need a statement Colin. We'd just like to have a quick look around *Ironside*. See if he left any clues although I don't suppose there'll be anything of any use since Maisie moved aboard. Do you know her surname? We only know her as Maisie.' Colin thought for a moment.

'Clarke, I reckon. Yeah that's it, Clarke.' It was mention of the name that caused Armstrong to knock his beer over.

'Bloody hell Doug, c'mon man, pull yourself together. Whatever is wrong with you?'

'Sorry guv. I know her. Her previous surname was Armstrong. She's my ex-wife!'

There was a stunned silence.

'How can you be so sure?'

'Maisie? Ex-con with Helen Blake? Surname Clarke? Give me some credit guvnor. I am a bloody detective after all.' Davies sat there, incredulous with his mouth wide open in disbelief.

Fresh beers were ordered and the DS related how he'd divorced his wife when he discovered she'd been having an affair with Graham Clarke, who she subsequently married and more than likely regretted it. He continued by describing how the abuse she suffered led to the GBH charge, Graham Clarke's disfigurement, and Maisie ending up in prison.

'Blimey! Better than the telly this is.' Colin was having his best night out in ages. 'He was here you know!'

'Who was?' queried Cartwright.

'Your man, Graham Clarke.'

'When?'

'Yesterday lunchtime. Ask Sid. Had to be him with the scars an' all. He and Maisie had a right ruckus, but he got short shrift from Maisie's friend, the woman who was with her. I reckon she must be the new owner of the *Ironside* and from the way she spoke I would guess she must be a lawyer; you know from what she said to him about seeing him in court.'

'Can you describe her?'

'Who? Maisie?' Cartwright was getting exasperated now.

'No, you fool, sorry Colin, the other woman, the one you thought was a lawyer.' After his description, Cartwright and Davies looked at each other and spoke in unison, 'Helen Blake!'

'I hate bloody coincidences!'

Chapter Nineteen

On the drive back to Kidlington, Lewis was humming quietly to himself. Davies sat alongside him in the front of the Capri, fast asleep. Neither the DI nor the DS in the back spoke until they were almost at St Albans on the A414.

'Sorry about all that nonsense back there guv. The prospect of seeing my ex-wife again after, what, it must be fifteen years, touched a bit of a nerve.' The DI looked at his friend and colleague with sympathetic eyes belying his curiosity.

'Obviously I knew you'd been married and divorced. Do you want to talk about it? What were the circumstances? Was it hard, painful?'

''Fraid so, couple of years after the war. Maisie was much younger than me and I was smitten, infatuated and impulsive. She wasn't ready for marriage and what with her gorgeous good looks, and me a young PC often on nights I suppose it was inevitable that she'd be playing away before too long. After the divorce – I filed against her for adultery, and she didn't contest it – I left Taunton and got a transfer to Oxford. I heard she got remarried to the bloke she been playing away with. Scout master he was, believe it or not. Goodness knows what went wrong for him to turn to the booze, lose his job, his respect and start beating up his wife. I'd heard a rumour that he'd been "interfering" if you get what I mean, you know, DYB DYB DOB DOB, want to play with my woggle, sort of thing. Anyway, he was taking it out on Maisie and when she did what she did to get her own back she was charged with GBH. I even offered to appear on her behalf as a character witness, not that

I was called. I suppose I'd quite like to see her again, because I guess I never really stopped loving her. With her appearing on the scene out of the blue – well it's all been such a surprise.'

'I can well imagine. If you ever want to talk about it… anyway, look, I apologise for wasting your Sunday. We're no better off really. Nothing new although I'm intrigued by the fact that Helen saw fit not to tell us that she acquired the houseboat where Jock had been living. I don't think it was an oversight on her part either. She's holding something back. What d'you reckon?'

'I reckon you're right guv.' Armstrong winked as he added, 'I reckon you should pay her another visit.' Cartwright blushed. 'I reckon I will.'

***

In Pin Mill, that same evening, Helen was now reading having spent some considerable time on the telephone to Ben, comparing and contrasting how their respective meetings with the police had gone. She knew only too well that Ben would have told the truth right down to the last letter and consequently there would have been no discrepancies in their statements. Helen was finding it all but impossible to concentrate on her novel *The Princess Bride* by William Goldman. Somehow she knew that Cartwright would be back again. She couldn't put him out of her mind and was hoping that when he did come again it would be for the very same reason that she wanted him to.

***

The next morning the last thing Cartwright wanted was a call from DCS Simons demanding to know what progress, if any, had been made since his last call.

'Well sir, we visited Helen Blake and her son again, interviewed them separately, independently in their own homes. Their "stories" are identical in every detail and we have no fresh evidence to go on as yet.'

'What do you mean as yet? How much longer do you need? How many more months do we have to wait? Maybe I should put someone else in charge of this investigation. Strikes me you're bloody useless Cartwright – no better than you were on the bloody Limehouse Basin Fiasco – speaking of which I hope you're on top of that particular cock up – the date's been set for the trial – can't remember the exact… early May sometime. So, what are you doing next? What's your next abortive line of time-wasting enquiry going to be? Eh? Speak up man!' Cartwright really wanted to tell the DCS to piss off and let him get on with the job, but he remained calm and in control.

'With respect sir, I've discovered that there's a letter – a letter from McClean to Helen Blake which possibly prompted the plan which led to his murder. I should have this letter within the next couple of days. I'm also sending DS Armstrong–' Simons barked down the phone, 'Armstrong? Another useless waste of bloody space…!

'Look sir, you know as well as I that this case is a real turd. In my experience you can't get a shine on a turd but we're trying our best.'

'Well, your best isn't good enough is it eh? We'll put you in charge of turd polishing instead, what? Eh? Now get on with it and stop buggering about swanning around East Anglia!' The phone went dead. Cartwright was incensed by the Detective Chief Superintendent's disapprobation of himself and of his team's efforts to the extent that the DI completely lost his customary indifference to his superior's remarks. Ordinarily he would give the DCS the benefit of the doubt by accepting his criticism as inappropriately framed expressions of encouragement and motivation. This however was too much and with an odious animosity he let rip whilst giving two fingers to the phone.

'You pompous arsehole – you pile of steaming excrement!'

'You called sir?' DC Ray Davies, in the next room, heard the vociferous proclamations and on entering his guvnor's office almost immediately restored Cartwright's good humour.

'Not you, you daftie!' A couple of seconds passed and they were both laughing.

'Well, don't just stand there giggling go and get us both some coffee – please!'

They discussed the previous day's lack of any real development and how it might be redressed. They needed sight of McClean's letter to Helen. If that could be traced back with any certainty, it could lead them to McFaddon. It could be McFaddon that held the key to the identity of the killer. Also troubling Cartwright was Helen's failure to mention *Ironside* and how she'd come about owning Jock's former residence. He had also determined that a fresh tack was needed. There could be no reasonable doubt that whoever shot McClean was also responsible for the shooting of PC Colin Harvey. Cartwright didn't accept Simons' assessment and description of the action at Limehouse Basin as a 'fiasco'. Certainly it hadn't gone to plan but It was highly likely that the members of the IRA involved in the incident and currently on remand in Brixton Prison might provide an insight.

'OK here's where we go. Ray, get on your bike and get yourself to Burton Overy. Interview Jamie Webster again and keep your eyes off his wife whilst you're at it. See if he can give us any more than Ben did yesterday.'

'OK guv, always happy to catch a glimpse of the lovely Diane. What will you be doing?'

'Well first I'll give Doug a call. He can go to Brixton and have a word with... what was his name?... Doyle. Michael Doyle. I'm fairly certain he led the Foxton ambush and if anyone knows the identity of the sniper, he does. I'm going back to Pin Mill.

'Thought you might!'

Chapter Twenty

Back in the day Thorpeness had been a small fishing community situated at a spot on the Suffolk coast. According to folklore, it was a preferred route into East Anglia favoured by smugglers. The village had since been developed in the early twentieth century by Glencairn Stuart Ogilvie. Ogilvie had made a fortune developing railways all over the world and he bought up a significantly sizeable piece of Suffolk including Thorpeness which he then regenerated into a private fantasy seaside holiday village. Be that as it may, it wasn't uppermost in the minds of the crew of the small trawler just a few nautical miles off the coast. *Harbour Lights* with skipper Maurice Read and deckhand, Matthew, his nephew, were hauling their net. It would be the last haul on what had been a not particularly bountiful day. It was always a risky business trawling in this stretch of water given the numerous wrecks littering the bottom not least of which was the *SS Magdapur* a cargo ship which struck a mine and sank in 1941, the wreck that he'd been dragging his net around for the last five hours. The last thing any skipper needed was to get his nets snagged on a submerged wreck or some other piece of maritime scrap. But the fishing had been poor on the regular East Lane grounds and Maurice had decided to take his chances a little further north. The hydraulic winch began to slowly wind in the wires and the trawl-doors clattered alongside the boat's quarters. Then as the bridles attached to the headline floats and the ground rope broke the surface the green mesh of the net became visible. For Matt, this was always the exciting part. The winch began to groan, the wire as taut as a piano string and the net bagged around whatever it was that had been scraped up from the seabed. Maurice applied the brakes to the winch and went to assist Matt pull the net inboard from where it hung suspended from the gantry at the stern of the boat. Pulling on the rope which tied the cod-end together, the catch spilled onto the deck. It was probably the best haul of the day. Skate, plaice, Dover soles, crabs, miscellaneous small shellfish, sea urchins, weed and – a golf bag.

'Well now, I'll be a-buggered!' exclaimed Maurice. 'I've hauled up some junk in me time, but this takes the biscuit eh lad?' Matt and his uncle busied themselves sorting fish into boxes. Then the deck was washed down and the undersized fish and unwanted stuff thrown back. Maurice returned to the wheelhouse and set the autopilot on a course back to the hamlet of Felixstowe Ferry, *Harbour Lights*' home port.

'What'll us do wi' the golf bag unc'?' asked Matthew.

'Well now, let's be 'avin' a look.' Matt filled a bucket with saltwater and gave the bag a swabbing down. 'Shame there ain't no clubs wi' it. Alus fancied playin' golf. Bag 'tain't bin in the sea for long by the look on it.'

'What's this then?' Matt had inverted the bag and as the mud and silt emptied on to the deck, the muzzle and barrel of a rifle began to slide out until the whole thing fell on to the deck.

'Bloody 'ell!' Matthew went to pick the weapon up. 'You tek care there lad, it might be loaded.'

For the rest of the trip home, Matthew sat on an upturned bucket cleaning the gun with fresh water, as advised by his uncle, and then drying it off with an old tea-towel. He proudly presented it to Maurice when he was satisfied with his efforts. Maurice was in the wheelhouse eating a corned beef sandwich whilst waiting for the kettle to boil.

'Look 'ere,' instructed Maurice, as he pointed to the engraved plate on the stock. 'Says 'ere it's a Remington M21A. An' look. telescopic sight an' all. Proper bit a kit this, 'ang on, what's this, look, serial number's bin filed off.'

'But what'll us do wi' it unc'?

'Dunno lad. I'll think a summat, I reckon.' A few moments later he added, 'Best say nowt about it lad. I reckon we should keep it secret.'

'OK unc' – can I 'ave me wages now please?' Maurice reached inside his oilskins into his trouser pocket. ''Ere y'are then Matt – three quid for the fishin' and an extra two for sayin' nowt about golf bag.' He tapped the side of his nose with his forefinger to imply confidentiality as he handed his nephew a £5 note.

Later that day with his fish gutted, packed in ice and in the cold-store, Maurice locked away the unexpected catch-of-the-day in his shed and went to the Ferryboat Inn as did most of the fishermen at the end of their working day. As they sat with their beers around the big table which Kevin the landlord always reserved for them, the talk followed the normal agenda of who caught what and where and the prices being fetched at the Lowestoft Fish Market auction. Notwithstanding his and Matt's 'secret', when Maurice announced how there had been an unexpected item in his last haul of the day, everyone around the table became hushed as they all listened intently to the tale of the golf bag.

'What'll you do wi' it?' asked one.

'Dunno mate. I'll think a summat, I reckon.'

'I reckons 'ow you should 'and it in at police station,' said another.

'Dunno, mate, I reckon mebe!'

'I reckon p'raps you could sell the bag to somebody at golf club?' suggested a third.

'If you hauled close to *Magdapur* it were prob'ly lost overboard somewhere to north off Lowestoft or Yarmouth and come down on longshore drift I reckon.' Fishermen did a great deal of reckoning. The suggestions kept coming, as did the beer and when closing time came, the only thing Maurice could be certain of was that the Remington and the golf bag would be hot gossip in and around the locality for the next few days. He was beginning to wish he hadn't mentioned it. When he finally got to bed, and for all that he was tired, he couldn't sleep for worrying about the rifle. 'I just knows it's going to be a problem. It'll cause trouble. I can feel it in me water!' he said to himself.

Chapter Twenty-One

A few days prior to the golf bag 'resurfacing' Brian O'Connor had woken on 13th March feeling better than he had in a long time. His room in the Alton House Hotel had proved to be most comfortable and he had slept soundly. He'd showered and dressed and gone down to the dining room for breakfast.

'Today' he told himself, 'is the first day of my "new" life. And whilst the death of my best friend is still on my mind I'll try not to let it dampen my mood.' Brian was feeling more positive than he had for a month. There were opportunities in abundance, places to go, people to meet, things to see and do. His past life was just that – past. Firmly in the past. He made a mental note to return to St Joseph's. Confession and the formal remission of his sins pronounced by the priest in the sacrament of penance. Whilst he wasn't particularly overburdened with guilt, to be absolved would surely set him on the straight and narrow for the rest of his days. But first, Watson's Estate Agency. He stepped out of the hotel and was greeted by that freshness in the air that one can only experience on the coast. Spring could not be too far away. The sun was shining. 'Think positively!' Brian instructed himself.

He couldn't have been out of school very long, the young man behind the desk in Watson's. Still, he was most obliging and better still he had a car and offered to drive him to inspect the property in Somerton; the cottage which Brian had noticed in the agency's window the previous day. The twin villages of East and West Somerton were pretty enough but the property was disappointing; damp, run down and requiring extensive repairs and refurbishment. Brian had absolutely no inclination towards DIY – in fact as far as he was concerned this particular household initialism stood for 'don't involve yourself' and he didn't intend to either. Neither was it his intension to spend money unnecessarily over and above the asking price to commission builders to make a place habitable. So, whilst this initial quest to find a place to spend the rest of his days hadn't lived up to expectations, Brian remained optimistic. After all, he told himself, there would bound to be a property in a location to satisfy every aspect of his self-imposed criteria. Back in Sheringham a billboard outside the newsagent's shop proclaimed, *'Lifeboat launched in Lightship emergency'*. Out of interest, Brian bought a copy of the *Eastern Daily Press* and read the article which reported the excitement he had witnessed the previous morning. Apparently, a member of the crew of Trinity House's *Dudgeon Light Vessel* had required emergency medical treatment and Sheringham's Oakley Class lifeboat had been launched to effect an evacuation. The article went on to extol the courage of the crew and the virtues of local hero, Henry 'Joyful' West, the lifeboat's coxswain.

It was approaching lunchtime and Brian decided a couple of pints might be in order. He walked down the High Street to the sea front and found The Crown public house on Lifeboat Plain. With an ample selection of local ales, he was spoilt for choice. He could get used to this kind of lifestyle. After an afternoon snooze back at the Alton House Hotel he finished reading his newspaper and decided he'd 'done' Sheringham and that maybe it wasn't for him. It was time to move on. He'd check out of the hotel tomorrow and resume his search for his own personal Shangri-la elsewhere. For all that his first attempt at East Anglian house-hunting had been frustrating he was far from downhearted.

Chapter Twenty-Two

The pressure on Cartwright and Armstrong had reduced a little whilst DCS Simons was totally preoccupied with the very real threat posed by IRA terrorists. The announcement on the breakfast news bulletin that Northern Ireland was to introduce trials without a jury for suspected terrorists would do nothing to de-escalate the violence. On the contrary. The assassination of PC Colin Harvey would pale into insignificance if more major incidents and bombings were to be carried out. During 1972, 467 people had died in political and sectarian violence in Northern Ireland. It seemed to Simons that the number of dead merely emphasised the hopelessness of the situation. He was determined that the perpetrators of any bombing campaign in London or other major cities in England would be brought to justice. They would know the full force of the law. His determination extended to averting violence wherever possible. But the quotient of the Intelligence Unit under his command was somehow sadly lacking. It had been as a result of the Ulster Workers Council strike in Belfast, that Northern Ireland was brought to its knees and led to the British government suspending the Northern Ireland government and parliament and introducing direct rule from Westminster. Simons and senior officers from the Metropolitan force and the Home Office suspected that this move to find a resolution to the Troubles by attempting to bring politicians together would end in disaster as similar efforts had done in the past. A backlash was feared and a bomb attack on Westminster was suspected. Security was tightened and the Palace of Westminster was put on high alert. Parliament's chief of security was quoted in the Times newspaper as saying, *The IRA will be keen to gather whatever targeting information it can, especially concerning our security measures, including closed circuit TV coverage, access arrangements and patrols.* Such was the unease and agitation that access restrictions were imposed with pass holders facing random checks with bag checks being intensified. DI Cartwright and DS Armstrong fully understood the importance of their role in bringing their IRA executioner to justice but at least, with DCS Simons off their backs, they could get on with their investigation without his intimidation and interference.

Since the interviews with Helen and Ben Blake, DC Lewis had been dispatched to Burton Overy to interview the landlord of the Old Greyhound, Jamie Webster. It was known that Jamie and Ben were the best of friends and that Jamie had been fundamental in the conspiracy with Danny McFaddon to kill Duncan 'Jock' Mc Clean. The investigating team also held the belief that there was no reasonable doubt that whoever shot McClean, also shot and killed PC Colin Harvey. The IRA cell responsible on that occasion was led by Michael Doyle and Ted Reilly and they were now in custody following the Limehouse Basin incident. Ray Harvey's trip to Burton was nothing more than a 'belt and braces' visit to establish that Jamie Webster's story was still consistent with Ben's and Helen's and to ascertain whether there might be any other detail that could help in the hunt for Danny McFaddon.

Doug Armstrong had been to Brixton to interview Michael Doyle.

'Well, it wasn't a complete waste of time, but I'm not sure it'll get us much further.'

'Come on then, report please Doug, let's hear it!' Cartwright was not exactly impatient but a little edgy.

'Well, did you know that Gerry Doyle, Michael's brother had died in hospital, here on our patch in the John Radcliffe Infirmary?' Cartwright turned to his DC.

'Did we know this Ray?'

'Don't think so guv.'

'Well that bloody Simons did!'

'What, and the stupid bastard never saw fit to tell us?' Cartwright exploded. He was incensed. Armstrong continued.

'Well, the prison governor had received a request from – guess who – none other than our friend Danny McFaddon to allow Michael Doyle compassionate release to attend Gerry Doyle's funeral.' This revelation drew gasps of exasperated incredulity from the DI as Armstrong continued. 'The governor, being obliged to seek approval for such requests when terrorism is involved, spoke to Simons and Simons declined and refused on the grounds that the murder of a police officer was on Doyle's charge-sheet.'

'What an arsehole! How the hell did he ever make DCS? He's not fit to take charge of a blasted school crossing patrol.' Cartwright's blood pressure was almost off the scale. 'And how the hell does he expect us to conduct this investigation with no manpower?' Cartwright's rant was gaining momentum.

'The Deputy Commissioner will hear of this – and all the time Simons is crazing my arse continually pestering me asking why we are not making headway – I'll tell you why you stupid fucking git – talk about a bloody nerve.'

'Anyway,' said Armstrong, 'All I got from Michael Doyle in response to every question was "No comment, no comment." All he said apart from that was,' Doug referred to his notebook, '"The feckin' bastard McClean deserves to be dead" They were the only other words he spoke.'

'Well done Doug!' Cartwright's blood was off the boil and down to a simmer. He sat for a moment during which no one spoke. Then after a bit more pencil-twiddling the DI stood and asserting his authority barked out a succession of orders.

'OK, we need to contact the infirmary, speak to the consultant or whoever. We want details of every visitor he's had, the date of death and anything else he can offer. We need all we can get on the funeral arrangements, who was the funeral director, when, where, burial or cremation, those attending, plus other details. I'll ask the Super to assign a couple of PCs to the case. I reckon we might well be up and running now. Simons you bleeding twerp!

Chapter Twenty-Three

Since the altercation with her erstwhile-husband and acting on Helen's advice, Maisie had filed a petition for divorce on the grounds of Graham's unreasonable behaviour and the irretrievable breakdown of the marriage. Helen was also communicating with her ex-employers in Ely, the firm of Meadows, Coleman and Pettegrew with a view to making an application to the courts for a restraining order against Graham Clarke if he continued to harass her friend. If he carried out his threat to sue Maisie for emotional distress or any other trumped-up claim, they would deal with that as and when the incidence arose. Maisie was happy and so glad she had found Helen again, a true friend as well as her landlady, not to mention her own personal legal adviser now as well. The bad taste that she had been left with after the encounter in the Anchor had, thanks to Helen, been sweetened and she had pushed the confrontation to the back of her mind. There was a matter of much greater importance with which to deal. She had to get a job.

Although she hadn't been living aboard *Ironside* for very long she had become good friends with Colin Smith on the *Mary Gloster* in a neighbourly sort of way. Nothing was ever too much trouble for Colin. He was always ready to lend a hand, do a favour or otherwise help out whenever assistance was required. He was always of a cheerful disposition and Maisie couldn't have wished for a better neighbour. It was mid-week and she'd invited him aboard for dinner by way of a thank you and merely as a neighbourly gesture. She had no ulterior motive. Colin was a lovely man but not Maisie's type. Maisie wasn't much of a cook and never had been, even before her prison stretch. Nevertheless, she'd come across a recipe in the *Observer*'s colour supplement at the weekend which didn't really involve much more than opening a tin and boiling some pasta. She felt she could cope and that had convinced her to extend an invitation, and besides which, the company would be nice for a change. Colin came aboard right on the dot of the appointed time. He'd brought a bottle of wine with him. It was all very convivial. Maisie had selected an album by Jacques Loussier, the French pianist renowned for his interpretations of Bach in a jazz idiom as suitable background music and it was well chosen. Together with Colin's chilled Chardonnay the music created exactly the right sort of ambiance. This was perhaps as well given that the penne in the tuna pasta bake had been overbaked and the accompanying broccoli just a little too 'al dente'. Still, it was tasty and Colin, ever the gentleman was not one to complain. After dinner they sat and chatted, about themselves, small-talk, houseboat life, and nothing much of any consequence. Colin had remained curious since he had witnessed the incident with the disfigured man in the Anchor, and Maisie, although a little hesitant, was quite prepared to reveal the background. She explained that the stigma of a prison record was not something she was necessarily ashamed of. Certainly, she was guilty as charged and the first to admit it. But she remained completely unrepentant. She still firmly believed that because of the mental and physical abuse that her drunkard of a husband meted out he thoroughly deserved what he got. Although the sentence was, in the opinion of many, excessive, Maisie bore her punishment with fortitude. In fact, she had reasons to be grateful for her time in prison. She'd met a kindred spirit; one who understood domestic violence, Helen Blake with whom she had shared a cell became Maisie's most trusted of friends. She was now her confidante and so much more. It had been at Helen's suggestion that Maisie had obtained a qualification whilst inside, something she would have been unlikely to do on the outside. She was hoping that her secretarial skills diploma from the Royal Society for Arts would stand her in good stead in securing meaningful employment, a job which she could enjoy and which paid enough for her to meet the costs of her very modest demands.

Throughout Maisie's loquacious discourse Colin had sat in silence and listened sympathetically to every word. It wasn't until mention was made of the need for a job that he spoke.

'I believe Potter's on the Market Hill might be looking for someone within the next week or so. I sometimes bump into a young bloke I used to work with, Keith Palmer, he did his apprenticeship under me. Now, his wife Sandra works there and I know she is expecting a baby and will be taking maternity leave. Why don't you go and see old man Potter and introduce yourself? Let him know you're interested.'

'What's Potter's?'

'Local estate agency – I know Sandra, she manages all sorts of secretarial stuff, typing and the like, producing details of properties for sale, you know? Sometimes she meets prospective buyers and shows 'em round. Be right up your street I should think.'

'Oh Colin, you star! Sounds like just the sort of job I need – and I could walk to work! I'll certainly go and see them first thing tomorrow.'

And she did. And she was appointed to a temporary position to cover maternity leave – a position which could possibly become permanent if 'things worked out'. She was to start in her new position on Monday 2nd April.

Chapter Twenty-Four

In common with all the other fishermen working out of Felixstowe Ferry, Maurice Read had a shed. The fishermen used their sheds mainly for baiting up long-lines in the winter, storing all manner of paraphernalia for boat maintenance and stuff used in the fishing business which to an average landlubber would appear to be just so much junk. Every day during the week since he trawled it up Maurice was reminded to do something with the golf bag and the Remington each time he went to his shed and saw it standing there in the corner partially concealed by an old green net. If ever there was something out of place in a fisherman's shed, it was a golf bag. If ever there was something out of place in a golf bag, it was a Remington M21A sniper rifle!

It was Sunday. If the weather was fit Saturdays and Sundays were just another working day. As was the custom and practice, Maurice arrived at the boatyard in the early hours except on this particular morning he was later than he would have normally been with the clocks having gone forward an hour to British Summer Time. Maurice had forgotten to alter his alarm clock. He knew immediately he parked his battered old Ford Anglia 307E van that something wasn't right. Where were the other blokes? He looked towards the moorings and the other boats were conspicuous by their absence. The rest of the fleet had gone. It was then that it dawned on him – almost literally. 'I forgot the bloody clocks! Sod it! There'll be no water over the bar now.' He walked towards his shed and it wasn't just the lost hour that wasn't right. There was something else; something was most definitely wrong. The shed door was open.

'Shit!' he cursed out loud. 'Did I forget to lock up? Bugger!' But then on closer inspection he noticed that he hadn't forgotten to lock up at all. The padlock was still closed and intact. The hasp and staple had been prised away from the door and stating the obvious, amongst an outburst of expletives, 'Some bugger's broke inta me shed!' He pulled the door open and straightaway knew what had been taken. The old green net was now sprawled across the floor.

With the ebbtide now well away the depth of water over the shingle bar at the mouth of the river would be insufficient for *Harbour Lights* to get out to sea so Maurice filled the kettle and lit the gas ring. He made a mug of tea and sat pondering. 'Who done it?' he asked himself. 'Which a them buggers done it? Thems were the only folks what knowed about it, 'part from young Matt.' The more he thought about it the more he wasn't prepared to accept that one of his fishermen friends would have broken into his shed and stolen the gun. He'd been at school with most of them. Their fishing community was a close-knit fraternity, a band of brothers who looked out for each other on the water and off it. They were his mates. So, Matt? Surely not? But his instinct told him otherwise.

He set to refixing the hasp and staple and with the shed now securely locked again he returned to his van and drove to his brother's house. Mervyn wouldn't be in. He'd be at sea in his boat *Three Brothers*. He was the sort of smartarse that wouldn't forget to put his watch forward. But then Maurice wasn't paying his brother a visit. Maurice wanted a word with his nephew. He parked the van and knocked on the door.

'Hello Barbara. Is Matt in?'

'Hello Maurice, thought you'd be fishin', Merv is.'

'Yes I know. I wants a word wi' Matt. Is he in?' he asked again.

'Aye, he's in – in bed.' Barbara shouted up the stairs and

after a few minutes Matthew appeared as Barbara disappeared into the kitchen. Even before Matthew had reached the bottom of the stairs Maurice asked him straight out.

'Why'd you do it lad?'

'Do what unc?'

'C'mon, don't get playin' the innocent wi' me lad!' For all that Maurice was angry and disappointed in his nephew, this was to be a reprimand, a severe reprimand. Even so he remained calm and softly spoken. After all, he was Matt's uncle. They spent a lot of time together, more like mates than relatives. Matthew knew that he would never get away with lying to his uncle besides which it would only make matters worse.

'It weren't me what done it, unc, 'onest.'

'Who were it then? C'mon, out wi' it. Who broke into me shed and pinched the golf bag?'

'I don't know unc, 'onest I don't.'

'Well, some bugger did. Who'd ya tell?'

'I was that excited unc I 'ad to tell somebody. Sorry.'

'So, who did ya tell then?'

'Alan 'igginson.'

Maurice could hardly believe his ears. He might have been willing to forgive his nephew for betraying his confidence, but to have told young Higginson? How could Matthew have been so stupid not to have considered what this could lead to?

The Higginson family had a certain local notoriety, a shady reputation. They lived on the Roughs Tower council estate near the docks. The Roughs Tower was a WWII installation some six miles off the coast, built to protect the ports of Felixstowe and Harwich. The estate couldn't have been more appropriately named and the Higginson house was in what many regarded as the rough end. It was invariably the police's first point of contact whenever there were any nefarious goings-on going on. But Maurice knew only too well that it would be imprudent to start making unsubstantiated accusations if one attached any value to the retention of one's kneecaps in working order. He could hardly report the matter to the police either. If the culprit had been one of Dickie Higginson's feral family, especially the eldest son, Maurice couldn't bring himself to think what Alan's big brother Ronnie might get up to with a sniper rifle. He was a nasty, malicious individual. It just didn't bear thinking about. So he didn't. Just one of those things. His unexpected 'catch' might have been worth a few quid to someone. Easy come, easy go. He might have netted a profit but guns were dangerous things. He'd somehow known this would be trouble.

'Oh dear, oh dear Matthew!' Maurice sighed in exasperation. 'How could you 'ave bin so bloody silly?' His patience was borne of sorrow rather than anger.

'Sorry unc, just dint think did I?' Matthew was beginning to understand the magnitude of what he had done and of what the consequences could be. But the unreproachful demeanour of his Uncle Maurice was demonstrative of a reluctance to punish. Matthew began to cry for the first time in years.

Chapter Twenty-Five

The early morning meeting at Kidlington had gathered in the CID briefing room. Present were DC Ray Davies, DS Doug Armstrong, PC Andy Lewis, PC Alex Hazelwood (who had stood most of the guard-duty outside Doyle's room in the infirmary's ICU) WPC Annie McKay and Chief Superintendent Timothy Adams. The Chief Super was taking a much more proactive role given that uniforms were now involved, not to mention the fact that DCS Simons had withheld vital information, whether intentionally or not. DI Cartwright looking ever so slightly flustered emerged from his office into the briefing room.

'OK, what have we got, what have we learned?' The questions were posed to no one in particular and everyone in general. It was PC Hazelwood who spoke first.

'I went to the John Radcliffe sir, I know my way about there after all the hours I spent…' Cartwright interrupted him 'Yes, yes, we know all about that, and well done by the way. What did you find out?'

'Gerry Doyle developed an infection after surgery on his leg. This led to pneumonia and that's the cause of death on his death certificate sir. According to the ICU Registrar Mr Christie – I got to know him quite well sir – Doyle had given up the will to live being faced with the rest of his life in a wheelchair.'

'OK well done. What about visitors? Did you check the visitors' log?'

'Yes sir, I did. The whole time he was in there he only had three visitors. DS Armstrong, Michael Doyle, twice, and a Father O'Connor – if you remember sir, I rang you about Father…'

'Oh yes I remember. Anything else?'

'No sir!

'OK very well done. Who's next?'

'Me sir, Annie McKay. I had a ring round all the funeral directors in Oxford and eventually came across the right one – a firm called Homewood, in Kidlington. The arrangements were all made and paid for by a Mr D McFaddon. The cremation took place on Monday 19th February at Oxford Crematorium. There were only three mourners. McFaddon, first name Daniel, Brian O'Connor – I assume that's the priest Alex referred to, and Ciara Doyle the deceased's niece – her dad is Michael, you know the guy in Brixton Nick.'

'Thanks Annie. Good work. Now we're getting somewhere at last, proper police work now we haven't got....' Cartwright stopped himself from mentioning Simons given that the Chief Super was in the room.

'Right what else have we got? Doug?'

'Not much else at the moment guv. Seems that after the cremation the three mourners checked into prebooked accommodation at the Killingworth Castle Hotel in Wootton using assumed names. The duty manager tells me the three of them got as pis... very drunk guv. They stayed two nights and booked a taxi to take them all to Luton airport. We know they flew to Belfast. I got in touch with the Royal Ulster Constabulary and there was a memorial service on the Friday at St Mary's Church in the Falls Road. Quite a big deal apparently. The RUC kept a watching brief on a procession lead by the three mourners, Ciara's boyfriend Tom O'Rourke and another priest as well as Father O'Connor. After the service which apparently was a full-on Requiem Mass, there was a knees-up at a bar on Springfield Road', Armstrong referred to his notes, 'The Blackstaff Bar which is run by Ciara while daddy's in Brixton. She and her boyfriend O'Rourke that is, who, coincidentally is the son of Maggie O'Rourke who you'll remember was Jock McClean's fancy woman.' There were murmurs of approval and hushed chat as the jigsaw pieces were beginning to be put in place.

'Right then, thank you DI Cartwright, and well done everyone.' It was Thames Valley's Chief Constable, David Worth who had now occupied centre stage.

'This investigation, which is the culmination of an investigation which was started when you young constables were still in school, has been impeded by a lack of cooperation and joined-up communication. It begins with bodies recovered from the Grand Union canal and our chasing spiv-cum-murder suspect, the late Jock McClean. Then there's his involvement with the IRA, gun-running and terrorist offences not least of which resulted in the death of one of our own and two prison officers. Several covert police operations have been – well, quite honestly, disastrous. The IRA had pre-empted our every move thanks to being tipped off by a bent copper and an ex-member of this force. Sadly, there has been a lack of cooperation from DCS Simons. This has been noted and referred to the Chief Constable and I now have every confidence that, under DI Cartwright we can bring it all to a close. Subject to the formality of approval from the Promotions Board, DI Cartwright is now Detective Chief Inspector.'

This announcement was greeted with a spontaneous round of applause and CS Adams left the room. Once the excitement had died down, the newly promoted DCI had more to say.

'OK, OK. Thank you all very much. But let's not forget this is a team effort and there's still a lot to be done. I don't even want to begin thinking how on earth on at least three occasions, McFaddon, the IRA brain behind McClean's assassination and possibly more, has been right under our noses, right here on our patch – on at least three separate occasions,' he emphasised, 'and we didn't even know. He's probably still here now.'

'Sir…' It was DC Ray Davies trying to attract his gov's attention.

'Ray?'

'OK, thanks sir, and congratulations by the way. What's been puzzling me is how did McFaddon know where to find Webster and Blake?'

'Good thinking Ray. Let's make that our next step. Let's find out. Oh, and by the way, after work, the Red Lion. Drinks on me!

Chapter Twenty-Six

Cartwright and Davies stood looking at the photograph pinned to the logistics board in the briefing room. It showed a man in a red sailing jacket, binoculars around his neck, lying in an area of shingle with clumps of what looked like a variety of cabbage. His eyes and mouth were open in an expression of surprise. There was a small black hole in the middle of his forehead. McClean.

'Hell of a shot!' exclaimed Davies.

'Has anyone spoken to the ferryman, what was his name, White, Reg White. Surely he would remember if he took anyone across to the island carrying a gun. I mean a rifle is not really something anyone can carry around and remain inconspicuous is it?'

'Dunno gov' was Davies' reply. 'Do you want me to go and question him?'

'No, I'll get someone local to do it. Of course, it also begs the question how did the gunman get off the island? There were no more ferry crossings on the day of the shooting.'

'Perhaps there was an accomplice in another boat waiting to pick him up,' Davies suggested.

'Good thinking again Ray – you'll make a detective one day! Get on to the local harbourmaster or the coastguard or whoever might have seen another boat in the vicinity at the right time.'

'OK gov, I'm on it.' Davies disappeared to carry out his orders.

Cartwright then telephoned his DS up the road at Oxford, St Aldates.

'Doug, I know I'm a bit nearer than you, but I'm snowed under with stuff. Can you run up to Burbage if you don't mind? Go and have a chat with Helen Blake's in-laws.' He paused whilst checking a file, 'Albert and Mabel. See if they can give us anything helpful. We particularly want to know how the IRA made contact with Helen. I reckon the answer to that might lead us to McFaddon.'

'Tomorrow be OK gov?'

'Yeah, sure. Do you mind taking your own car? We can't really spare a driver or a car come to that.'

'No problem – if it starts.'

'OK, Good. Just drive carefully in that ratty old Avenger!'

Cartwright was convinced that McFaddon was the key. By another monumental omission from DCS Simons, Cartwright had only recently been informed that since the Troubles had escalated, the English police shared a control room with the RUC in Belfast although the RUC ran the show. He found the telephone number and dialled it. After a few seconds came an abrupt response from a distinctly Ulster dialect.

'RUC. Sergeant McGovern speaking.'

'This is Detective Chief Inspector Cartwright of the Thames Valley Force. I wonder if you could help? We're currently investigating the murder of a Duncan McClean and a local constable and the name McFaddon, Danny McFaddon keeps turning up. Is this a name familiar to you?'

'Oh yes, very much so. A bloody Republican and something important in the IRA. He's on our wanted list. Elusive bastard though. We could have had him a couple of weeks ago. Seems he was here in Belfast for a Requiem Mass of one of their own, Gerry Doyle. You know all about the accident and McClean's involvement with the American arms shipment of course. We didn't bloody well know. He could be anywhere. We think he may be associated with an IRA cell in London somewhere. If we knew where, we'd have had him by now. He is a friend of Gerry Doyle's brother Michael Doyle who you've got banged up on remand. Have you not tried talking to him?' McGovern paused for breath. Cartwright thus far had experienced great difficulty getting a word in. The telephone connection was a bit sketchy as well and that didn't help. He'd just formed a question in his mind which he was about to pose when Sergeant McGovern, clearly one of the RUC's finest, started up again.

'Still, I'm glad that bastard McClean has gone to meet his maker. He was also on our wanted list. Anyway, look, I'm sorry sir but I have to go. Best of luck finding McFaddon and if you do, let us have him after you've finished with him.' The telephone line went dead.

Cartwright scribbled down some notes. He was tempted by the Laphroaig bottle but was distracted as Davies knocked on his door and re-entered.

'Yes Ray, what've you got?'

'Well, I spoke to a lovely sounding lady the National Coastguard Operations Centre, and she put me in touch with the Coastguard Station closest to our place of interest, Walton-on-the-Naze. Apparently this is a few miles down the coast but it covers all the North Sea traffic southwards towards Dover and north towards Great Yarmouth. I spoke to the Station Officer Archie Turnbull.'

'And?'

'Well not a lot really. On 31st January there were the usual ferries in and out of Felixstowe and Harwich.' Ray referred to his pocketbook. 'A few trawlers and the *Samson*. *Samson*'s up and down the East Anglian coast quite a lot, small deliveries, salvage operations, moving navigation buoys for Trinity House, that sort of thing.

'So, what do you reckon? Could our sniper have been evacuated from the island?

'I s'pose it's a possibility gov. Shouldn't think the fishing boats would have been involved but the other one, *Samson* might have, yes that might be a possibility.'

'Good work Ray. Can we find the owner or the skipper of *Samson* and have a word?'

'I s'pose so.' He ventured. 'Must be registered or licensed or something somewhere. I'll get onto it.' Ray Davies took himself off to his own desk again. Cartwright thought again about resorting to the Laphroaig bottle but didn't. He called in WPC Annie McKay, seconded to his team for the duration of the investigation.

'Pop to the post office please Annie. Get a £3.50 postal order and send it to Gail Read.' He handed her the cash and the envelope he'd already addressed.

Chapter Twenty-Seven

Brian checked out of the Alton House Hotel, and travelling light with all his worldly goods and a couple of changes of clothes in a holdall made his way to the railway station where he caught a train back to Norwich. He'd previously decided over breakfast that since he wanted to be close to the coast, he'd take the train to Norwich and change tracks and return to Lowestoft. He recalled his railway journey to Norwich from London a couple weeks earlier. 'What was that guy's name?' He searched through his jacket pockets and found the envelope. 'Ben Blake, Lobster Pot Cottage, Orford.'

'Orford!' Brian was totally stunned by the sudden realisation. He hadn't previously put two and to together. 'Orford!' he exclaimed again. Even though it had been six weeks ago the memory of his last commission came flooding back in every detail. 'Lowestoft!' – of course. He smiled. Not at the recollection of the last hit, although he admitted to himself it was a terrific shot from a precarious perch in that concrete pagoda thing, built in the '50s for atomic weapons research. He smiled in the knowledge that the £1000 fee for the job had been paid in cash into his bank account, the secret account under his *nom de guerre* (literally). He'd forgotten how lucrative the job had been. He smiled in the knowledge that it was all behind him. He didn't think of himself as a murderer, or as callous. He wasn't insensitive, quite the opposite if anything. Although he did however regard himself as armour-plated, indestructible, a hard man. He was the consummate professional. He had the aptitude and the attitude. He practised. Lying prone in wet grass or adopting other awkward or difficult vantage points required fitness and patience. He was fit and patient. Staring, unblinking and without moving for long periods required special skills. A deep, steady rate of respiration and a heartrate to match were physical and mental prerequisites. Knowing how and when to caress the trigger was the ultimate in mastery of the snipers' art. Maybe they were extra-special faculties, God-given gifts. Although if God knew the manner in which such gifts were used he would not have been best pleased. Brian had always been a loner and maintained an anonymity which verged on invisibility; assets which were absolutely fundamental to becoming successful in such a career. In a sense he was proud of his success. But now, that was all behind him. No more would he take another person's life.

At Norwich station, Brian studied the pictorial representation of the map once more. If he couldn't find what he was looking for in or near Lowestoft he would have the option of the coastal route via any of the stations at Oulton Broad, Beccles, Halesworth, Saxmundham, Wickham Market, Melton and Woodbridge, places from where he could get a bus to Suffolk's coastal villages. He could remember some of the place names that he'd heard on passage to Lowestoft aboard *Samson*. So, Lowestoft was to be the first stop and he boarded the next train. Arriving in Lowestoft, it all looked different in the daylight. He walked from the station in a vaguely familiar direction towards the bascule bridge and the sea front. He stood and watched fishing boats coming and going to and from the Trawl Dock where he himself had first set foot in Lowestoft. He decided to take a room at the Victoria Hotel again. From there he could explore for as long as he wanted.

Chapter Twenty-Eight

Detective Sergeant Doug Armstrong was still fretting about his erstwhile wife appearing on the periphery of the investigation. He wasn't at all sure how he felt with his emotions churning in some sort of turmoil. It was a relief in many ways that Cartwright had assigned him to the trip to Burbage to talk to Mabel and Albert Blake. At least that would take him out of the office for the day and give him an opportunity to try and get his head straight about Maisie. Since the divorce and Maisie's imprisonment Doug had lived alone. He'd sold the three- bedroomed semi and after renting for a while whilst his new posting to Thames Valley was being finalised he'd taken out a mortgage on a two-bedroom flat in Sunnymead, a suburb to the north of Oxford. Officially he was stationed at St Aldates Police Station in Oxford, but he was spending more and more time at HQ in Kidlington as part of DCI Cartwright's Murder Investigation Team. Doug Armstrong was self-sufficient, and he liked living alone although if he was to be honest with himself he still had feelings for Maisie.

Whilst eating breakfast on Wednesday 28th March, he had his road atlas on the table to check the most expeditious route to Burbage. Given his current state of mind he decided to adopt the more expedient itinerary. He didn't want to get back to the office to be given something else to do. This excursion could take all day, in fact he'd make it take all day. He reckoned on about two hours to get there, about an hour for the interview, an hour for lunch and two hours back should see the day out.

Passing Bicester he had recollections of his interview with Tom Wenzl who had turned out to be Ahmed abu Moussa, a terrorist and member of the extreme Palestinian organisation, Black September. It all seemed so long ago. There had been quite a lot of water under the bridge and through the locks since then. He turned his Hillman Avenger on to the A43 and it was easy going towards Towcester and the A5. His forecast of about two hours to cover the eighty miles or so to Burbage wasn't far out and it being a reasonably small village he found the address without too much difficulty. He rang the doorbell. No answer. He rang again. This time an old woman appeared though a side-gate, carrying an empty laundry basket.

'Sorry, I could hear the doorbell, but I was in the garden hanging out the washing,' she explained. 'I doubt Albert would've heard it. He don't hear much these days. Don't say much either – in fact he don't do a lot of anything. He's not a well man any more I'm afraid. I don't reckon he'll be with us for much longer.' Mabel gave an enormous sigh.

'Still, hark at me going on. I don't suppose you're the doctor come to visit are you? Can't get a visit these days – always too busy. Like me really, up and down the stairs all day looking after 'im, cooking and cleaning., having to change the sheets and stuff and he's only got two pairs of pyjamas. Good job we've still got Frank from the farm. He does all my shopping for me you know…' Before she could launch into yet more of the trials of an octogenarian's life, Armstrong interrupted.

'Mrs Blake? Look Mrs Blake, can we talk inside? I'm from the police.' Mention of the police took Mabel by surprise.

'Why, what's happened? Yes, yes of course, sorry how rude you must think I am keeping you stood here with me gassing on. Come on round the back.' Armstrong followed the indomitable Mrs Blake through the side-gate and they went into the house through the kitchen door. Armstrong instantly detected that distinctive odour. What was it? A combination of old-age, boiled cabbage, and, oh yes, urine.

'Come into the front parlour – shall I make you a nice cup of tea?' Why are cups of tea always referred to as 'nice'? he wondered. He'd drunk more than several in the line of duty that were anything but nice. Mabel disappeared back into the kitchen and he heard the kettle being filled notwithstanding his having made no response to the invitation. Mabel returned after a little while with a tray on which there were the best china cups, teapot, sugar bowl, but with the milk still in the bottle.

'The milk jug got broke,' she explained. Armstrong was quick off the mark as Mrs Blake poured the tea.

'Now, Mrs Blake, I'm detective Sergeant Doug Armstrong and I'm here to see if you can tell me about anything which might have involved your daughter-in-law, Helen and a Scotsman – you'd have known him as Jock McClean I think.'

'He's a bad 'un.' Mabel was there, sharp as a new pin and with more than a liberal dose of malice. 'Our Helen should never have got mixed up with him.'

'Did you know he'd been murdered?'

'No I didn't. Still, I know I shouldn't speak ill of the dead but I hope he rots in hell. Who killed him? I'd like to shake his hand – if you know what I mean. You said murdered so I'm assuming he got killed and that it wasn't natural causes.'

'Well that's just it Mrs Blake. We don't know. All we do know is that it was more than likely a member of the IRA.'

'The IRA, you mean the Irish who keep bombing stuff?'

'That's right. Now this is where you might be able to help us.'

'Of course, I will if I can but I'd say let 'im go, whoever killed 'im, he's done the world a favour!'

'If we can't find him, we might have to. But, Mrs Blake, as I'm sure you realise, the law's the law and we can't let people take it upon themselves to dish out their own kind of justice when and wherever, can we now?' Mabel gave the detective a sort of 'sideways' look.

'No, I s'pose you're right.' She thought about it for a while longer as she poured more tea which by now had far exceeded the 'nice' stage. 'We got a letter from Belfast. That's near Northern Ireland isn't it?'

'Yes Mrs Blake it's very near!'

'Call me Mabel for goodness' sake. Anyway, it seems that the no-good Scotchman had been living in Belfast with a woman who died. Her son, let me think, Tom, I think his name was, yes that's it, Tom O'Rourke. Anyway, when the son Tom was clearing out his mother's house so he could sell it, he found a letter. Well, his mother was asking him if he would post another letter and some other papers and stuff to our Helen. Problem was they didn't know our Helen's address but she, Mrs O'Rourke that is, knew mine 'cos Jock must have told her 'cos 'e'd been here once you see, maybe twice I can't remember. I'd ask Albert but he can't remember his own name half the time these days.' Armstrong looked up from his notes believing he could work the rest out.

'Is that it then?'

'Oh no, dear, there's more. In the letter from Tom, he asked us to ring him and to let him have Helen's address. Well, I couldn't, could I?'

'Why not?'

'Well, I didn't know it, did I? I tried to tell him but when I rang it was a woman who answered. She was ever so rude. She kept on at me asking about people I'd never heard of and about guns and car crashes and stuff. Any road up, in the end, she writes down our address here again and says we're going to get these important papers for our Helen and they'll be sent here to our address that she's written down. Then she slams the phone down. Well, I never did.'

'You mean you didn't give the papers to Helen?'

'No, silly, I mean, well I never did! Albert would say "Well bugger me!"'

'Oh, I understand – you were shocked.'

'That's right. I was. She was so rude. Can't be doing with folks what's rude, can you?'

'No indeed Mrs Blake, Mabel.'

'Then, and it might even have been the next day or the one after that. There's a knock at the door, and I'm thinking now who can that be? When I opens it, there's a bloke in a suit. Ever so polite. Wants to speak to Mrs Blake but not me.'

'Did he introduce himself, give you his name?'

'No, I don't think so. If he did I've forgotten it.'

'Could you describe him? Short, tall, slim, fat, dark, fair?'

'Yes well,' she thought for a moment, 'sort of ordinary but in a suit. I thought it were the man from the pools at first. He was ever so nice. He says it's very important that he speaks to the young Mrs Blake and wants her address. Well, I couldn't tell him could I?'

'Because you didn't know it.' Armstrong is beginning to get just a little weary of the long-winded telling of the story.

'That's right. Well to cut a long story short…' Thank goodness for the abridged version Armstrong thought.

'I told him how to get in touch with her through Jamie in his pub. You know Jamie? But before I could explain any more, he'd gone – just like that.

And I thought, well that's a bit rude. I'll go to the bottom of our stairs I thought!'

Armstrong didn't ask.

After another ten minutes of protracted pleasantries, Armstrong left Mabel Blake on the doorstep.

'I hope Mr Blake doesn't get any worse,' he said knowing full well that it was a stupid thing to say. Even if Mrs Blake didn't realise it, Armstrong did. Poor old Albert had probably got dementia and unlikely to improve. DS Armstrong returned to his Hillman with the intention of finding somewhere for lunch and then a layby maybe for a snooze.

Chapter Twenty-Nine

In her home in Kirton near Felixstowe, Gail Read, Matt's younger sister had received a letter. Gail never received letters. Fashion catalogues, perhaps, if she'd sent for them but letters? Never. Her excitement lasted only as long as took to open the envelope. The Postal Order for £3.50. She put it in the inside pocket of her blazer and went off to catch the school bus. Gail was a bright girl, not exactly what one would describe as stunningly good looking, but far from a gawky teenager. She was pretty in a certain way and not unattractive in the slightest. For her age her figure was well-developed and with her skirt at least three inches shorter than school regulation knee length she had no difficulty in attracting the boys with her innate sexuality. She certainly knew how to flaunt it. After the geography field trip she had completed the questionnaire and her O-level project submission on migrating birds, long-shore drift and coastal erosion. When it came to types of vegetation indigenous to coastal shingle her comprehensive answer included some of the photographs she'd taken during the Havergate study trip. One of the photographs was the one featuring the dead man. She'd intended this as a joke, but Mr Ross wasn't amused. Mr Ross had marked her work prior to sending it off to be moderated. He'd given her an A– but with a comment 'see me' in red. At the end of the next geography class, she waited by her teacher's desk.

'I don't think the exam moderators will be interested in this photo,' he said, handing the offending snap back to her.

'It was only a joke, sir. Sorry sir.'

'Yes, I know, I know. You did very well.'

'Thank you sir.' As she turned, Mr Ross was very tempted to give her a pat on the bottom. He resisted.

After school, as usual there was a gaggle of boys hanging around at the school gates, not necessarily boys from school either. Older boys, boys with apprenticeships or jobs as well as boys with neither. There would be young men with motorbikes and motorcars. Gail hardly ever bothered with the school bus home. She was never short of a lift being, as she was, one of the principal attractions amongst the other girls who were also regular attenders at the afterschool 'socialising'. It was no wonder that her dad, Mervyn worried about her. Mr Ross, her geography teacher was concerned as well. He'd been a teacher for longer than he cared to remember and all too often he'd seen decent kids go off the rails by keeping the wrong company. He had a soft spot for Gail. She was basically a good girl, doing well at school with good prospects of a university education and a decent career. But she had begun mixing with the bad company.

Mr Arthur Ross had obtained his BSc degree and teaching diploma six years before WWII was declared. He took up his first teaching post in 1933 and being in a reserved occupation he avoided the 'call up'. Forty years on, such was his experience that he could assess the character of a pupil within a few days, in some cases a few hours, of meeting children for the first time. He could spot the boy or girl with the potential to achieve three good A-levels in six years' time. Equally he could predict those that had no chance; those who would end up in juvenile court, wasters, illiterate and innumerate or worse. Over the years it had become clear to him that more often than not a child's prospects had much to do with their upbringing; the sort of home they came from. This determination of their destiny was never more apparent than when he was introduced to certain children, the parents of whom he had taught, or tried to teach years earlier. The Read family lived in a modest three-bedroom semi-detached house on the Woodvale council estate. The family was decent and hardworking. Not poor but certainly not affluent either. Dad, Mervyn, was a fisherman and his income was dependent on the price of fish and how much he caught. Mother, Barbara, was a housewife who took in mending, sewing, alterations and the like. She was looking forward to the day the instalments on Mervyn's trawler had been paid off, the day when their financial situation would improve to the extent that her supplementary income would no longer be required. Mr Ross knew the family. He had also taught Gail's elder brothers, David, Michael and Matthew. All good kids and properly brought up. None of the brothers were ever going to set the world alight academically, hardly Nobel Prize winning material. David had been a nice enough lad, not daft but not too much up top. Sadly, whatever potential he might have had was never realised when his life was cut short in a motorbike accident. Michael was apprenticed to Frank Knightley's boatyard business and having passed all the aptitude tests went on day-release to the boatbuilding college in Lowestoft with the aim of becoming a shipwright. Matthew, only just out of school aged sixteen worked weekends for his uncle Maurice, Mervyn's elder brother, on his trawler. During the week he was a trainee manager at the Co-op supermarket. Gail on the other hand had the potential to shine. A-levels, college or even university, and who knows, a profession, a lawyer or doctor perhaps.

Matt Read had begun to get quite pally with Alan Higginson. Older than Matt by almost a year Alan had been working at the co-op for almost three months, replenishing the fruit and veg shelves when Matt got the trainee job. The diet in the Higginson household had improved significantly during those three months. Alan had an elder brother, Ronnie. Ronnie had been expelled from school and hadn't held a job down for more than a few weeks before he was either sacked or just stopped turning up. But for all that he never seemed to be short of cash. Not only did he not have a job but he wasn't very bright either. Mr Ross recalled a staff room comment on one occasion which referred to Ronnie Higginson as being about as bright as a five-watt lightbulb. However, what he lacked in intellect and intelligence he more than made up for in brawn. He was a big lad with a physique and ego to match. Even as an eleven-year-old he'd been selected to try out for the rugby team. He never turned up. Ronnie had a car. An old car. Cruising around the town, posing, he fancied himself. He liked to think that the girls fancied him as well and one of his trawling grounds was outside the school gates around 3.30 every afternoon.

For all her common sense, Gail enjoyed the attention she received from the boys, especially Ronnie and it was on the Friday afternoon when Mr Ross was on duty in the playground seeing pupils safely on to their respective busses home and off the school premises that he witnessed Gail Read getting into a car with Ronnie Higginson. 'That's it!' he thought to himself. 'She's throwing it all away.'

The following Monday morning the friendly and respectful relationship between teacher and pupil was terminated when Mr Ross attempted to give Gail some paternal advice. He hadn't intended to speak to her in any admonishing manner nor that any dialogue between them should become confrontational, but Gail was not going to be dictated to.

'Listen, you sad old man, I am not going to be told what I should or should not do or how to behave or who I can and cannot see, especially out of school.' In short Mr Ross was told in no uncertain terms.

'So, you can fuck off and mind your own business!' It was probably the most unpleasant, uncomfortable, and disagreeable encounter of Mr Ross' entire teaching career. He was hurt, mortified even, and extremely worried for the future of a girl he had been very fond of.

At 3.45 when the bell rang for the end of the school day, Mr Ross watched Gail from the staffroom window as she strutted across the playground like a model on the catwalk and straight into the arms of Ronnie Higginson then his car.

'Yes, that's it!' Mr Arthur Ross said out loud to no one in particular as he made a note of the make, model and registration number of the car, an old black Ford Prefect CKY 279A.

Chapter Thirty

In Lowestoft Brian had spent a couple of leisurely days enjoying his newly found lifestyle and the spring sunshine. He'd enjoyed most of the seaside resort's leisure attractions (he didn't bother with the zoo) but the prospect of summers when the town and its beaches would be heaving with tourists and holidaymakers didn't appeal to him. He'd walked the short distance to Oulton Broad. Very pretty again with family leisure facilities and water-based attractions but when considering the place as a permanent home, it was the commercial and tourism industry aspects which prompted Brian to disqualify it. Taking the train further down the line, he'd had a good look around Beccles. This was different. This small market town had great appeal. It was picturesque and unspoilt with the River Waveney running through it. Although when he considered the price of properties for sale in the estate agents' windows, Beccles too was crossed off Brian's list. Sitting on the train as it made its way south towards Halesworth he began to realise that living in this part of the world was always going to be expensive. Beautiful it certainly was and no mistake but surely there were alternative, easier ways distinct from the way 'ordinary' people managed to find a place to live. His cottage in County Antrim had met his needs. Admittedly the owner was reluctant to let the cottage to him initially, but the rifle had helped him to see sense. But it was rented. Brian considered renting to be a waste of money. He was very much of the opinion that a tenant had nothing to show for his weekly expenditure apart from a place to lay his head. At the end of the day a tenant was paying the owner of a property to look after a place for him. To Brian's way of thinking it should have been the other way round. Anyway, this was all very slightly depressing, especially after he'd initially thought that he would have sufficient cash reserves to see him through to the end of his days. The train pulled into Halesworth from where he had planned on taking the bus into Southwold. He was hardly out of seat and reaching for his holdall from the luggage rack when the train moved off again. From his pocket, he took out his list and crossed off Southwold, Walberswick and Blythburgh. This was nothing to do with 'sour grapes' of course. The train had made the decision for him. He resumed his seat and thought to himself 'be just as expensive there anyway.'

It was late afternoon and his thoughts turned to finding somewhere to stay for the night. He'd been through Woodbridge those few weeks previously when he was travelling to Orford to fulfil his last contract. From what he could remember of what he saw through the train windows and judging by the number of passengers that got on and off, Woodbridge looked like the sort of town that would have a reasonable hotel. So there, out of his hands, the second decision of the day was made for him.

As he walked away from the station the lights in the Anchor, the pub over the road looked inviting; an invitation too good to refuse. There were already several people in the bar, the surroundings and atmosphere of which were warm and welcoming. The natives were friendly as well. After a couple of pints, chatting with a few locals and in response to his enquiry Brian was directed to the Crown Hotel where he took a room for just one night. After a supper of 'takeaway' fish and chips, he sat on the bed and laid out the contents of his holdall. Not much to show for almost fifty years. Amongst his bits of paper, receipts, and train tickets he found the envelope addressed to Ben Blake with his telephone number scribbled on it. 'Worth a shot,' Brian thought. 'He might know someone or be able to point me in the right direction. As he climbed into bed, weary from doing not a great deal apart from sight-seeing, he determined that he'd take up Ben's offer and give him a call. Tomorrow was Saturday. Chances were that he wouldn't be going to London and might have time to show him round.

Chapter Thirty-One

DC Ray Davies was at his desk with several telephone calls to make. The first was to County Hall in Ipswich, the base for the Suffolk Constabulary. After having his call diverted from one office to another to another and another he finally managed to speak to someone who could authorise an officer to go to Orford Quay and get a statement from Reg White, the Havergate Island ferryman. Davies requested that a DC Turner, the detective instructed to go to Orford, should liaise directly with DCI Cartwright. His second call was to a number in London, Lloyd's Register of Shipping.

Detective Chief Inspector Cartwright was reading through DS Armstrong's report of his interview with Mabel Blake. He wasn't sure whether Doug Armstrong, not just a colleague but a good friend, had intentionally written the report verbatim or not. Either way, it made him smile even though it didn't really get them any further forward. He sat and pondered. Had Doug got over the revelation of his ex-wife turning up? Should I go and see Helen Blake? Had the man at Mabel Blake's front door been McFaddon? Highly likely he thought, since from Burbage he'd then gone straight off to Burton Overy and we know he met Ben and Jamie in the pub. His private deliberations were interrupted by the telephone.

'DCI Cartwright please.'

'Speaking.'

'I'm DC Turner sir, Suffolk Constabulary based in Ipswich. I was instructed to go to Orford and talk to Reg White, the ferryman who runs the boat to and from Havergate Island.'

'Yes I know. What'd you get, anything useful?'

'Well sir, he remembers the woman – blue anorak and bobble hat – and he remembers the dead bloke in his red sailing jacket with the binoculars. He doesn't remember anyone else, in fact he didn't seem to remember much at all apart from the schoolgirl who found the body – very pretty, by all accounts.'

'Thanks, DC Turner. He didn't spot anyone carrying a gun then, a rifle I would have thought?'

'No sir.'

'What about the number of passengers? Apart from the dead man, did he take anyone out that he didn't bring back? Surely he must keep a head count otherwise how's he going to know if he's left anyone behind after he stops running for the night?'

'I know what you mean sir, and I did ask him that exact same question. Seems that because the woman – blue anorak and bobble hat – was in such a state, like shock he described it, he was anxious to get her back to Orford and he forgot to do his daily tally. Didn't even realise he hadn't taken the bloke in the red jacket back 'til it dawned on him the next morning when the party of school kids found him.'

'Terrific!' The dismay in Cartwright's response was evident.

'Sorry sir.'

'Not your fault, Turner. So we still don't know how the gunman got on and off the island. Did he say anything at all about a gun, has a gun been found on the island since?'

'He didn't mention it sir and I didn't ask. But I'm sure he's the sort of fellow who would report finding a gun. He'd realise it was probably the murder weapon.'

'Yes, you're right. OK. Well done and thank you DC Turner.'

'Pleasure sir – let me know if you need anything else sir. Don't often get the opportunity to get into something juicy.'

'Hardly the description I'd use lad, but yes I will. Thanks.'

Cartwright had just replaced the receiver when DC Davies entered the office.

'Good news?' Davies enquired.

'In a word? No!' The DCI wasn't in the best of humour. 'That was Ipswich, the young DC who has interviewed the ferryman for us. Doesn't remember anyone apart from some pretty schoolgirl – I reckon it was the girl who took the photo, Gail somebody. Now, how did you get on?'

'Well guv, I've been in touch with Lloyds of London. They keep a register of all commercial British shipping so I've got the contact details for the owners of the boats we were told about by the coastguard.'

'Have you called any of them yet?'

'Well, no guv. If you remember we discounted the trawlers. I've tried to get hold of Sam Reynolds though but only managed to speak to his wife.'

'Who's Sam Rey…?'

'Sorry guv, forgot to mention. He's the owner and skipper of the *Samson*. According to Mrs Reynolds he's at sea. They don't get to spend much time together. All she could tell me was that he had a couple of passengers to pick up and take to Lowestoft. From there he had a cargo to deliver to Nieuwpoort…' Cartwright interrupted his DC's report.

'Newport eh? Well let's get on to the Cardiff police and …'

'No guv, Nieuwpoort, Belgium. He'll be long gone from there by now I should reckon. But we will need to find him.'

'Get about, don't they these seafaring types. What I'm thinking is, two passengers, Belgium? What do you reckon? Did *Samson* pick up McFaddon and the mystery gunman and take them to bloody Belgium?'

'I see your thinking guv, but no. I spoke to the harbourmaster in Lowestoft. The *Samson* arrived in Lowestoft late on 31st January – the day of the shooting. She came up the coast during a gale apparently. On board were Sam the skipper, his son Joe, the mate, and two blokes, the passengers. The two blokes booked into the Victoria Hotel in Lowestoft.' Cartwright's initial excitement bubble burst.

'I don't suppose we know…?'

'Yes we do guv. A Mr D Ellis and a Mr B Miles. I rang the hotel and spoke to the receptionist. She had been on duty that night and remembered them distinctly, with good reason. Two Northern Irishmen, just arrived by a small boat through a storm, both a bit worse for wear – she wasn't sure whether it was booze or the effects of seasickness. Although the kitchen was closed the receptionist managed to find someone to prepare them some sandwiches. The rooms had been prebooked and paid for by credit card that turned out to be stolen.'

'Bloody well done Ray. That's great police work. We'll certainly make a detective out of you.' With his excitement bubble reinflated Cartwright gave his DC a congratulatory slap on the back.

'Don't suppose we know what was in the sandwiches?' Cartwright joked, back in good humour.

'Well, surely they have to be our suspects don't they? Mr bloody McFaddon and Mr bloody Mystery using false names, after they've been picked up from Havergate Island and taken to Lowestoft by Sam Reynolds' ship. We'll nick him as soon as we can. Aiding and abetting will do for a start. Ring his wife again let's see where and when he's expected.'

Even with this recent probability of a step forward on the trail left by McFaddon and the gunman, Helen Blake remained at the forefront of Cartwright's mind. He desperately wanted to see her again but could hardly use the case as a subterfuge. Or could he?

Chapter Thirty-Two

The weather on Saturday 31st March was absolutely appalling. After breakfast Brian dialled Ben's number from his room in the Crown Hotel. He was less than sure what he might say and with the weather the way it was, it was hardly suitable for a day of sightseeing. Even as the number was ringing, he was rehearsing some words in his head. The rehearsal ended abruptly when his called was answered.

'Hello, this is Tina Blake…'

'Good morning. I'm sorry to disturb you. My name is Brian O'Connor. I was hoping to have a word with Ben if that's possible, please? I think he'll remember me.'

'Ben's out in the woodshed, I'll just give him call.' Brian heard the 'clunk' as Tina put the receiver down on a hard surface. In the distance he heard her call out, 'Ben, Ben there's someone on the phone for you, Brian someone, sounds like an Irishman to me.' A few seconds later Ben was on the line.

'Hello Brian, this is Ben. How are you, any joy with house-hunting yet?'

'Sorry to bother you Ben, but you did say… on the train…'

'It's no bother. I wouldn't have said anything I didn't mean. Now, how can I help?'

Although he didn't mean to, Brian went through chapter and verse of what he'd been up to since their chance encounter on the train from Liverpool Street back in February and when his rather nervously presented discourse was becoming protracted Ben interrupted him.

'Look, you've obviously got a lot to tell me. Why don't we meet for lunch?

Where are you right now?'

'I'm in Woodbridge at the Crown Hotel.'

'Well I'll meet you in the Anchor on Quay Street, do you know it? Back towards the station.'

'Yes, I was in there last night – nice pub for sure.'

'Say 11.30? I've just got a few chores to finish up.'

***

The windscreen wipers on the Hillman Avenger were struggling to cope with the rain and spray. Doug Armstrong had made an impulsive decision to drive to East Anglia to see his ex-wife. Not only had it been an impulsive decision he hadn't really thought through the full implications of his visit at all. He hadn't even bothered to find out if she'd be at home or care to see him when he turned up unannounced. 'What if she's with another bloke?' Doug thought. He was half a mind to turn back.

***

Tina Blake had made herself some coffee when Ben announced he was going out to meet Brian. They had planned on going for a walk together but the weather was hardly conducive to that kind of pursuit and she was quite happy to sit and read the newspaper, something she very rarely had time for. Holding her attention as Ben was about to leave was a piece on women being allowed into the Stock Exchange for the first time.

'I'm not sure when I'll be back, but I shouldn't be late. I promised to help out this Irishman so I'd better keep my word,' Ben explained.

'Uh huh,' was the only reaction.

***

It was 11 am and at the Anchor, Sid had just opened up and the usual few of early regulars were getting served before taking their customary positions to study form in the *Racing Post*.

'Morning Colin, usual?'

'Yes please Sid. What a terrible day!'

'Ain't it just? Still forecast reckons it'll brighten up a bit around now. On yer own? Where's yer new lady-friend?'

'If you mean Maisie, she's my neighbour that's all. There's nothing going on if that's what you're thinking.' The banter was all in good humour.

'Are yo' sure about that?' Sid nodded towards the door and Colin turned to see the dripping form of Maisie.'

'Oh Colin, thank goodness. I was hoping I'd find you in here.'

'Watchya Maisie, what'll you have?'

'Well, I wasn't going to but, oh, go on then. G&T please Sid.' Maisie took off her wet coat and hung it up and the two houseboat neighbours perched on barstools in the corner. As Maisie was explaining to Colin about a slight problem with the float switch on *Ironside*'s bilge pump, Brian entered the bar.

'Hello again. How was the Crown?' asked Sid. After a minute or two of small talk, Brian took advantage of the bar being fairly clear of customers and took a walk around to study the photographs mounted on the walls. One early picture of the Quay when it was a regular working port he found particularly fascinating. Noting Brian's obvious interest and having such a friendly disposition Colin commented, 'Imagine what that must have been like, barges in and out on every tide. Good job it's not like that now eh Maisie?' Brian was genuinely interested.

'Why's that then?' Brian enquired. Colin laughed as he replied,

'We live there, me and Maisie here, my neighbour.'

'What you live on the boats in the dock by the quay?'

'Colin's been there forever,' quipped Maisie. 'I've only been there for about a month now. I'm getting used to it and I love it.' Colin noticed the way Maisie had looked at Brian as she spoke to him. Was there just the slightest pang of jealousy there? An easy-going three-way conversation ensued with each of participants contributing little facets of themselves.

'I'm waiting for a friend,' announced Brian. 'Well, I hardly know him yet, I met him on the train from London and he agreed to show me round. I'm looking for a place to live somewhere locally.'

'Is he local?' asked Colin.

'Not Woodbridge, he's from Orford.'

'Oh yes, lovely there. Bit of excitement there a couple of months ago.'

'Go on.'

'Some bloke got shot, murdered, across on the island on the other side the Orford River.' Before any further questions were asked or comments made a fourth person had approached the corner of the bar.

'Hello Maisie. It's been a while.' All eyes instantly focused on the newcomer.

'I do not believe it!' Maisie stared with eyes and mouth wide open in surprise. 'Doug Armstrong. I do not believe it!' she repeated with incredulous excitement. 'You could knock me down with a feather! Sorry, Colin, Brian, this is Doug Armstrong, my ex-husband. Doug's a policeman, where are you based now Doug?'

'Thames Valley, Detective Sergeant.' He answered proudly. Brian slid from his stool as inconspicuously as he could.

'Excuse me, I have to go to the toilet,' he said quietly.

'You two must have a lot to talk about – I'll leave you both to it. I'll go and have a look at your bilge pump Maisie. See you later.' There was something of a resigned disappointment in the tone of his voice as Colin finished off his pint and disappeared.

Even as Colin walked out the door, Ben Blake walked in. He looked around the room and approached the bar and spoke to Sid.

'I'm supposed to be meeting a fellow here, has he arrived?'

'Well, I'll need a bit more of a clue than that,' answered Sid with his customary genial grin.

'Excuse me, it's Ben Blake isn't it? Doug Armstrong, Thames Valley,' he announced. 'We met at your mother's house in

Burton Overy.' Out of context, Ben hadn't recognised the DS at first.

'Of course, hello sergeant. How's the investigation going?' DS Armstrong ignored the question and introduced his ex-wife.

'This is Maisie Clarke, my ex. Maisie this is Ben Blake, I think you know his mum Helen?'

'Of course. Hello Ben, how's things, how's your mum?'

'She's fine as far as I know although I get the impression she's a bit smitten with Detective Armstrong's boss!'

'Really? responded Armstrong. 'Well, I reckon your mum's feelings might well be reciprocated,' he laughed. 'So, what brings you here on such a dreadful day?'

'I'm supposed to be meeting a chap I met on the train last month and offered to give him a guided tour. He's been looking to buy a place in Norfolk but decided maybe Suffolk might be better. He's moving here from Northern Ireland to get away from the Troubles. Has he been in?' DS Armstrong all but choked on his beer. It was Maisie who replied.

'Oh right, that'll be him me and Colin were chatting with. Seems like a nice chap. He's just gone to the toilet.' No sooner had she said so that Brian reappeared. He greeted Ben and taking his arm guided him towards the door as he bade a hasty farewell to Maise and the DS.

'Oh, that's a shame,' said Maisie. I was taking rather a shine to him.

DS Armstrong didn't hear her. He stood in suspended animation staring after the two men who had just left. 'Couldn't be could it?' he half whispered to himself.

'Couldn't be what?'

'Oh never mind.' Ordinarily he would have gone chasing after them but today was his day off and he had other things on his mind.

'Another G&T?'

Chapter Thirty-Three

It had been during World War II in 1943 that the Royal Air Force established RAF Sutton Heath, a base just north of Woodbridge on the edge of Rendlesham Forest. At that time the base's primary purpose was to accept distressed aircraft returning from raids over Germany, low on fuel, perhaps with undercarriage or other problems from being hit by flak or whatever. During the last years of the war RAF Woodbridge handled in excess of 4000 emergency landings. The base was also used by the United States Air Force as home to the B17 'Flying Fortress' bomber. After the war, Lancaster bombers from Woodbridge flew experimental bombing missions over Orford Ness. And, as a result of an escalation of the Cold War, the Americans stayed on. More recently in 1970 the base was in use by the USAF and their 67th Air Rescue and Recovery Squadron and the sight and sound of the Lockheed 'Hercules' aircraft and the 'Jolly Green Giant' helicopter became familiar locally.

With so many American Service personnel and their families stationed at the base an American High School was built. This became a great attraction for Ronnie Higginson and his associate ne'er-do-wells. For reasons best known to themselves, teenage American girls were fascinated by English boys and vice versa. Inappropriate liaisons and relationships were formed and prohibited sorties into the more isolated spots in the forest were commonplace. It was on Friday 30th March that Gail Read was enticed by Ronnie Higginson to take a ride to Rendlesham Forest on the pretext of a party with some of his American friends. It was during that evening that Gail's virginity was stolen.

***

With there having been a few days earlier in the month which promised an early spring it was almost a case of back to midwinter. There had been an overnight frost and the north-easterly force eight was howling down the North Sea coast delivering hail, sleet and snow showers. It was most certainly not a day to contemplate getting out of bed, never mind going to sea. 'Fish'll still be there tomorrow,' thought Mervyn as he rolled over in bed. Meanwhile, the Read's youngest son Matthew had got up at the crack of dawn and biked down to Felixstowe Ferry to meet his Uncle Maurice. It was the standing arrangement for a weekend. Had the Reads been on the phone, maybe Maurice would have called Matt to tell him not to bother but then he could find him something to do in the shed.

By the time Matt got to the yard he was wet through and bitterly cold having cycled across the golf links into the teeth of the gale. He was relieved to see the Ford Anglia van already there. Maurice had the gas ring lit upon which there stood a saucepan containing the contents of the discarded Heinz Tomato Soup can, warming up.

'Come in, come in yer daft bugger. Yer might 'ave knowed we wunt be goin' in this weather.' Matt was shivering and made no response.

''Ere sit yer down lad and get some o' this soup down yer neck.' After a few minutes, Matt was thawing out. He'd removed his wet coat and trousers which were steaming on the nail which served as a hook and he'd put his oilskins on which had dried out since the last trip.

'I reckons we'll just 'ave a bit of a tidy-up then We'll stick your bike in the van an' I'll run yer 'ome.'

'OK unc', that'll be great.'

'So, what d'you know? 'Ow's work? Everything OK at the Co-op?'

'It's OK unc. Tell yer what though… Alan Higginson got the sack. Manager told me he were lucky not to get reported to the police.'

Bob Bennett

'Go on? What'd he bin up to?'

'Nicking stuff.'

'Don't surprise me in the least. Serve the silly young bugger right! Like 'is elder brother. I bet it were 'im as nicked that rifle.' Matt didn't care to be reminded of his indiscretion, breaching his uncle's confidence. He changed the subject.

'Cor, our Gail didn't 'arf get a roastin' last night.'

'Oh arh? Tell us more.'

'She din't come in from school 'til gone nine o'clock.'

'Where'd she bin then?'

'Told me dad she'd bin round a friend's from school, but 'e knew she were lying. Me dad went b'listic. An' there were mud on her skirt and blazer and she 'ad no tights on when she come in. But she wouldn't say nowt. The more 'e shouted, the more she cried an' screamed an' stuff.'

'Oh dear oh dear. Silly girl. I thought your sister were a bright kid. I 'ope she ain't done owt stupid.'

'Yeah. Me dad's goin' to see 'eadmaster on Monday.'

'Right lad lets sort that mess out in the corner. I reckon we'll 'ave to chuck that net. Don't look like it's worth mendin'.'

Nephew and uncle set to the task. All manner of paraphernalia, none of which was totally out of place in a fisherman's shed, got moved from one place to another. As they manhandled the old net out of the door Maurice picked up a small carton, trodden flat, and hastily put it in the pocket of his smock. Whilst it might not have been out of place in certain fishermen's sheds, it had no place in Maurice's.

After an hour or so, the shed was not really looking any tidier than when they started, apart from there was now a space where the net had been.

'OK lad, that'll do for now. Get yer gear an' yer bike an' I'll run yer 'ome.'

'OK unc!'

It was what he'd found on the floor and what his nephew had said about his niece that Maurice decided there was something pressing that he should attend to.

143

The Ford Anglia van pulled up outside the house in Kirton. Matt collected his bike from the back of the van and pushed it up the path to put it away in the garden shed. Maurice knocked on his brother's front door which was subsequently opened by his sister-in-law Barbara.

'Hello Maurice, terrible weather isn't it? Thanks for bringing Matt 'ome.'

'Watchya Barb! I came to see our Merv' as much as bring the lad 'ome. Is he in?'

'Oh aye 'e's in. In bed.'

'Oh, well don't wake 'im on my account. Tell 'im I need a word, White Horse at lunchtime? "Ow's Gail by the way? I ain't seen her fer a while.' Matt told me there were a bit of a ruck.'

'Gail who? We don't 'ave a daughter anymore!'

'Oh dear. Bad as that is it?'

'She's in disgrace and not allowed out of 'er room until we get the truth.'

'Oh, well, don't be too 'ard on 'er. She's only a gal.'

Maurice liked a pint on a weekend, or at any other time come to that, but especially on a weekend when he wasn't at sea. The White Horse at Kirton was one of his favourite pubs.

'Eh up Bert. "Ow's it 'angin'?'

'Hello, Maurice. Usual?' Maurice looked around the bar. There were a couple of youths playing on the one-armed bandit.

He hadn't got down his first pint very far when the front door opened and another customer came in accompanied by a draught of wind. Perhaps it's just human nature, but when someone enters a pub, those already present look around to see who the newcomer might be.

'Ay up Arthur', greeted Bert. 'Don't see you up 'ere very often. You lost?'

'Hello Bert – no I'm not lost I've come to Kirton to see Mervyn Read but now I'm here I think I need a drop of Dutch courage.'

On hearing his brother's name, Maurice's ears pricked up and he turned to face the man he now knew as Arthur.

'Hello Arthur, I'm Maurice. Maurice Read, Mervyn's brother. He'll be 'ere in a bit. I'm meetin' 'im 'ere. Let me buy you a drink while you wait. What'll it be?

'I'll have a Mackeson please. Very kind of you, thank you.' They took their drinks and went and sat in the snug. Before long they both knew sufficient about each other to enable free and easy small talk, even though Maurice had never married and had no children therefore no connection with the school.

'I've met Mervyn and Barbara more than several times at parents' evenings and school functions and the like. I've taught all his children. Oh dear, this is very difficult for me.' Arthur was getting a little agitated. 'Can I ask your advice Maurice; you know your brother better than I? It's Gail, his daughter.'

Instantly Maurice put two and two together. Arthur began to relate his recent confrontation with the girl he had held high hopes for and just as he was doing so the draught of wind through the front door announced the arrival of Mervyn.

Fresh drinks were served and Arthur Ross nervously launched forth on his tale of woe. The brothers sat quietly listening. When Arthur got to the part where Gail disappears into Ronnie Higginson's car Mervyn leapt to his feet, apoplectic with rage. The drinks went flying over the snug's already sticky carpet and it took a full five minutes for Maurice to calm his brother down.

'Eh up, lads, easy now, what's up?' It was Bert come to see what the ruckus was about.

'It's OK Bert,' assured Maurice, 'he'll be alright in a minute.' Maurice was unsure whether to add further fuel to the flames which had now died down but thought, better to get it done in one.

'We all know the bloody Higginsons, what they're like. Look, and 'ang on to yer 'at Merv.' Anxious looks, including those from Bert behind the bar, were now cast in Maurice's direction. I'm pretty certain it were Ronnie Higginson what broke into me shed last week and I found these on the floor when we was tidying up this morning.' He took the squashed packet of contraceptives from his smock pocket and tossed them on to the table. There was a stunned silence. Mervyn was speechless. He picked up the packet and threw it down again.

'No!' he shouted the word in a long-drawn-out roar. He began to cry with rage. Arthur's eyes were closed and he sat slowly shaking his head from side to side waiting for the eruption. The storm brewing in the snug looked like being every bit as violent as the one that had prevented the brothers from fishing that morning. It was Arthur Ross who spoke first.

'Now look, let's not jump to conclusions. This doesn't mean…'

'Of course it bloody well does Arthur. What else can it mean? My daughter comes home from school at nine at night covered in muck and no tights on after you've seen 'er gettin' into a car wi' that bastard Higginson, 'im what carries Durex around wi' 'im? I'm not bloody stupid!' Had Mervyn had a safety valve it would have blown by now, such was his ferocity of his rage

'I'll bloody kill 'im!'

With that, Mervyn Read, incensed with pain and in a revengeful temper the likes of which his brother had never previously witnessed, left the pub. Maurice didn't know whether he should follow him or not. He decided not to. Besides which, through the window he could see that the rain was torrential. There was every chance that Mervyn would explode when he got home and Maurice was concerned for his niece's welfare. He was also worried by the threat directed at Ronnie Higginson. Surely it was an idle one? Or was it? Merv's mood at that moment was uglier than the weather but the rain would douse any potential fire and fury… wouldn't it?

Chapter Thirty-Four

The news that the *Samson* was expected to arrive in Felixstowe on Saturday 31st March was music to DCI Cartwright's ears. He had been looking forward to interrogating Sam Reynolds ever since his DC had discovered that it had more than likely been his boat *Samson* which had ferried two men to Lowestoft on 31st January; two men who had prebooked reservations at the Victoria Hotel and prepared to make the trip through a gale. 'Would anyone in their right mind travel up the coast in a small boat through a gale in the dark unless they had to? Or unless they were trying to escape from something or somewhere?' Cartwright was hypothesising. Surely these were his wanted men. Not only would this trip to Felixstowe hopefully provide some answers but it would also present an opportunity for him to look up a certain woman. He could use the excuse of an unannounced visit as being a sort of pastoral, social call, checking on her welfare after the trauma of witnessing a fatal shooting. He rang PC Andy Lewis to ask if would like the overtime again.

When they arrived at the Felixstowe Dock and Railway Company's port, the *Samson* was already berthed on the recently extended Landguard Container Terminal. There was one large, partially loaded, or was it partially unloaded ship on the quay. It was hard to tell since there wasn't much in the way of any activity and none of the three cranes were in operation. Lewis then spotted a small vessel berthed beyond the ship.

'I reckon that could be it guv.' Lewis nodded in the direction of the small ship he had seen. He drove the length of the quay and parked the car adjacent the boat, the name *Samson* emblazoned across the transom. Cartwright got out of the car and recalling a distant memory of something he'd seen in a film once-upon-a-time he shouted up towards the open wheelhouse door.

'Permission to come aboard?'

A hatch-cover on the afterdeck opened and Joe Reynolds appeared from the engine room wiping his hands on an oily rag. 'Who are you? What'd you want?'

'Are you the skipper, Sam Reynolds?'

'No, I'm the mate, Joe, his son. Skipper's gone to sort out the paperwork at the dock office. He shouldn't be too long. What is it you want?'

'I'm DCI Cartwright of Thames Valley Police. I need to talk to the skipper, your dad.'

'Well you'll have to wait 'til he gets back then won't you?' Joe disappeared back into the engine room. So, Cartwright went and sat in the car with Lewis.

'He mentioned paperwork. That's encouraging, well it is if there's a record of all his trips and cargoes and such.'

'He'll surely have a logbook of some description?' suggested Lewis.

After a frustrating wait of almost half-an-hour a man who Cartwright assumed was Sam Reynolds approached the *Samson*. Cartwright was out of the car and intercepted him.

'Are you Sam Reynolds?'

'Who's asking?' Cartwright was not impressed. The evasive response from the skipper was just as unhelpful as that from the mate.

'I am. Detective Chief Inspector Cartwright of Thames Valley Police.' He asserted.

'This is the bloody Orwell. You're on the wrong river. Bugger off and leave us alone.' Reynolds made to climb the gangplank onto his boat.

'I need to ask you a few questions in connection with a murder enquiry. We can either do it here or at the police station in Ipswich. You're choice!'

Lewis had heard the exchange so far and got out of the car knowing that the presence of a second officer might well prove to be sufficiently intimidating to prompt a little cooperation.

'OK you'd better come aboard then.' Reynolds' invitation was reluctant to say the least. Skipper and mate, DCI and PC descended the companionway into *Samson*'s saloon and they sat around the table.

'I'm interested in the two men you took to Lowestoft on 31st January.'

'What two men?'

'Look, we know you took two men to Lowestoft on 31st January. This has been confirmed by the harbourmaster at Lowestoft. Let me remind you, you sailed through a gale…'

'Ah, those two men,' said Reynolds, miraculously recovered from his amnesia. 'Joe, pop up and get the logbook.' The book was placed on the table, simulated leatherbound and embossed in gold with the words Ship's Log. Reynolds opened the book and flicked back through several pages.

'Here we are. That's right, I remember now. Two blokes. A Mr Ellis and a Mr Miles. They'd booked and paid for a trip up the coast. Booking was done through the dock office here. I was to pick 'em up off Orford and take 'em to Lowestoft.'

'Did it not strike you as strange that they wanted picking up off Orford? Wouldn't it be more usual to pick up passengers from a dock, a port, a quay or some such?'

'Aye it would that, but I don't ask questions. I just deliver. As far as I'm concerned passengers are just self-loading cargo. I'll pick 'em up anywhere.'

'Did you speak to them?'

'Of course, just a bit, not much. It was a rough trip. They were below drinking scotch most of the time.'

'Is there anything else you can tell me? A description perhaps? Did they have any luggage?'

'Nothing really. Just ordinary fellers really, average sort of blokes. One of 'em had his golf clubs with him. I thought that was a bit strange. I reckon he must have had a bad round 'cos he threw them in the sea!

'Weren't they Irish dad?' asked Joe.

'I reckon they might have been. Anyway, I dropped 'em off at the Trawl Dock in Lowestoft and they went off to the Victoria Hotel. I reckon they'd got rooms booked.

The dialogue had been enough to convince Cartwright that *Samson* had indeed taken McFaddon and the gunman to Lowestoft. Reynolds could have been a little more forthcoming perhaps, but he no more knew who Ellis and Miles were than anyone else. Cartwright doubted that there was anything he could be charged with. OK he'd assisted a murderer to escape the scene of his crime but there was no way he could have known that.

'OK Mr Reynolds, Joe, thanks for your help. Oh, just one thing more, would you recognise them if you saw them again? If we manage to apprehend these men we may need someone to identify them.'

'Doubtful, that.'

'OK Lewis, Pin Mill if you please.'

'Guv,' he responded with a knowing smile.

Chapter Thirty-Five

'What's the rush?' Ben was more than a little taken aback to be dragged out of the pub. When they were outside Ben explained.

'I'm sorry about that for more than one reason as well.' Ben was straining to hear what was being said. The traffic on Quay Street seemed to be much heavier than normal, and some drivers were sounding off their frustration and annoyance with their horns. The rain had eased off, but it was still drizzling as they walked up Quay Street passed the queuing traffic.

'Look, here's my hotel. Let's stop here, at least we'll be able to hear ourselves think.' They took a couple of stools in the public bar of the Crown. Brian was served with a bottle of Guinness whilst Ben waited for a coffee.

'So, what was all that about then?' asked Ben.

'Now look Ben, firstly let me say how much I appreciate you giving up your time to act as native guide to someone you only met briefly...'

'Not a problem, a pleasure,' interrupted Ben.

'No, you don't know me and there are things in my past that you don't want to know either. I'm not sure whether that policeman back there might be looking for me – whether he was or not, I didn't want to stay there to find out.'

Ben was intrigued.

'You're not on the run are you, a fugitive?'

'Better you don't know – can we leave it there please?'

'Well, I'm not sure. Didn't you tell me you were a consultant for the military? You're not AWOL are you? I don't want to be associating with a criminal.'

'I'll just tell you this – there are things in my past I'd rather forget. I was involved on the periphery of the Troubles in Northern Ireland. I had sympathy with the Republican ideal. I still do but it's a lost cause. It was all getting way too heavy. It's why I decided to move here and start afresh. You don't know me, the police don't know me, in fact nobody here knows me and that's how I'd like it stay until I make new friends. I'd like you to be my first.' The look on Ben's face expressed a hesitant uncertainty and after a long moment of silence the hint of a smile suggested he might accede to Brian's friendship invitation.

'OK then – friends!' They shook hands and it was if some kind of bond had been established.

'Did you know that woman, the woman in the pub? asked Brian.

'Maisie? Well not really, I've met her before. She's a friend of my mother's. They were in prison together.' The minute he'd said it he regretted having done so.

'Ah, so I'm not the only one with a shady background!' Brian laughed.

'I suppose you're right. It's a long story. Maybe one day. For now I'll just say that my mum's conviction was grossly unfair. The bloke that should have been convicted disappeared. He's dead now though. Got shot! Anyway, enough of that. Where do you want to go, what do you want to see?'

'Could this have been…?' Brian wondered.

Brian explained what he was looking for, in terms of location, his budget and his intentions but his mind had just been jolted back by two months – although it seemed longer. Ben clapped him on the back in a matey gesture which brought him back to the present.

'Right-ho. If the rain's stopped I suggest we have a walk down the Thoroughfare. There're a couple of estate agents down there we can take a look at and see what they've got to offer.'

'Fine by me. Let's go!'

Chapter Thirty-Six

By the time Mervyn was almost at home having walked from the White Horse oblivious to the torrential rain he was soaked. Every stitch of clothing he was wearing was wet through. He had wept all the way. He was an emotional wreck, a soul in torment. He was hurting to the point of despair. His little girl, sexually abused, violated by a child-molesting yob, a feral degenerate. He blamed himself. If only… What would he say to her? Who was he angrier with? His daughter, Higginson, or himself? Should she be scolded, or reprimanded or even disowned? He let himself in and went directly to the bathroom where he stripped off his wet clothes and washed. He stared at himself in the mirror, his eyes red from weeping. He pleaded with himself to find the right way to deal with the situation; to find the right words. As he dressed he determined that there would be no repetition of last night's raging anger. Getting worked up again would do neither of them any good. At the end of the day, Gail would still be his daughter, the apple of his eye. Could he find it in his heart to forgive her?

He crossed the landing and quietly tapped on his daughter's bedroom door.

'Gail,' he whispered, 'it's dad. Can I come in in?' Without waiting for an answer he went into her room. Gail was lying on her bed. She turned to look at her father and immediately gave in to the compelling urge to hold him, to hug him. With her arms grasped tightly around his neck she whispered in his ear.

'I'm so, so very sorry dad. I was very stupid. I should have realised what he wanted.' Father and daughter sat together on the edge of the bed.

'Tell me,' requested Mervyn. Gail wiped her eyes with her handkerchief. She took a deep breath, sighed, and hesitatingly began her account of all that had happened since the end of school on the previous day.

'Ronnie Higginson and a load of other lads were hanging about outside the school gates. They were all going to a party in Rendlesham Forest, to meet up with some American kids from the high school on the base. I shouldn't have gone. When I think about it now I'm not sure I wanted to go anyway. But Ronnie kept saying things like "C'mon Gail, it'll be great, the Yanks have booze and stuff, we'll have fun, it'll be a laugh, I'll take you home after, don't be a spoilsport." So I went. Everything was OK to start, one of the American kids had a portable record-player and he was playing that new Pink Floyd record, *Dark Side of the Moon*. Some of the kids were dancing and getting friendly, if you know what I mean. There was a load of booze. The Americans get it cheap from the BX store on the base even though they're underage. I told Ronnie I didn't want any, so he gave me orange juice. I guessed he was putting vodka in it.' Gail paused, then began to cry. 'It was awful dad. I didn't want to. I kept telling him, no Ronnie, stop. I was fighting him, trying to punch him, kick him, screaming "No" but he was too strong. The other kids were just laughing.' Her tears were now in full flow as she sobbed uncontrollably. Mervyn was fighting back tears of his own as he sat stroking her hair. The paternal affection and tenderness he was feeling at that moment outweighed by far his loathing of Higginson. Gail's weeping abated sufficiently for her to manage to say, 'I was raped, dad.' Mervyn held his daughter in a desperate embrace; her tears diluting his own.

After a while he stood up. 'I'll make it right love, don't worry. I'll make it right.'

Barbara had returned from delivering some mending she'd been doing and was surprised to find Mervyn sitting at the kitchen table staring into the oblivion of the middle distance, seemingly miles away.

'Merv? Merv, what's up?' Barbara was filling the kettle.

Mervyn began to tell his wife of Gail's experience as told to him, of the emotional wringer he'd been and was continuing to go through, of how he was full of remorse and sorrow for the manner in which he'd flown into a rage without knowing the facts and for thinking the worst of his own daughter. Barbara's reaction was to rush upstairs to Gail's room and with a heartrending outpouring of compassion and tenderness she comforted her daughter.

The two women in Mervyn's life came downstairs together.

'We're going to the hospital,' announced Barbara. 'Best we get her checked out if you follow my drift. Then whilst we're in Ipswich, we're going to the police station.'

'OK, I'm coming with you.'

Chapter Thirty-Seven

A bridge over the river Orwell would have made the drive from Felixstowe to Pin Mill a much shorter and quicker journey without requiring the need to negotiate a way through Ipswich's congestion.

'OK Andy, make yourself scarce for an hour. Where'll I find you?'

'I'll have a bit of a walk then a snooze in the car if that's OK guv?' Cartwright was nervous. He'd never had a great deal of success with women although this woman would be different. He could sense it. He approached her cottage and even as he did so the front door opened. His pulse was racing. She looked amazing.

'I knew you'd be back,' she said. And they were the only words that were spoken. It had been his intention to behave in a gentlemanly manner, with chivalry and courtesy, with a display of gracious good manners and tactful suavity. Cartwright had rehearsed it all in his mind. He'd played it over and over like a cinefilm, with Helen and himself starring as Ali McGraw and Ryan O'Neal. As it happened, the rehearsals proved to have been superfluous. Helen ran towards him and to Cartwright it seemed the most natural thing to do was to open his arms to receive her embrace. The mutual attraction that had been evident previously was now something much greater. Mutual affection. They kissed and far from there being even the slightest notion of any illicit desires they both knew where this was heading. Helen took his hand and led him into the cottage.

Lewis had observed all of this from a discreet distance and knew he would be in for a long wait. He didn't mind. There was no reason for him to be rushing back to an empty flat and the overtime payments on a Sunday were more than adequate compensation for the imposition. After an hour or so, Cartwright, minus his necktie, tapping on the car window woke Lewis from his snooze on the back seat.

'Would you mind an overnight?'

'Guv?'

'Drive into Ipswich, find yourself a bed and breakfast and pick me up at eight in the morning.'

'OK guv.' Lewis' responded in a matter-of-fact manner but had difficulty supressing a big grin.

'And don't forget to get receipts for everything!'

'Guv.'

***

In Woodbridge, Doug Armstrong had spent the best part of the day with Maisie, his ex-wife. He'd also spent the best part of a week's salary behind the bar of Anchor. They hadn't seen each other in more than several years and, rather more in the manner of long-lost friends than a divorced married couple they had idly and pleasantly whiled away the hours hearing of each other's fortunes and misfortunes. After the Anchor had closed on the Saturday afternoon Maisie had given her erstwhile husband a guided tour of *Ironside* and Doug had been well impressed. She made him a cheese sandwich and they sat in the saloon watching the rain until both of them had fallen asleep.

'They're open!' It was Colin from the *Mary Gloster*. Since becoming neighbours, it had almost become a Saturday evening tradition that Colin and Maisie would go out for a drink and then on to a restaurant.

'Sorry Colin, we both dozed off. Do you mind if Doug tags along tonight?' Maisie was hurriedly applying little makeup.

Freshened up after the lunchtime session Colin suggested a walk to the Cherry Tree.

'You know what they say, a change is as good as a rest, besides which, the walk will do us good.' Neither Maisie nor Doug had the energy to argue. Several drinks later they descended on the recently refurbished restaurant, the Galley. During their meal conversation was stilted until Colin asked if Maisie had heard any more from Graham her second husband further to the threats he made. Maisie hadn't mentioned any of this to Doug earlier in the day and she would rather Colin had not raised the subject at all in Doug's presence. She was sure that he would be bound to interfere, interference that would be unwelcome. She made light of it and steered the conversation on to her new job.

All the misgivings that Doug Armstrong had when he'd first got wind of his ex-wife being involved on the periphery of the investigation into McClean's murder had proved to be unwarranted. Together, even with the ubiquitous Colin, the day had been most convivial. Doug was more than just a little anxious about how to address his imminent predicament. He didn't want to create the wrong impression or send out misleading signals.

'Maisie, I was wondering… look it was never my intention… I don't mean that we should… oh bugger! Look I'm a bit pissed and in no fit state to drive. Can I stay the night on *Ironside* please?' Colin looked on with interest waiting for Maisie's response.

'I'm not sure. I don't really think that would be appropriate. It would be better if you stayed with Colin on *Mary Gloster*. Is that OK with you Colin?'

'Of course, no problem. The spare cabin is always made up.' Colin was immediately released from the slightly jealous feelings he'd been harbouring. Colin was playing the long game.

***

At Thames Valley Constabulary Headquarters in Kidlington, Chief Superintendent Tim Adams was on the prowl.

'Where the hell is DCI Cartwright? Where the hell is DS Armstrong?' He was vexed about something. From amongst the blank faces in the detectives' room came a response from DC Davies.

'He's gone to Felixstowe sir.'

'Who has, Cartwright or Armstrong?'

'The DCI sir.'

'What the bloody hell's he doing there? He's supposed to be investigating a murder.' The Chief Superintendent was not happy.

'He is sir. I mean, yes he is investigating, not yes he's supposed…'

'I know what you mean. What's in Felixstowe? It's a port isn't it?'

'Yes sir it is. We believe the murderer and his accomplice may have made good their escape by sea after the shooting. The boat that picked them up was due to dock at Felixstowe today.' With the wind taken from his sails Adams' attitude moderated somewhat.

'At least he's on official police business then?' The question was rhetorical. 'What about Armstrong? Is he in Felixstowe as well?'

'No sir. He's in Ipswich.' The Chief Superintendent's exasperation rose again.

'What's he doing there? Do tell.' The sarcasm had a sharp edge to it.

'I believe his gone to interview the principal witness again sir, Helen Blake.'

'Well, I'm glad they've both seen fit to inform you of their whereabouts DC Davies. Shame they couldn't be bothered to keep their Chief Superintendent informed. I want to see them both the minute they return!'

'Yes sir.'

Adams left the room mumbling something to no one in particular. 'Might as well move the whole bloody investigation to East bloody Anglia. Save time and money!'

Chapter Thirty-Eight

Ben and Brian walked casually down the Thoroughfare, the town's main shopping street. It was fairly busy with Saturday afternoon shoppers. They stopped outside Mortimer's and peered through the window at the photographs of the various properties they had for sale. Many were captioned with 'estateagencyspeak' alongside the price. '£9500 Scope for improvement,' '£10,950 Well-proportioned town-house,' '£16,000 Stunning views,' '£14,500 Older-style cottage property'.

'I quite like the look of that one,' Brian said, but without much enthusiasm.

'Which? That one at Capel St Andrew, south-facing garden? Let's get the details then.' Brian had lost impetus even before they'd barely started.

'It's a bit remote. Small village close the River Butley. There's a ferry across the river and a nice walk to Orford. You could come and visit.'

'Oh, I don't know…' For all that Ben was trying to generate a modicum of interest, very little was forthcoming.

'We could take a drive past at least. Have a look at it from the outside? What do you say?'

'OK I guess so.'

'Let's just see what Potter's has got. There might be something else that takes your fancy in the same area.' Ben was clearly having a much better time than Brian.

'How about that one – look, £14,000 Fully refurbished cottage, no chain' -

right up your street, meets your spec, price is right. Only eight miles away. Let's get the details.' As Ben was about to open the door he noticed the schedule of opening hours.

'Closed! Seems Potter's doesn't open Saturday afternoons. You'll have to come back on Monday. Still, we can have a look. Boyton's not far from Capel, and it's got a pub, The Bell.' Was that a spark of enthusiasm thought Ben to himself?

They walked back down Quay Street towards the railway station car park and got into Ben's MGB and took the B1084 towards Butley before turning on to the minor road to Capel St Andrew. They located the property easily enough, with the agent's 'For Sale' board erected on a stake in the 'south facing garden'. Neither Ben nor Brian was particularly impressed.

'Needs quite a bit of restoration by the look of it,' Brian commented. 'I'm not really a hands-on sort of bloke. In my book, DIY stands for Don't Involve Yourself.' Where's this other one?'

They drove on to Boyton and the 'feel' of the village, the atmosphere had a much more sociable disposition. Once again the cottage was conspicuous by the agent's board. Ben parked the car and he and Brian took a peek through the windows. Brian liked what he saw even though the view was restricted. As far as they could, they walked around the property. Ben noticed Brian making various gestures of what he took to be approval.

'I like this one. This would do, I think. I'll get the details from the agent on Monday and take a proper look. I'll need some transport.'

'Can't help you on Monday, I'm afraid. I have to go to London. I'm sure the agent will be happy to drive you out though especially if he thinks there might be a sale in the offing.'

The house-hunting, such as it had been, was done for the day and Ben dropped Brian back at the Crown before returning home to Orford.

***

Was it merely coincidental or ironic? But there in East Anglia and just a few miles from each other were two police detectives and a PC, miles away from their own postings in the Thames Valley force with neither detective aware of the presence of the other nor of their close proximity of the elusive suspect. The Detective Sergeant slept uneasily feeling guilty that he had taken a day off from the murder investigation he should have been working on. Little did he know that his clandestine liaison with his ex-wife would soon involve the man who stole her from him. The Detective Chief Inspector didn't sleep very much at all in the shared bed. Little did he know that his clandestine liaison with an important witness in the murder investigation would soon involve him to within a whisker of making an arrest in the Harvey and McClean cases. The police constable slept soundly in a budget hotel.

***

'It's important to remember that it's not your fault.' A kindly policewoman was speaking gently to a very tearful Gail at the hospital. Barbara, her mother was sitting with her daughter on the bed. Mervyn was idly flicking through the pages of an out-of-date magazine in the waiting room. Julia Robinson, the WPC had been called to the hospital by the nursing sister who had examined Gail. The examination had revealed some bruising in the groin area and on the girl's breasts and arms. Having consulted with the nurse at some length there was no doubt in Julia's mind that Gail had indeed been raped. She continued.

'Sexual violence is a crime no matter who commits it. You didn't actively consent and he forced himself on you. You now feel defiled, violated. You feel dirty no matter how many times you bathe. I know, I know'. Julia's sympathetic and caring manner, her warm and tender kind-heartedness were working wonders on Gail's fragile condition and easing her mental anguish and distress. Addressing Barbara, Julia asked,

'How old is Gail Mrs Read?'

'She'll be 16 in August.'

'So, she's currently beneath the age of consent as well. I would imagine that the rapist will likely get eight to ten years.'

'They should cut his tackle off as well,' Barbara pronounced with malicious acerbity.'

Turning back to Gail, Julia asked, 'Who was it? Do you know him?' It was Barbara who answered. 'Oh yes, we know him all right!' Julia made a note of Ronnie Higginson's details in her notebook.

Chapter Thirty-Nine

On the Roughs Tower Estate, Ronnie Higginson expected that it would only be a matter of time before someone came calling regarding the 'party' in Rendlesham Forest. Even so, he was convinced that he'd done nothing wrong. Such was his highly developed sense of chauvinistic bravado and tyrannical arrogance that he was certain he could talk his way out of the situation.

'If she 'adn't been gaggin' for it, why'd she come wi' me in me motor? She knew what the fuckin' score were; a party in the woods. What were she expecting, ice cream and jelly? Weren't much of a shag neither!' Higginson was mentally rehearsing his arguments. It barely crossed his mind that Gail Read might not have reached her sixteenth birthday. She may have looked older, or acted older than fifteen but she was under the age of consent nevertheless. Ronnie Higginson was guilty of statutory rape whether Gail had consented or not. But he wouldn't have known that. There was a knock at the door. He looked out of his bedroom window and was relieved not to see a police car. He went downstairs and opened the door. It was not one of Ronnie's mates, more of a hanger-on really, a bumsucker by the name of Donald Hetherington.

'What do yo' want Toady?'

'I come to tell ya summat.'

'What?'

'I were in White Horse on Sat'd'y right and there were a right ruckus kicked off in the snug right? I 'eard yer name mentioned right? And a bloke, I reckon he were a fisherman from down The Ferry right? Well, this bloke right, 'e screamed "I'll bloody kill 'im" as 'e slammed out o' the pub. I reckon 'e meant you an' I thought y'ought to know right?'

'OK right, thanks Toady. I'll buy yer a pint right? Now piss off. I've got stuff to do.'

Ronnie closed the front door and went back to his bedroom.

'Bugger! I weren't expecting that.' He was ever so slightly rattled. He thought of the gun under his bed and laughed.

'Goin' to kill me is 'e? Not if I fuckin' kill 'im first!'

He pulled the golf bag from under his bed and took the rifle out. He'd had a Diana .177 air rifle once that he'd stolen from a sports good shop, but this was something else. A proper sniper's rifle. A Remington M21A with a Zeiss telescopic sight. He held the gun in an 'aiming' pose, with the crosshairs of the sight centred on the lightbulb suspended from the ceiling rose and pulled the trigger. Click. He mouthed several onomatopoeic noises. He lay in prone position on his bed and repeated the mime. Then it occurred to him he'd need ammunition. He carefully placed the rifle on his bed and picked up the golf bag. 'I wonder,' he thought as he unzipped the pocket in the front of the golf bag. 'Bloody bingo!' he exclaimed as he withdrew a full magazine of twenty rounds of high ballistic centre-fire cartridges. He unzipped two other pockets on the sides of the bag and stacked up a pile of five magazines. From that moment Ronnie was Michael Caine in *Too Late the Hero*, the film he'd seen at the Regal Cinema. He replaced the weapon and the magazines in the golf bag, put on his US Army surplus parka. He loaded the bag into the boot of the Ford Prefect and drove off to Rendlesham Forest for some target practice.

The detritus from Friday's party was still there. Litter, empty bottles and cans, cigarette cartons and the ash and embers from the fire that had been lit. Ronnie set up some cans at a range of about the width of a football pitch. He removed the rifle from the bag and clipped in one of the twenty-round magazines. He took careful aim with the rifle's stock tucked into his shoulder. He gently squeezed the trigger. Nothing! 'Safety catch,' he thought. He took aim again and nervously squeezed the trigger. As the firing pin made contact with the centre-fire cartridge the barrel shot upwards, the tins remained where they had been placed and the wannabe sniper was forced on to his back by the recoil with the cartridge case lying beside him on the ground. After several more attempts Ronnie actually hit a cola can. As far as he was concerned he'd mastered it. Ronnie Higginson was now, or so he considered himself, an expert marksman. He packed the gun and drove home.

Airman First Class Shultz was on duty in the gatehouse at RAF Woodbridge and had heard the shots. Later that afternoon when he was relieved he took a walk into the forest and came upon the rubbish left behind after Friday's party. The empties were mostly American brands. 'Damn kids been in the BX again,' he surmised. Then he spotted the cartridge cases. He picked one up. 'Don't get these in the BX.' Later, back on the base he asked his sergeant to take a look at the spent cartridge case.

'Nope, no sir. Our Armalite AR15s use .223 as well you know. This here's a .308. I'd say maybe an M14 or an M21. Where'd you get it?'

'In the woods sarge. From the crap that's lying around. I reckon it's kids. They got no respect these days.'

'Where in hell they'd get these from? Time somebody had a word with the school principal.'

Chapter Forty

For all that it was a budget hotel Lewis couldn't remember the last time he'd eaten such a fantastic breakfast. Fortified for the day he drove to Pin Mill and was at Helen's cottage with the engine ticking over on the stroke of eight o'clock as instructed. He didn't have to wait. DCI Cartwright appeared at the front door with Helen Blake at his shoulder still in a dressing gown or was it a housecoat – not the Lewis knew the difference. Cartwright got into the car.

'I know what you're thinking so stop it! Get us to Kidlington and don't spare the horses.'

'Guv!' Lewis smiled. 'I bet my breakfast was more nourishing than yours!'

Cartwright blushed.

***

In Woodbridge, Armstrong's breakfast consisted of a slice of toast and a cup of coffee and two paracetamol tablets.

'Thanks for your hospitality Colin. God, I feel rough! Say cheerio to Maisie for me?'

'It's been good to meet you Doug. See you again soon?' Armstrong hurried the short distance to the station carpark hoping his elderly Hillman Avenger would start without any bother.

***

It was mid-morning by the time the two detectives had returned to their Thames Valley HQ. They'd barely had time to get through the door of the CID room when they were accosted by DC Ray Davies.

'Slim's been on the warpath!' Slim, otherwise Chief Superintendent Tim Adams, not nicknamed for his svelte physique, but quite on the contrary.

'Oh bugger. What does he want?'

'I reckon you'll find out soon enough. He told me to tell you both to report directly to his office the minute you showed up this morning.'

'OK, so you've told us.' Cartwright disappeared into his own office. 'Slim can bloody well wait!' He initialled Lewis' receipts and signed his expenses form in order that his favourite driver could submit his claim and not be kept waiting unduly for reimbursement. This, Cartwright estimated, was far more important than anything Slim would have to say. But then, the DCI wasn't to know that on this occasion he'd underestimated.

Cartwright and Armstrong stood on the carpet in front of the desk at which sat the corpulent figure of Chief Superintendent Adams. They were both expecting an upbraiding to come down from on high.

'Now then, I wouldn't have known where the pair of you have been all weekend if your DC, what's his name…?'

'Davies, sir.'

'If DC Davies hadn't told me. I suppose I should be grateful that somebody had been kept informed. When I first started here as CS I did so with the same intention as Sir Robert Mark when he took over the Met.'

'Sir?' Armstrong enquired. Cartwright didn't need to, he heard it before.

'To arrest more criminals than I employ.' Cartwright responded with indignation.

'With respect sir,' he hoped his sarcasm wasn't too obvious, 'I hope you're not implying what you seem…….'

Although Adams already knew the answer he interrupted Cartwright with the question anyway.

'So, where have you been then and what've you been up to?'

Cartwright gave a report on how they were now confident that McFaddon and the gunman had escaped from Havergate Island by sea as had been confirmed in the interview with Reynolds, the skipper of the *Samson* the boat that had picked them up. He phrased the report in such a way as to imply that his DS had also been with him. Armstrong was relieved that he didn't have to fabricate a story to cover his liaison with his ex-wife.

'Very well! It's a small step, but at least it's almost in the right direction. Now look!' Adams leant forward on his desk as if he were about to impart something in confidence.

'I've been discussing the case with DCS Simons and the Deputy Commissioner and we are all agreed that since this whole investigation seems to be now centred on East Anglia you're both being transferred to the Suffolk Constabulary on a temporary secondment until this bloody case is resolved. With the escalation of incidents in this country involving the IRA it's absolutely essential that those responsible for the assassination of... what was his name?'

'McClean, sir.'

'... For the assassination of McClean are apprehended and brought to justice. You're both to be working out of the Ipswich headquarters. It's all been cleared with my counterpart there...' he referred to his notes '... Chief Superintendent Gibson. He will supply whatever you need in terms of grunt or gofers. So, get out there and get it bloody well sorted. That's an order!'

'Sir, if I may?'

'What is it Cartwright?'

'May I take Lewis, sir? PC Andy Lewis, my driver.'

'If you must.'

'Thank you sir.'

The two detectives returned to Cartwright's office. It was time for a Laphroaig moment.

'Well, I'll be blowed! That's a turn up!' exclaimed Cartwright. 'Get on to Lewis and let him know what's going on – oh and I think he knows of a decent hotel. Just the two rooms, one for you and one for himself. I think I'll be OK elsewhere.'

Chapter Forty-One

Maisie Clarke was up bright and early. After a shower, a bowl of cornflakes and a cup of coffee she stood in front of the long mirror trying on a succession of outfits – not that she had that many. Deciding what to wear was proving to be a challenge. She finally opted for the matching navy-blue jacket and skirt that had been the first she'd taken from her closet. Over a crisp white blouse she did look the business. With a little makeup applied she left *Ironside* for her first day at work. Arriving at the shop ten minutes early she took the time to acquaint herself with the properties for sale which were advertised in the window.

'Hello, you must be Maisie. I'm Sandra!' The heavily pregnant Sandra took a keyring from her handbag and unlocked the door. They entered the office and Sandra turned on the lights.

'Mr Potter has asked that I stay on this week to show you the ropes.'

'I'm glad of that, otherwise I'd have been floundering, I'm sure.'

'Oh, you'll soon get the hang of it,' Sandra reassured her, 'now let me show you round. This is the ladies'; you can hang your coat in there. There is Mr Potter's office and just beyond that is the kitchenette. Opposite is Jeremy's office.'

Maisie was coming to the end of the guided tour when the doorbell tinkled announcing the arrival of someone in the office.

'That'll be Jeremy. Mr Rogers, Jerry, is the valuer and surveyor.' He and Maisie were introduced. In concluding the introductory briefing to the world of Potter's Maisie was then thrown into the deep end of the filing systems of properties for sale, valuations, potential clients, and various other intricacies.

'Right, that'll be your desk for this week. If you'd like to make a start on these I'll go and get some milk.' Maisie was handed a sheaf of papers to file.

She had barely got started when a man she recognised came into the office.

'Hello again,' she said with a slightly nervous smile. 'How can I help sir?'

'Hello' responded the man with surprise in his voice. 'I didn't know you worked here.'

'It's my first day,' Maisie admitted. 'You're the first person through the door that I've had to look after. Now, how can I help sir?'

'Well, you can start by dropping the "sir" business. I'm Brian O'Connor, remember? We were introduced in the pub on Saturday.'

'Oh yes, I remember very well.' Maisie cheeks reddened.

'I'd like the details for the cottage you have advertised in the window, the one in Boyton,' requested Brian. Maisie instantly recalled the property from her earlier study of the window.

'Yes it looks nice doesn't it. £12,500. Boyton. Fully refurbished period cottage with vacant possession.'

'That's the one.'

Maisie went straight to the 'properties for sale' filing cabinet. Property details were filed in order of price with the cheapest at the front of the drawer. She pulled the correct page from about a third of the way back.

'Would you like to view the property?'

Brian explained how he and Ben had made a fairly careful inspection of the exterior and all that he needed was to see the inside.

'I'll just check with Mr Rogers to see what the viewing arrangements are.'

Bob Bennett

As Maisie disappeared down the corridor to Jeremy's office, Sandra returned with the milk. 'Are you being looked after sir?'

'Oh yes, most efficiently thank you.'

Maisie returned with a broad smile and announced that Mr Rogers would be free to show Mr O'Connor the property that afternoon. Brian left with the full specification of the cottage and blew a kiss in Maisie's direction.

'Friend of yours?' queried Sandra with a smirk.

Later that afternoon, after his trip to Boyton and inspection of the cottage, Brian returned to the office. Sandra had gone home with backache, Mr Rogers was out with another client and Maise was single-handed.

'Hello Maisie. Mr Rogers has kindly showed me around earlier this afternoon. I liked what I saw and I'd very much like to make an offer to purchase.' Maisie couldn't believe it. A sale on her first day!

'Oh, I am pleased. Would you like to take a seat and I'll get the preliminary paperwork started?' It was like she'd been doing the job for years and the initial form filling was soon completed. As Brian got up to leave, he looked around and seeing that they were alone he mimed tipping a glass to his lips. Maisie nodded enthusiastically. As he was leaving, an elated Brian almost bumped into an older gentleman coming into the office as Maisie held the door open.

'Ah, you'll be Maisie then. I'm Gerald Potter.'

'Yes of course Mr Potter, sir. We met at my interview.'

'Of course we did. Silly me, getting forgetful in my old age. So, how has your first day been?'

'Well, I sold a house sir!'

'Splendid!'

Chapter Forty-Two

Barbara had done her best with Gail's school uniform. In fact, given the state it was in she'd done remarkably well. At least it could wait now until Easter for the dry cleaners. The school holiday was only a couple of weeks away. Not without good cause Gail was apprehensive about returning to school. One or two of the boys in her year had also been at the party in the woods and would more than likely have been given chapter and verse by Ronnie on his conquest. To be considered by the boys as 'easy meat' or 'up for it' was the last thing in the world she wanted. In equal last place on her wanted list would be the girls thinking of her as a slut or slapper.

On strict instructions from her dad the first thing she had to do on that Monday morning was to apologise to Mr Ross and she did. Her apology was heartfelt and sincere and accompanied by a few tears. Mr Ross was more than prepared to accept the apology. He would really have liked to have given her a cuddle, but to have done so would not only have resulted in him being disciplined but it would have exacerbated Gail's situation as well. What he did do however was to insist that she wait by the staffroom after school and he would drive her home. That way she would be spared the embarrassment of having to run the gauntlet at the school gates.

'We'll get you through these two weeks up to the Easter holidays. By the time the summer term starts it'll all be forgotten.' Gail was reassured by Mr Ross' kindly words and determined to get her head down and study. She really wanted to make amends for her conduct by getting good grades in the forthcoming 'O' level exams.

***

That evening, Brian met Maisie in the Anchor. Little did he know, but since opening time she'd been keeping an eye on the front door of the pub from *Ironside*'s wheelhouse, watching and waiting for him to arrive. She didn't want to be there before him. She locked the boat and hurried across the road.

'Evenin' Maisie. Usual?'

'Yes please Sid, G&T, ice and a slice.'

'I'll get that,' Brian insisted. Together they went and sat in a discreet corner. Maisie was secretly hoping that if he should come in Colin would have a little tact and understand and appreciate that this wasn't an occasion for a threesome.

There was a certain uncertainty and nervousness about their conversation initially as if they were sounding each other out. Brian particularly was having difficulty in conversing in an easy and relaxed way. But, as time wore on, and with the aid of lubrication the chat from both became self-confident and unreserved.

'Have you instructed a solicitor?' Maisie enquired.

'Wasn't sure I needed to,' Brian answered. 'Do you recommend anyone?'   'Well, I'm told it's not ethical for Potter's to make recommendations, but I believe that Crean & Berry are fairly good, and they're local which helps. When it comes to exchanging contracts and that sort of stuff, we can just pop up the road rather than have to wait on the post.'

'Makes sense. I'll go and seek out Crean & Berry in the morning.'

As the evening wore on Brian, who had previously never been comfortable talking to women, was sufficiently emboldened to enquire about Maisie's past. For her part, Maisie had nothing to hide. There was nothing to be ashamed of as far as she was concerned, well, mostly anyway. She didn't dwell on her marriage to Doug Armstrong nor the reasons for the subsequent divorce but she did go into great detail of her second marriage and how it led to her being imprisoned.

'Living with Graham was becoming hell. Drunk every night, drinking the housekeeping money. Shouting and swearing, verbal and physical abuse. I was his punchbag. I was always covered in bruises from the beatings, the pushing and shoving. I was ashamed to go out sometimes. I'd call the police but they wouldn't do anything about it. In the end I decided that I'd get some of my own back.'

Brian was clearly horrified. He reached out and took her hand in his.

'What did you do?'

Maisie went on to explain how she exacted her revenge.

'Serves him right. I'd have shot the bastard!' After a while of just sitting and smiling at each other Brian asked, 'Do you still see him?'

'Not if I can help it!' she laughed. She went on to explain how he had tracked her down and was threatening to file a claim for compensation for his suffering and disfigurement.

'Would you like me to get rid of him for you?' The words seemed to linger in the air for a moment and Maisie looked at him in disbelief.

'How?' she asked. Brian now regretted making such an offer.

'Goodness, is that the time? Quickie for the road?' Brian hurried away to the bar and left Maisie's question hanging. After Sid called time, Brian walked Maisie across the road to her houseboat. 'Will I see you again?'

'I certainly hope so!' She kissed him on the cheek and tottered up the gangplank.

Chapter Forty-Three

Andy Lewis had always wanted to be a policeman for as long as he could remember. Ever since that day he and his classmates had sat cross-legged on the floor of the school hall listening to a talk by the local community policeman Andy's mind had been made up. When he left school he went straight to the police training college at Hendon and did his thirteen weeks basic training before being posted as a cadet to the Thames Valley Constabulary's police station in Oxford, St Aldates. It was there that he first met Doug Armstrong. It wasn't long before his superintendent had been sufficiently impressed with Lewis' dedication, conscientiousness and commitment above and beyond the line of duty that he joined the ranks as a fully qualified police constable. Andy, resplendent in his uniform even though he only just made the minimum height requirement of 5' 10" cut a dash as an authoritative and imposing figure. When an opportunity came to train as a specialist driver Andy was at the front of the queue. This was the realisation of an ambition he had held since joining the force. After the initial assessment, Lewis was deemed proficient enough to leapfrog the basic course and go straight to 'response' status and then on to becoming an advanced driver of high-performance vehicles. That was the extent of his ambition. Having driven a certain DI Cartwright on one occasion, Lewis was requested by the recently promoted DCI to transfer to Kidlington and become his first-choice driver and unofficially his personal assistant and chauffer, not that he minded.

When he got news of the temporary posting to Ipswich his initial reaction was one of disbelief at the extent to which Cartwright could engineer a scam to be near his new girlfriend. When he heard that he would be responsible for a new unmarked Jaguar XJ12 disbelief turned to amazement. 'Fantastic. Good old guvnor!' Lewis thought. When he heard that he'd got to take care of the hotel reservations... 'What am I now, his bloody secretary?'

The hotel in Ipswich where Lewis had previously stayed was fully booked. Using his initiative he thought that accommodation a little closer to the hub of the investigation would make sense and thus it was that that he booked three rooms at the Red Lion in Martlesham despite having been told to only book two. 'If he thinks I'm going to run him to and from Pin Mill everyday he can think again!' The white XJ12 was probably the finest car he had ever driven. It was claimed by Jaguar that at 140 miles-per-hour it was the fastest production car available in the UK. There would hardly be an opportunity to reach even half that speed on the roads of Suffolk, but Lewis was happy enough with the consolation of the luxury.

At the headquarters of the Suffolk Constabulary the officers from the Thames Valley Force were not exactly made welcome with open arms. If anything, the Chief Superintendent felt their presence to be something of an imposition. However, he did pledge to be cooperative. Cartwright's team were provided with a small office space in the basement which served as the archive for old cases and it had only been a matter of hours before someone had referred to the intruders as 'The Three Stooges' – a nickname that was to become widely used.

On the first day from their new base Cartwright was convinced that some vital piece of evidence had been missed somewhere along the line. He decided that the three of them should revisit the scene of the crime. The XJ12 purred onto the quay at Orford and, with the car parked, the policemen pulled on their wellies which Lewis had had the foresight to put in the boot of the car and joined the queue of twitchers for the ferry across the River Ore to Havergate Island.

'Hello again Reg.' Cartwright greeted the ferryman and Island warden like an old friend. 'Can you spare us half-an-hour or so?'

'Inspector – din't think we'd be seein' yo' agin.' Cartwright explained that since the investigation hadn't got very far they were going back to basics and the scene of the crime. When they disembarked they allowed a few moments for the birdwatchers to disperse and get a little local knowledge from the warden. Reg led them to the spot where the body was discovered. Lewis and Armstrong, working together again for the first time in a long while, conducted a fingertip search of the few square feet in the immediate area. Nothing! Cartwright had been pondering.

'Now, look, I've been thinking. McClean was only a little bloke. The shot that killed him hit him dead centre...' Doug, Andy and Reg laughed at the unintentional pun '... of the forehead. Where would the gunman have been to make that shot? What was the trajectory?' It was Reg that made the suggestion'

'Over there, yonder.' He pointed towards one of the 'pagoda' buildings on Orford Ness that had been built for the Atomic Weapons Research Establishment.

'How come?'

'Well niow, as I recall,' In his drawn-out Suffolk dialect, Reg proceeded to explain the rationale for his thinking. 'I keeps a diary, see, an' on that theer day, the day o' the shootin' I mean, it started owt wi' a good breeze o' wind nor'east. 'E musta bin a'shelterin' in the lee up theer. Nobody woulda seed 'im an' up theer.'

'But that's what, five or six hundred yards away, even half-a-mile.' Lewis observed. Armstrong replied,

'If it's the same gunman as we believe carried out the Foxton Ambush, we know that whatever the gun he's using is, it has one hell of a range.' I say we go and take a look, guv?'

'Nothing to lose. Reg, you stay here if you don't mind, on the spot where the body dropped, just to give us a sense of perspective. Right, come on you two.' Cartwright strode off across the shingle in the direction of the nearest of the pagodas. He stood at the edge of the stream which ran between the island and the Ness but left it to Armstrong and Lewis to wade across the mud and onto the Ness. From the mound inside the pagoda they had a clear view to where Reg was representing the target and gave him a wave.

'It's a possibility. Right let's spread out and see what we might find,' Armstrong suggested. Slowly, step by step in a diligent and meticulous search they combed the area. Back and forth. Every few minutes one or the other of them would look towards Reg and imagine the trajectory of the fatal bullet, then back to the ground. A startled hare darted from a patch of gorse and almost immediately disappeared into another. And then, there it was.

'Here sarge.' Lewis's excited call over the few yards that separated them startled the DS as much as their presence had startled the hare a few seconds earlier. There, lying beside a patch of vegetation resembling cabbage and smelling like Brasso was a spent cartridge case. The detective came over and the two of them stood staring at the find in wonderment.

'Bloody bingo!' exclaimed Armstrong as he pulled on a clean pair of latex gloves. He gingerly bent down and picked up the discovery and dropped it into an evidence bag. Lewis shouted across the small stretch of water to Cartwright and gave him a 'thumbs-up'.

Reg ferried the policemen and a few bird spotters back to the mainland.

'Thanks to you Reg we may just have found a crucial piece of evidence which could ultimately lead us to the killer.'

'Yo'm more 'an welcome Inspector. If yo' need any more 'ssistance you'll noo where to find me.' The Jaguar purred across the quay, out of the village and direct to Ipswich and the forensics department at their temporary headquarters.

Chapter Forty-Four

The Ford Prefect with Ronnie Higginson in the driving seat was on its way to Rendlesham Forest again. The golf bag containing the Remington was in the boot. Alan Higginson was in the front passenger seat with two admiring fifteen-year-old schoolgirls in the back. As had become his custom and practice Ronnie was intending to drive into the forest and park close to the airfield perimeter. But the Prefect coughed, spluttered, and died. So, he, his brother and the girls got out of the car and between them carried the blanket, the picnic box and the various other things from the boot, including the golf bag, deeper into the forest. Shortly they came to the place which, judging by the number of dented drinks cans and the amount of broken glass, Ronnie's aim with the Remington had been getting better. Whilst this evening was principally for showing off his prowess as a marksman, he was anticipating a walk in the woods on a nature ramble of sorts with the girls.

He set up his targets on the trunk of the fallen tree as he had on his previous visits. He then paced out 60 strides back towards the perimeter fence. He removed the Remington from the golf bag.

'Blimey Ron, that is one awesome rifle,' admired his brother.

'Ooh Ronnie, what a big weapon you've got,' said one of the girls giggling at the inuendo whilst making a fair impersonation of Little Red Riding Hood. He took aim and with the first shot a Coca-Cola bottle was shattered to smithereens as a flight of rooks rose into the air from the tops of the trees. Another two rounds hit their mark in impressive style. Happy with his performance Ronnie decided that was enough for the day. He knew this sport would only be a temporary activity given that he only had a limited amount of ammunition and no idea where he could source any more from. He replaced the gun in the bag and the four of them, carrying all the gear, walked off into a denser part of the forest but not before Alan had picked up a couple of cartridge cases and put them in his pocket. Over at the Airbase gatehouse AFC Shultz had been on duty again and heard the shots but didn't worry too much about it. Later that night only three of the four people who had come to the forest were hitching a ride home.

***

It was always a duty that no one was keen to perform – a visit to the Roughs Tower Council Estate. The police Ford Anglia panda car pulled up outside the Higginson dwelling. The fronts of the houses on the estate all had an area intended by the council to be developed as garden. The front of this particular house was more of a scrapyard. Various car body parts were lying about going rusty as was on old bedspring. There were bags of rubbish variously split and littering the whole area and an old Elswick bicycle with the back wheel missing was doing little to enhance the view. From the car, WPC Julia Robinson and PC Clive Randall were surveying the scene. Their car had already attracted the attention of a number of kids who should have clearly been in school. They had gathered around the panda and just stood looking in a variety of menacing and intimidating poses. The officers got out of the car and made their way through the debris to the front door followed by a procession of kids.

'You going to arrest 'im, mister?' asked one.

'Mind your own business. Now clear off before I arrest you for not being in school.' Randall's threat worked but only to the extent that the group assembled back on the pavement, lined up as spectators.

Julia knocked on the door. Her knock was answered a few seconds later by Dickie Higginson, bare-footed and wearing nothing more than jeans and a vest. A hand-rolled cigarette hung from his lips and it appeared he hadn't shaved for a number of days.

'What's 'e done now? Tell me what 'e's done and I'll clip 'is ear when 'e comes in.'

'I'm afraid it's more serious than that. We need to take him in for questioning.'

'Well, 'e ain't 'ere, is 'e?'

'Where is he?'

''Ow the 'ell should I know? On the bloody golf course I shouldn't wonder.' The officer took this remark to be facetious.

'Does he still drive that Ford Escort CKY 279A?' asked the WPC, referring to her notebook.

'Well, it ain't 'ere is it?

The two constables looked at each other and with a mutual understanding knowing that they'd get nothing out of Dickie.

'OK, thanks for your cooperation Mr Higginson.' The sarcasm was lost on him.

Returning to the panda car Julia asked one of the juvenile spectators 'Does Ronnie still have that black Ford Prefect?'

'Not tellin' – now fuck off pigs.' Before Randall could catch a hold of the boy they had all scarpered.

Chapter Forty-Five

'If that was our man, our gunman, it's the first mistake he's made, leaving a cartridge case like that,' DCI Cartwright stated. The Three Stooges were loitering in the lobby of the Forensics Laboratory.

'It might not have been our man. Maybe it was someone just out to bag himself a duck for a Sunday roast?' suggested Armstrong as an alternative justification for the cartridge case. Lewis had been quiet so far, until he asked something obvious that maybe had been missed.

'Did anyone check the ground after the Foxton ambush? Could the shooter have left a cartridge case there as well? And what about the bullets? Where are they?' It was Lewis posing the questions. Although forensic science had been around for a very long time it was becoming ever increasingly sophisticated. Forensics had been an integral part of Lewis's more recent training and he had considered the fact that his older and longer serving colleagues might not have been quite so well informed.

'Explain your thinking here Andy,' Cartwright requested.

'OK but forgive me if I'm out of place. If the bullet that killed Colin Harvey in the Foxton ambush was fired from the same gun as the bullet that killed McClean, the forensic process should be able to get a match from them. You see, in the barrel of a gun is what they call "rifling". This causes the bullet to spin when it's fired to improve accuracy and leaves what they call striations, like unique scratches on the cartridge cases. The forensic guys can match a cartridge to a specific weapon.

Then there's always the possibility of there being fingerprints on them…'

'Yes OK and thank you Professor Lewis for the lecture. Very informative I'm sure.' Cartwright interrupted whilst thinking to himself that this was something he should have thought of. 'Right then who was that uniform sergeant that helped us out at Foxton?'

'Do you mean the old bloke? He was Sergeant Cuthbertson, from Leicester as I recall, tipped us off about the IRA outside the pub,' said Lewis.

'Get that DC Turner to ring Leicester and ask Cuthbertson to take a team and see what they can find in that field – it's a long shot I know…'

'Ha ha, very good guv!'

'Yes, yes, calm down now, and let's get hold of the respective pathology departments as well – they'll still have the bullets won't they?'

'No guv. I already requested that they be forwarded here,' replied Armstrong.

'Good thinking Doug. What a team eh?'

'I hadn't finished guv.' Lewis was anxious to conclude imparting his knowledge. 'If it's the same gun, there will be unique marks on the cartridge made by the firing pin and the ejector, marks left by the firing process.'

'I think we can be sure it's the same gun in both shootings, but you're right of course, we'll need more than our suspicions in court. The forensic evidence will be important. OK me hearties! We're closing in.' The door from the laboratory swung open and an otherwise fresh-faced attractive young female, had she not been chewing a wasp, stepped into the lobby.

'Which one of you is Cartwright?' she snapped abruptly. The DCI stepped forward extending his hand in a greeting which was snubbed.

'I'm Hannah Hamilton, in charge of forensics and ballistics.'

Cartwright could only just supress his surprise. 'Pleased to meet you Miss Hamilton.'

'That's Doctor Hamilton to you, Inspector.'

'Oh indeed. My apologies Doctor, and that's Detective Chief Inspector to you Doctor! This is Detective Sergeant Armstrong, and this is Police Constable Lewis.'

'You'll receive my written report in due course but I thought that since you're here I could let you know my findings so that you can get on with your investigations.'

'That's most helpful, thank you Doctor.' Cartwright was attempting to thaw a way through the Doctor's icy demeanour.

'I've had chance now to examine the two bullets germane to your enquiry. From my preliminary examination, the one from the brain of a PC Harvey and the other from the back of McClean's skull, I have been able to rule out a number of weapons, that is to say several guns that didn't fire these bullets may now be excluded from your search.'

'Oh that's good,' said Cartwright sarcastically. Undaunted the arrogant ballistics Doctor continued.

'The make and model of the weapon inferred by the characteristics, the calibre and the rifling twist, suggests almost irrefutably that both bullets were fired by the same weapon. The right-handed clockwise rifling leads me to believe these bullets were fired from a Remington, that's an American manufacturer – maybe a 700 or one of the models developed for the American military based on the 700. My belief can be further substantiated by the marks left on the cartridge case you've found, marks from the firing pin and the ejector mechanism.'

Lewis, who had been frantically taking notes asked, 'So, if we find you the gun you'll be able to say without a shadow of any doubt that the bullets and the cartridge case…' the Doctor didn't wait for Lewis to finish.

'On the balance of probabilities, yes. Now, if you'll excuse me gentlemen.' Doctor Hamilton turned on her heel and with a haughty toss of her auburn locks disappeared back into the laboratory with her nose in the air

'Snotty public-school bitch. Still, she seems to know her stuff. We now know what we're looking for. But where do we start?'

Chapter Forty-Six

Brian was early for the appointment he'd made with Vanessa of Crean & Berry. He'd been given a cup of coffee whilst he was waiting in reception. The *East Anglian Daily Times* was lying on the occasional table and he idly glanced through its pages. Tucked beneath an article on a charity fund-raising event in Claydon, wherever that was, Brian was drawn to a piece with the headline *'Police Breakthrough in Havergate Shooting'*. He read through it but, as far as he was concerned it was of no significance whatsoever. A spent cartridge case. That was it. How could that possibly implicate him, never mind secure a conviction?

'Mr O'Connor? Good morning. I'm Vanessa Crean. Would you like to come through?' Brian was led the short distance down a corridor and into Vanessa's office. He explained how he was buying a cottage but totally unfamiliar with the formalities. After Vanessa had helpfully explained how conveyancing worked, Brian requested that she accept his instruction and to 'Get on with it as quickly as possible.' Brian didn't want to be haemorrhaging his savings as a guest of the Crown Hotel for longer than was absolutely necessary.

As he was escorted back down the corridor Brian could hear voices raised in an argument. He came into reception and there he witnessed a man looking like a tramp remonstrating with another wearing a pinstriped suit. He assumed this to be a dissatisfied client seeking redress from a solicitor. He was about to leave the offices when he overheard what he took to be the subject of the dispute. The solicitor, Mr Berry presumably, was trying to explain.

'But Mr Clarke, your claim is frivolous and vexatious, and it will never stand up in court.' The shouting continued and Mr Clarke's contributions to the argument were becoming abusive. 'Was he drunk?' wondered Brian. He certainly sounded it, even at this time of the morning.

'Sorry about this Mr O'Connor,' Vanessa was looking anxious. 'I think I'd better call the police, excuse me won't you?' Without waiting for an answer, Vanessa had disappeared back to her office. 'Mr Clarke,' thought Brian. He turned and discreetly looked back at the altercation. The skin grafts and scarring on the side of the man's face were quite hideous. 'Mr Clarke! Of course!' Could he, should he loiter and eavesdrop some more?

'If yo' aint goin' to tek me case, I'll find some bugger that will. I needs compersation. Call yo'sel' a s'licita? S'licita my arse. I'll get compersation from 'er meself if I 'as to, even if I 'as to beat it owt on 'er.' Brian had heard enough and at the sight of uniformed PC running towards the office, Brian walked back in the direction of his hotel.

From his hotel room, Brian telephoned Potter's. As he had anticipated it was Maisie who answered the phone.

'I need to see you. There could be a problem. I'll explain later.' Brian didn't want to distract Maisie from her work so restricted his call to making an arrangement to meet. He spent the rest of the day looking through the 'Motor Cars For Sale' classified advertisements in the hotel's copy of the *East Anglian Daily Times*. He'd completely forgotten the *'Police Breakthrough'* piece.

Brian was waiting for Maisie outside Potter's when the estate agency closed at five o'clock. They walked arm-in-arm towards the quay as Brian recounted what he had seen and heard earlier that day. Maisie' expression showed her concern.

'After what Helen had said to him in the pub back in March, I really didn't think he'd go through with it.'

'Go through with it?'

'Yes he threatened to make a claim against me in court.'

'Well from what I overheard this morning, that won't be happening. In fact, I should imagine he got carted off for disturbing the peace. I'm sure he was drunk. No. What worries me is he was saying he would get his compensation himself even if he had to beat it out of you.'

'Oh dear.'

They called in at the Anchor. The ever-genial Sid was polishing glasses.

'Evening you two. Usual is it?' They took their drinks and sat in the corner where they hoped they wouldn't be spotted by Colin if he happened to come in. After a couple more, any worries about Graham Clarke had been dispelled and they were happily chatting about conveyancing and buying a car.

'Look when I live in Boyton I'm going to need wheels to get in and out of Woodbridge to see you. I'm not going to walk it!'

'You could always stay.' There was a stirring in Brian's loins. 'C'mon, finish your pint and I'll cook you something to eat on *Ironside*.'

Once aboard she sat Brian down in an armchair and gave him glass of Chardonnay whilst she set about her 'signature' dish, tuna pasta with broccoli. She hoped it would turn out better than when she'd cooked it for Colin.

Brian had enjoyed the meal and the wine and the company. He was convinced that had he been brave enough to make such a suggestion, he'd have been sleeping aboard the *Ironside* rather than in the Crown. But then, he was a gentleman and he didn't want Maisie to get the wrong impression of him. He couldn't stop thinking about her. The threat from her erstwhile husband was troubling him and he knew exactly how the threat could be permanently removed. Hadn't he done something similar on many occasions?

Chapter Forty-Seven

After his encounter with Hannah Hamilton – 'Doctor to you!' – Cartwright was in need of some friendlier female company and he knew exactly where he could find some.

'Drive me over to Pin Mill please Andy. You and Doug can then have the night off.'

The XJ12 was an absolute dream to drive with its magnificent 5343cc engine pushing out 250 brake horsepower through Borg Warner's latest model 12 automatic transmission. It really was the ultra-refined luxury motor car. He didn't mind at all. Neither did Doug. He went along just for ride, like royalty sat in the soft leather back seats. The plan was that he and Andy could check out a few likely hot spots on the way back to the Red Lion.

'What time in the morning guv?'

'Pick me up at eight please.'

'Guv.'

'Have I nice evening and don't wreck the car.'

Helen, standing at the garden gate gave the Two Stooges a wave.

'Right, Doug. Where to?' Doug explained his thought process.

'I'm thinking Friday night, start of the weekend, seaside, funfair, kiss-me-quick hats, candyfloss, brandy snap, fun-time girls, fish and chips and a few pints. How does that sound?'

'You need to get out more!' retorted the DS's junior.

Forty minutes later the Jaguar was parked on Sea Road in Felixstowe and judging by the comings and goings along the promenade at least some of the items on Doug's list would be available. They walked past an amusement arcade and stopped at a fish and chip shop. Sitting in a shelter like a couple of pensioners they unwrapped their supper. Doug was wondering out loud,

'Why are they called amusement arcades? I don't think it's very amusing seeing your money disappear into a slot in exchange for pulling a handle to watch three reels spin round and get nothing back!'

'You're right Doug. That's why they call them one-armed bandits.' With supper finished they continued down the prom. With Easter approaching this was the start of the summer season and there were plenty of people out and about.

Driving a dodgem car was slightly different to the XJ12 but Lewis was having fun and rather than dodging, he was doing the opposite. Between them, Lewis and Armstrong had soon bumped a car with two likely ladies into submission and they had willingly accepted the invitation to go for a drink.

In the Buregate Arms, there was room for the four of them to sit by the window.

'What'll it be ladies?' Andy had been on nights out with Doug before. He recognised the chivalry and knew what was coming next.

'Get 'em in then Andy!'

The ladies, perhaps in their early twenties, were not much more than girls really and they were content to sit and debate whether Gilbert O'Sullivan's *Get Down* was a better song than Donny Osmond's *The Twelfth of Never*. One of them went and selected both songs on the jukebox in order that their debate could be better informed. At the next table were a couple of likely lads if ever there were. A fine thing, a highly sensitively tuned policeman's nose, or so Cartwright always said.

Lewis was discreetly observing what was going on.

'Gis a look then Alan,' one lad was insisting.

'Only if yo' get the beers.'

'OK, but gis a look first!'

The one called Alan rummaged in the pocket of his jeans and pulled out something wrapped in an old piece of towelling.

'Ere it is. I knowed you din't believe me Matt. Now get the bloody beers in while I polish it up a bit.' The one called Matt went to the bar. When he returned, with two bottles of light ale, there, standing on its end on the table was a shiny cartridge case. Lewis gave Armstrong a dig in the ribs with his elbow and with a slight tilt of the head indicated the exhibit on the next table. The policemen nodded to each other and simultaneously stood up and went at sat the lads' table. Doug took out his warrant card and flashed it before the two very surprised young men.

'I'll have that thank you!' and before either of them could protest Doug had snatched up the cartridge case and put it in his pocket.

'Now you're going to tell me where you got it from.'

'Nah, piss off pigs.'

Doug didn't take too kindly to being spoken to in such a way and grabbed the one called Alan by the front of his jacket.

'Now you're going to tell me where you got it from,' he repeated. 'You'll tell me now or you'll tell me from a cell in the nick. Your choice.'

Matt wasn't feeling so good. This was the very first time he'd had any kind of confrontational experience with the police

'Tell him Alan!' Lewis didn't relish the prospect of having to take two young scruffs anywhere in the Jaguar. He went to the lobby to use the public telephone and requested a local uniformed plod. The two boys sat saying nothing and staring at the table.

Lost your voice?' asked Lewis.

The Twelfth of Never had long since faded out and Donny Osmond had disappeared down the hole in the middle of the record. The girls had found another pair of likely lads, more their own age, and were flirting. One of them, Donald Hetherington, had always got on with girls much better than he did with boys. When the imposing form of PC Clive

Randall strode into the pub, Toady Hetherington edged over to a vantage point where he was able to eavesdrop. Lewis briefed Randall on the situation in the pub and the significance the cartridge case had on the ongoing investigation with as much background as he needed. Randall took off his helmet and pulled up another chair.

'Right then Alan, are you going to tell this officer wants he wants to know, or shall I be giving you another ride in the panda?'

'It's me brother's.'

'And where did he get it from?'

'Dunno.'

'You know these lads constable?' asked Armstrong.

'Yes sir. This here's Alan Higginson. He's known to us. In fact, the whole family is. There's currently a warrant out for his brother's arrest. This other lad is a Read. Matthew is it? He's alright I think but his sister's in a bit of bother. Poor lass got raped and it's Alan's brother, Ronnie Higginson, who's in the frame.'

'E din't do it!'

'That'll be for the judge to decide. Now where'd you get this cartridge.'

"I've told yo' already. Yo' bloody stupid or summat?'

Randall had heard enough. He collected Alan Higginson by the scruff of the neck. 'On your way Matthew.' Higginson was then unceremoniously bundled into the back of the panda.

'Whose idea was Felixstowe for a good night out?' queried Lewis.

'Ah but think how pleased the guvnor will be.'

The Jaguar purred back to Martlesham and the Red Lion where the two colleagues evaluated their seaside encounter with the younger Higginson until the landlord called time.

Chapter Forty-Eight

As punctual as ever, Lewis brought the Jaguar to a stop outside Helen Blake's rented cottage in Pin Mill. Cartwright appeared at the front door, Helen helping him on with his jacket. Lewis got out of the car and walked around to open the front passenger door. With his tie untied, top button of his shirt undone, a piece of buttered toast in one hand, Cartwright got in the car.

'So, Andy, how was your evening?'

'About as exciting as yours I'd imagine, probably more productive though.'

'I think you'll need to explain that.'

Lewis gave a synopsis of the earlier part of the evening, omitting the dodgems and the two girls. When he came to the Buregate Arms incident he recounted the details in full.

'And you say the Higginson family is known to the local police?' Cartwright asked.

'Oh yes guv, quite notorious by all accounts. There's a warrant out for the arrest of the elder of the two brothers.'

'Yes, so you said.'

'What about the other lad, Read was it?'

'Pretty average sort of lad, decent family. His dad's a fisherman, so's his uncle. It's Matt Read's sister that was raped, allegedly, by the elder Higginson. She's expected to go on to university when she leaves school.'

'Where's Doug?'

'I dropped him at HQ so he could get forensics to look at the cartridge case. Looked identical to the one we picked up on the island to me.'

'We'll let Hard Hearted Hannah determine that.' Cartwright considered this latest development as Lewis negotiated the early morning traffic through Ipswich.

'Right, let's go and talk to Matthew Read. You know where to find him?'

'He's a trainee manager at the Co-op store in Felixstowe, but sometimes on a weekend he helps his uncle Maurice on his trawler so he may not be there.'

'I'm feeling lucky – get us to Felixstowe.'

Twenty minutes later Cartwright and Lewis were outside the Ipswich and District Co-Operative Store, quite close to the railway station. Cartwright went in. A few minutes later he returned to the car with the young man that Lewis had seen the previous evening. The DCI and Matthew both sat in the back and Lewis prepared to take notes.

'Now then Matthew, or shall I call you Matt? We thought you might be out on your uncle's boat today.'

'No sir, he's not gone today. There's a problem with the winch. It's the hydraulics he thinks. we're going tomorrow if he gets it fixed.'

'Now I want you to tell me everything you can about that cartridge case that young Higginson had last night. It could assist us to solve a murder. You're not in any trouble but if there's anything you know that might help us and you don't tell us, you will be. Understand?' Matt nodded.

'Will you tell my dad, only he's warned me about seeing Alan. He reckons the Higginsons are a "no good" family and mixing with Alan will only lead to trouble.'

'Well, from what I've heard, your dad is absolutely right. There'll be no reason for us to talk to your dad if you tell us what we want to know.'

'Alan picked it up in the woods the other day. He'd gone there with his brother and a couple of girls.'

'The woods? Which woods?'

'Rendlesham Forest, sir.'

'So, Alan has a gun does he?'

'No sir, but his brother does, Ronnie. His brother's been doing target practice up there. In the woods.'

'What's so special about this cartridge case you might be wondering? Why this one when there must be hundreds lying about if folks go shooting in these woods?' Matt hesitated. He was about to tell the DCI about the unusual catch from three weeks previous but thought better of it realising that any mention of the gun in the golf bag would get Uncle Maurice involved, and if Uncle Maurice was involved, he would tell his dad.

'Where are these woods exactly?'

'Near to the airbase past Woodbridge. We used to bike there when we were kids and watch the planes and stuff. There's a place by the fence where we'd make a camp.'

'Are these the same woods where Ronnie took your sister?'

'I think so.' Matt's bottom lip began to quiver.

'Mmm, upsetting business.' Cartwright paused with his questioning and then asked, 'When did you last see Ronnie Higginson?'

'I saw him in his car a week or so ago, but I don't like him. He's a bully, a show-off and he really fancies himself. I try to avoid him.'

'Quite sensible. I suggest you steer clear of Alan as well.'

'Yes sir.'

'OK Matt, that's all for now. If we need to talk to you again we can find you here at work, yes?'

'Yes sir.' Matt got out of the car and went back into the store and Cartwright resumed the front passenger seat.

'What do you reckon Andy?'

'I reckon we liaise with the locals and find this Ronnie Higginson. Sounds like he could be our man.'

'Indeed it does. What a break eh? Good job I gave you the evening off eh?'

'Guv!'

'Right let's get to HQ, see if Hard Hearted Hannah's got anything for us, find out who's leading the investigation into the Read girl's rape and pick up Doug.'

As they were about to pass through the front office of the police station, the desk sergeant handed the DCI a note. *Ring Sgt Cuthbertson, Hinckley Road. 0533 7296.* From the cramped space in the basement Cartwright dialled the number on the note.

'Sergeant Cuthbertson, Hinckley Road Police Station speaking.'

'DCI Cartwright sarge. How're you doin'?'

'Hello sir. I've got some news. I marked off that field in like a grid, you know, and I had ten of my lads do a fingertip search. The farmer wasn't too happy about it, said we were upsetting his sheep. Still when I told him how it was part of a murder enquiry... Anyway, we found it, the cartridge case,' Cuthbertson announced triumphantly.

'Brilliant! That's terrific, well done you and your lads. Can you get it down to us here at Ipswich HQ?'

'It's already on its way by motorcycle courier.'

'Sergeant, you are a star. Thank you.' As Cartwright finished the call Armstrong squeezed himself into the room.

'Just been to see Snotty Pants.'

'A little respect, if you please Doug, Doctor Snotty Pants to you. And?'

'As I was about to say, I've just been to see Snotty Pants and she confirms that the cartridge case we took from the Higginson youth matches the one we found on the island.'

'Now then, there's a turn up. The plot thickens. Can't believe they've found the one from the Foxton ambush as well. It's on it way. I'll bet my pension that's a bloody match as well!'

'Where to then guvnor? The wood? asked Lewis.

'Ad silvam!' responded the DCI in his best schoolboy Latin.

Chapter Forty-Nine

The leaky union in the hydraulic feed had been replaced and *Harbour Lights* was back at sea. Maurice decided to try his luck trawling outside the Whiting Bank and set a course to the northeast and put the kettle on.

'What'd yo' get up to yes'd'y then lad?'

'Went to work.'

'Somebody said they saw you down the seafront in the afternoon.'

'Yeh, I was. The boss gave me the afternoon off 'cos I wasn't feelin' so good after… '

'After what?' Matt decided to be straight with his uncle and take the consequences. 'I got picked up by the police yesterday morning. They fetched me out of work.'

'Don't tell us, let us guess, summat to do wi' that 'ooligan 'igginson I bet!'

'Yeh. I was with him on Friday night. He said he had something to show us, so I met him in the Buregate Arms. Two blokes came in and sat close to us on the bench seat in the bay window, you know? I thought they were just ordinary blokes, 'cos they had a couple of girls with 'em. Anyway, turns out they were coppers, not local plod either.'

'What were it that 'igginson wanted to show yo'?'

'A cartridge case. Anyway, one o' the coppers snatches it up off the table. Then Randall arrived, you know the plod that's always down the front. Alan wouldn't answer any questions, so he got carted off in Randall's panda. I got told to go home so I did.'

'So, what 'appened on Sat'd'y mornin' then?'

'One o' the two as Friday night turned up wi' another, a Detective Chief Inspector. I had to sit in the car – right posh Jaguar – and answer his questions. He reckoned the cartridge could help solve a murder and he wanted to know where Alan got it from.'

'Did yo' tell 'im?

'Of course I did. Well I had to didn't I? It was in Rendlesham. Then he tells me he knows all about Ronnie and our Gail.'

'Let us guess. The cartridge were from that gun we trawled, the one in the golf bag that got nicked? I bloody knew that'd be trouble! Did yo' say owt about the gun in the golf bag?'

'No unc', honest I didn't.'

'OK then, good lad. Let's shoot the nets.'

Chapter Fifty

For all that it had only been a couple of weeks or so since he'd been introduced to Maisie, Brian had grown extremely fond of her. He'd never known a close friendship with a woman before and now he was worrying about the threat to the one with whom he hoped he would have a relationship. Graham Clarke was clearly a down-and-out, vindictive, and with nothing to lose, a chancer who thought he could stitch up his ex-wife. Sure, he was full of smouldering resentment, having to live with such hideous mutilation and disfigurement left by the caustic burns but that was his legacy for the months and months of physical and mental abuse he had inflicted on Maisie. For her part Maisie had been incarcerated for ten years. By Brian's reckoning she had more than paid for what she did and didn't owe Graham a penny nor an ounce of pity.

Back in the day Brian wouldn't have given a second thought to dispatching a character like Graham. Whenever there had been an itch, Brian scratched it. Any unwelcome irritation he would remove with the aid of the Remington. He was now beginning to regret the pledge he'd made to himself. He was certainly regretting having disposed of the gun. 'Just one more shot,' he was thinking.

The receptionist at the Crown Hotel was busying herself with whatever hotel receptionists do when Brian returned from a walk. He'd been looking at possibilities on a second-hand car lot on the edge of the town.

'Mr O'Connor, sir, Mr O'Connor...' she called after him. Brian turned and smiled. 'Mr O'Connor, your solicitor rang with a message. I think you must have been out,' she giggled, 'Silly me, I can see you have! Could you call in and sign a contract?'

'I surely will. Thank you.' Without returning to his room, he made an about-turn and headed off to the offices of Crean & Berry. With his contract signed and the prospect of exchange and completion happening simultaneously by the end of the week, provided of course that the balance of the purchase price was paid, he was advised that the Boyton property would be his and he could pick up the keys on Saturday. This was exciting news and Brian walked back towards the Crown. As he walked past Potter's he saw through the window that Maisie was occupied with a client otherwise he'd have gone in to share his news. He would meet her after work as she left the office. At the hotel the same receptionist was on duty and he requested that she make up his account until Saturday when he'd be moving out after breakfast. He was thinking about everything he would need before he could move in. A list. He would make a list.

***

By the time they arrived at the edge of Rendlesham Forest it was early afternoon. Between them, the Three Stooges had no idea where to start looking or even what they were looking for amongst the trees and woodland which covered in excess of 3700 acres.

'Maybe we should have waited for DI Whatsisname' suggested Doug.

'I'm not sure DI Whatsisname would be any the wiser,' said Cartwright.

'That's DI Brinkley, John Brinkley,' interrupted Lewis.

'Whilst those involved with the rape enquiry know the offence was committed hereabouts I don't think they're aware yet that Ronnie Higginson uses the woods for his target practice. We only found out from our chat with Matt Read.' At a walking pace Lewis drove on a little further. Suddenly the ear-rending roar of two Phantom F-4C aircraft taking off shattered the silence.

'Of course! Young Read told us didn't he. A place by the fence where they'd make a camp.' As the sound of the Phantoms faded, the Jaguar was crawling by the entrance to the airbase.

'Pull in here Andy,' Cartwright instructed. 'I'll just have a word with the sentry.' Cartwright got out of the car and walked towards the gatehouse where a barrier extended across the road. An airman or was it a soldier (Cartwright wasn't sure) stood at ease holding the Armalite rifle across his camouflaged tunic. Cartwright took out his warrant card and identified himself. It was the hapless AFC Shultz who was on duty yet again. Cartwright explained what they were looking for.

'Damn kids. Always here creating a mess and a nuisance. The locals say it's the American kids from the base but it's just as much you Brits, 'specially when they get together. Campfires and crap left all over. It's a wonder they ain't burnt the forest down by now. Then there's that bastard who comes here for target practice with a bloody Remington. A Remington for God's sake. Where'd a kid like that get a Remington from? He's bloody scary!' AFC Shultz continued to complain but Cartwright did manage to get some idea of where the place was that the parties generally took place.

With the Jaguar parked in a layby Lewis and the detectives went exploring. It didn't take long to find the site they were looking for. Following a fairly well-worn trail they came upon the ring of stones with its ashes and burnt-out embers of previous fires. It was just as Shultz had described, empty drinks cans and bottles, Coca-Cola, Budweiser, Tolly Cobbold, cigarette cartons and packets, Lucky Strike, Embassy. More than enough evidence to prove an Anglo-American gathering. Lewis had wandered further on and discovered tyre tracks up by the fence around the perimeter of the airfield. There were places where the fence had been breached. Beyond there was obviously the shooting gallery. He put on a latex glove and carefully picked up several cartridge cases and dropped them into an evidence bag. He walked some considerable distance deeper into the forest and with his penknife managed to dig out a bullet from the fallen trunk of the tree which supported the tins and bottles used as targets. He dropped it into the evidence bag and returned to where the detectives who didn't seem to have detected very much at all if anything were still standing around the dead campfire.

***

Brian was waiting outside Potter's at five o'clock.

'Brian,' gushed Maisie, 'we can't be doing this every day. People will be talking. They'll think we're a couple.'

'I'd like that.' Brian managed to say.

'Really?'

'Yes really.' Maisie immediately linked her arm through Brian's, looked up at him and with a melting smile said, 'Then we are!' Had they walked down Quay Street just a little more slowly they would have noticed the white Jaguar XJ12 on its way back to Ipswich.

'Usual?'

'Yes please Sid.'

Brian paid for and carried the drinks over to their favourite table as the Jaguar cruised past the Anchor. Brian told Maisie his news at which she became just as excited as he was.

'Can't wait for the weekend!'

'Hello you two. You been hiding from me?' It was Colin. He leant over to give Maisie a peck on the cheek. Brian gave him a withering look. Colin brought fresh drinks over and listened to Brian's news.

'Is it furnished?' asked Colin. 'I can probably help you out there. Mate o' mine's got an antique and second-hand furniture place up New Street, opposite the Bell and Steelyard. I'll have a word if you like?'

The conversation then moved on to cars and unsurprisingly the ever-enterprising Colin also had a mate in the trade who would be only too happy to do Brian a good deal. After a couple of hours it had become painfully apparent to both Brian and Maisie that they were highly unlikely to get any time alone, so they made pretence of saying goodnight and going their separate ways – together.

Colin went back to the bar to gossip with Sid.

Chapter Fifty-One

Chief Superintendent Nigel Gibson, head of the Suffolk Constabulary was everything that Tim Adams, his counterpart in the Thames Valley force wasn't; fit and friendly, unobstructive, constructive and helpful in his criticism, and generally in good shape. Gibson, Cartwright, Brinkley and Armstrong were in Gibson's office for a case conference. Also present was DC Turner. He'd been seconded to the team given that he knew a little about the case being the detective who'd interviewed the River Ore Ferryman. Every detail of Gail Read's rape, Ronnie Higginson's disappearing act, the murder of PC Colin Harvey, the assassination of Duncan McClean and now the Rendlesham Forest connection were being scrutinised. They had been looking for the common denominator and believed they may have found it, as confirmed by the cartridge cases and AFC Shultz. It had to be the Remington.

Gibson took the lead. 'Let's get a forensic team up to the forest, see what they can come up with. A cast of those tyre tracks your PC Lewis discovered would be useful. It could put Higginson in the woods and help to substantiate the rape case as well as establish him as the gunman.'

It was then Cartwright's turn to make a suggestion. 'If the manpower can be spared, let's stake out the party venue in the forest. According to our witness at the airbase, AFC Shultz, English kids from the comprehensive in Woodbridge and American kids from the new high school on the base like to mix and mingle on a Friday. We know Higginson likes to show off and he fancies himself as a ladies' man, picking up schoolgirls.

He might well show up for a spot of shooting practice just to impress the girls before getting another one of them drunk and taking advantage, if you follow me.'

'Oh, we follow you alright. In fact, we're ahead of you.' It was Brinkley now holding forth. 'We know he drives around in an old black Ford Prefect. He's been observed with girls still in school uniform in the back. We also doubt whether the car is roadworthy or that he has insurance or road fund licence. Wouldn't surprise me if he didn't have a driving licence either. The car's not been seen for the last few days. I think since the alleged rape and the warrant being issued for his arrest he's been lying low. According to his dad, he's not been at home for days. Can we stake out his address on the Roughs Tower estate?'

'I can't see there being a queue of volunteers for that duty' the Chief Superintendent responded. 'I don't think we'll need anyone up there. Ronnie maybe thick but he's not stupid. He'll know that we'd be watching the place. If anything, it'll be the younger brother Alan that'll be a go-between if he needs anything from home.

***

Ronnie Higginson couldn't get used to being woken up every morning around five o'clock by the dawn chorus. He couldn't get used to sleeping on flattened carboard boxes under a makeshift shelter either. Life in the forest was hard but he realised it was something he'd have to put with for the time being at least until he could sort out something a little more permanent and as far away as possible. Although at first he'd thought it was some kind of April Fool joke, it had been the visit from Toady Hetherington that had convinced him of the need to leave home. He knew that the fishermen at the Ferry were all good mates, a sort of band of brothers, all for one and one for all. If Gail's dad was after him, they all would be and that's before any of them knew that he'd nicked the gun in the golf bag from Maurice's shed. Ronnie stumbled his way out of the shelter and took a leak in the same spot he had been using as his lavatory since he'd set up camp. It was beginning to stink and there were flies starting to swarm. Ronnie had never been a cub or a boy scout and his camping skills ranged between minimal and non-existent. Prepared he certainly wasn't. He was almost out of food and water and drinking light ale all the time, especially first thing in a morning was a taste he hadn't yet acquired. He was down to his last two bottles anyway. He unwrapped one of the few remaining Hershey bars that one of the American kids had given him, sat on a tree stump and wondered what he was going to do. Apart from the racket created by the birds it was quiet and peaceful.

He began to chew on his breakfast when he thought he heard something in the distance disturb the stillness. A drone, like when just for the hell of it he used to trap bees in a jam jar. It was barely audible but then it seemed to get louder before fading away again. This broken silence went on for more than several minutes and it was definitely getting louder. When the thrumming got closer it was the revving up and down that Ronnie recognised, but what was it doing here in the densest part of the forest? He ducked into the shelter and took the gun from the golf bag and hid behind a clump of trees. The Lambretta stopped by his shelter and the rider dismounted. He started rummaging around in the shelter. Ronnie crept around behind the kneeling figure looking through his stuff. He pushed the barrel of the Remington into the back of the figure's neck.

'Geddup an' put yer hands in the air!'

'Don't shoot, don't shoot – Ronnie it's me, Toady!'

Slowly Toady got to his feet and removed his crash helmet. 'Bloody hell, Ronnie, I near shat mesel' right?'

'What yo' doin' 'ere an' 'ow'd yo' find me?'

'Weren't 'ard right? I seen yer car on the verge. I knew yo'd be 'ere abouts somewhere, right?' Ronnie had worried about leaving his car on the side of the road, but he hadn't had much choice when it ran out of petrol.

`'Anyway, right, look I brought yo' some stuff I thought yo' might need right? Toady had two plastic carrier bags secured with elastic straps to the rack on the back of his Lambretta. In one of them there were some groceries including bread, milk, some apples and two lemonade bottles filled with water. In the other were a clean pair of socks and pants, a toothbrush and paste, a roll of toilet paper and five packs of Embassy Filter cigarettes and a box of matches. For once, if not the first time ever, Ronnie was pleased to see Toady. He was even more pleased to see the provisions.

'Bit of a whiff round 'ere, right? Chucking up summat rotten ain't it, right?'

'Yeah, I think I'll move today – specially now yo've gone an' left bloody tyre tracks right to me camp yo' stupid bugger!'

'Sorry Ronnie. I thought yo'd be pleased to see me right?'

'Well I am, but I'm a fugitive now,' he announced with pride. 'Can't 'ave folk jes' wand'rin' in can I?' He brought the stock of the Remington up to his shoulder and mimed picking off the imaginary intruders.

'Still got the gun then right?' Toady observed. 'It'll get yo' in trouble you know right?'

'How?' Toady related the conversation he'd overheard between Lewis and Randall in the Buregate Arms. He described how Alan had been taken away in the police panda car, all for the sake of a cartridge case. Ronnie opened a packet of the cigarettes and lit one. He thought twice about it before offering one to Toady.

'Did they let our Alan go?'

'Yeah. I seen him day afore yest'd'y right? It's 'ow I knew yo' weren't at 'ome. 'That's why I knew yo'd be 'ere an' might need some stuff right?' Then he emphasised what he knew of the gun from what he'd learnt from Alan. 'Look Ron, that there rifle is goin' to get you in a whole load o' bother right? Cops knows about it an' it's prob'ly bin used in a murder. Do yo'sel' a favour and get rid, right?' Then, returning to 'lad talk' he asked,

'Did yo' really shag Readie's sister?'

'Course I did,' Ronnie bragged.

'What's it like?' Ronnie laughed but didn't answer.

After a while Toady announced he'd have to get back otherwise he'd be late for work.

'Can yo' come again in a couple a days wi' some more stuff?'

'I'll need some money.'

'I'll sort yo' out proper, soon as. Get a can a petrol for me car an' all. An' next time, 'ide yer scooter an' walk. If the pigs know about the cartridge case, Alan's prob'ly told 'em I come 'ere for target practice. Readie's sister will have told 'em she got screwed here an' all. They'll 'ave the bloody forest staked out I bet.'

'Does this mean we're mates now?' Toady asked hopefully.

'No! Piss off.'

***

Maisie answered the phone. 'Good morning, Potter's Estate Agency, Maisie Clarke speaking, how may I help?'

'Ah, Mrs Clarke, WH Smith's here. The book you ordered is in if you'd like to collect it. Or, if you like we could post it for you.'

'I hadn't thought of that. As it's a gift it'll be much more of a surprise coming through the post. Could you put a card in it for me as well please, just say 'Lots of love, may it last forever, Maisie' and post it to Brian O'Connor, 7 Mill Lane, Boyton?'

'We'll happily do that for you.'

Chapter Fifty-Two

'Forecast's not lookin' so clever for the weekend,' predicted Maurice. *Three Brothers* and *Harbour Lights* were rafted up alongside the jetty at Felixstowe Ferry, much to the annoyance of the ferryman who was having to navigate a passage around the trawlers to disembark his foot passengers from across the river at Bawdsey. 'Shan't be many minutes Charlie, just unloadin' and there ain't much to unload neither.' Maurice and Merv had both been at sea all night and the fishing had been mediocre at best. They'd been out pair-trawling because Maurice wanted to keep an eye on his brother. It was his first time back at sea since the 'incident' with Gail and even yet, he wasn't himself.

'Look yer me brother an' I care about yo', an' yer wife an' Gail. Look, next weekend's Easter. Why don't yo' tek Barbara an' Gail away fer a few days? I'll keep an eye on Matt. Get away from 'ere and get it all out o' yer system.'

'I wish it were that easy,' responded Mervyn. 'It don't seem to matter what I do, I just can't get that shitbag and what he did to our Gail out o' me 'ead. Goin' away, even wi' a basket full a choc'late eggs ain't going to mek it any easier. I s'pose it's some cons'lation that Gail seems to be getting over it at least.'

'Well that's good, innit?'

'S'pose so.' Merv was clearly dejected and not himself at all.

'C'mon yo' pair of buggers,' yelled Charlie as he approached the jetty again. 'Stop yer yacking and get off the bloody jetty!'

'Yeah alright yo' cantankerous git, 'old yer bloody 'orses a minute!' Maurice shouted back. 'C'mon Merv, let's get finished up 'ere and I'll buy yo' one in the Ferry Boat.'

With their catch packed in ice and in the cold store and their trawlers back on their respective moorings, the two brothers made their way across the green to the pub. As they sat nursing their pints Maurice recalled something Mervyn had threatened in the White Horse when news of the 'incident' broke.

'I 'ope yo' din't mean it.'

'Mean what?' asked Merv.

'I 'ope yo' ain't plannin' on doin' owt stupid.'

'Such as?'

'Well, yo' did threaten to kill 'im.'

'Yo' know me Bruv. That were just 'eat o' the moment talkin'. Why're yo' worryin' yersel' about that?'

'Well, I din't tell anybody else, an' afore I tell yo' I don't want yo' takin' it out on Matt. I've dealt wi' 'im.'

'I'm not sure I knows what yer on about.'

'Yo' remember a few wiks agoo me an' Matt trawled up that golf bag wi' the rifle in it? I told youse all in the pub? Well, it were Matt what told Alan Higginson an' he told 'is brother. It were Ronnie Higginson as what nicked it out o' me shed. Ronnie Higginson's got a rifle.'

'What makes yo' so sure it were 'im?'

'I just told yo'. Matt told Alan and Alan told Ronnie. 'Ad to be 'im. Couldn't 'ave bin anybody else. Wouldn't surprise me in the least if yo' went after 'im that 'e dint turn the gun on yo'.'

'Nah! 'E ain't got the balls!'

With the second round of drinks the conversation reverted to the weather and the likelihood of them getting to sea the following day or Friday.

Chapter Fifty-Three

The faces of the Three Stooges were becoming familiar around the police headquarters. The logistics for the Rendlesham Forest Stakeout were being meticulously planned. Efforts had been made to get a photograph of Ronnie Higginson for circulation to those who would be involved but the only picture they'd managed to obtain, thanks to Arthur Ross, was an old school photograph showing Ronnie as a smiling freckled-faced fourteen-year-old looking angelic and as if butter wouldn't melt in his mouth. It was decided not to bother with it. Ronnie would be readily identifiable as the big guy with the rifle. Gibbo was very pleased with the codename he'd come up with, 'Operation Axeman'.

Camouflaged and weapons-trained officers would be deployed around the area reconnoitred by Cartwright where it was known the Friday parties were held. Higginson was the prime target, and the plan was that on a given signal from Cartwright the police would move in and ring-fence everyone who would then be taken away and interviewed. As part of the preparations, DI Brinkley made a visit to the Airbase just with the intention of keeping the commanding officer informed of what was planned. In the event the CO offered a detachment of American military to supplement the police operation and provide backup if required.

The day before Operation Axeman Lewis took the DCI and the DI on a drive-by.

'There!' shouted Brinkley. Lewis applied the brakes and the Jaguar pulled up alongside the black Ford Prefect on the grass verge. 'CKY 279A – that's Higginson's car.' Although it had been there, the Three Stooges hadn't really paid it much heed when they'd driven by the previous day. Brinkley got out of the Jag and opened the driver's door of the Prefect. 'The keys are still in the ignition!' he called. Turning the key, the needle of the fuel gauge flickered and returned to 'E' where it settled. He removed the keys, put them in his pocket and got back in the Jaguar. 'Proves he can't be far away. We won't need that tyre cast now.' Brinkley's excitement was mounting although Cartwright was being slightly less optimistic.

'I know kids like to party and stuff but have you seen the weather forecast for tomorrow? Blowing a gale and lashing down by all accounts. I wouldn't be too sure many will turn up – if any. I certainly wouldn't if I were them, but then I'm older and wiser.' Lewis laughed.

'Even so,' Brinkley chipped in, 'I think we should deploy Axeman. One can never be certain.'

'What of, kids or weather?'

'Both!'

***

For all that it was almost a fortnight since his daughter had been violated, Mervyn Read had been totally unable to come to terms with the seething hatred he had for the abomination of a human being that he considered Ronnie Higginson to be. The severity of his wrath was merciless and his thirst for revenge would never be quenched. Despite the best intentions of everyone close to Gail it was inevitable that news of the assault she had been subjected to would become common gossip. The meddlesome and morbid curiosity that the attack was now attracting was exacerbating Merv's malicious enmity. When he got wind of the rumour that Higginson had gone to ground and was hiding out in Rendlesham Forest Merv decided it was time to take the law into his own hands. The police had had two weeks to capture this sexual predator and so far, all they'd managed to do was issue a warrant for his arrest. Merv was hell-bent on exacting retribution for his little girl.

It was early evening. He'd borrowed Maurice's Ford Anglia van and was parked on the edge of the forest some 100 yards back from where he could see the Ford Prefect abandoned. His thinking was that Higginson would come back to his car sooner or later. So, it was to be a waiting game. When the police tow-truck arrived and took the Ford Prefect away, Merv set about rethinking. He rooted around in the back of the van for a weapon. Taking the twelve-inch stainless steel barbed fishing gaff he ventured into the forest.

This was it. This was the day of reckoning. Resolute and intent on inflicting pain he made his way quietly and cautiously into the increasing density of the trees reliant on his own sense of self-preservation. The ground had a thick covering of leaves and pine needles through which wood anemones and primroses were just beginning to show. There were areas of sweet woodruff and fern which cushioned his footfall. The snap of a dry twig could ruin everything. Every few steps he stopped and listened. Silence. Above the canopy of the trees the sun had been obscured by cloud and in the fading light now it seemed that the almost mythical surroundings were coming to life. It was silent. Strangely silent. No more the woodland idyll, no more the Shakespearean fairy glen. He'd never known such stillness. It was menacing. The air felt malevolent. He stopped and peered into the gloom. Conscious of his heavy breathing he tried to bring it under control. Deep breaths, calm down, slow. But the supreme contempt with which he held his quarry edged him onward. The execution of vengence on the degenerate scum who had defiled the purity of his daughter would be carried out. He stopped again. Run away. Escape while you can. He listened to one side then the other with intense concentration on the silence. It was eerie. His heart continued to pound. Something was not right. He turned and…

Like a startled muntjac he took off. Completely spooked by something, he was no longer worrying where he ran, or where he trod. Which way to go? He hadn't run anywhere in years but was now running as fast as he could, in a cold sweat as the brambles tore at his clothes, his hands, his face. He glanced back without breaking his stride and ran straight into a low branch which split a deep gash across his forehead. The thick roots of ivy were trying to trip him, still he didn't stop. Run, run, faster! He was panic-stricken and overcome with the desperate need to escape from this place of perdition. His breathing was now out of control. He was gasping for breath, his heart racing, the palpitations driving him on until in the same instant as he heard the crack of the rifle shot, he fell forwards, heavily. He tried to move but couldn't. There was blood. A lot of blood. Where was he bleeding from? He couldn't tell. There was pain. Where was the source of the pain? He couldn't tell. As he tried to move again he screamed in excruciating agony. The gaff was impaled in his thigh. Blood was pumping. He tried to move his arm but the pain from the bullet wound in his shoulder wouldn't let him. He was also bleeding from the savage laceration to his forehead. He lay still as the spring tide of his lifeblood ebbed away from the massive lesion to his femoral artery. This was it.

***

The figure in the old army greatcoat had witnessed everything; the man with the gaff, the hunter hesitating as he crept through the trees. The man with the rifle, prone, watching and waiting. He saw as the hunter became the hunted, the frantic flight of a frightened man. He heard the shot, the scream, the silence descending and restored. The figure in the old army greatcoat moved with an agility that belied his posture. He manoeuvred himself into a position where he had a clearer view. He watched as the man with the rifle laid the weapon on the ground whilst he then scraped a hollow clear of leaves and bluebells. With some apparent difficulty he rolled the body into the hollow. He watched as the burial proceeded with the corpse being covered with earth, rocks, leaves and with ivy and the fallen limbs from trees finally disguising the grave. He watched as the man picked up his rifle and disappeared from view in the direction from which he came. The figure in the old army greatcoat returned to his own hideaway, the kind of camp that Baden Powell would have been proud of.

***

When Merv hadn't come home on Thursday night, Barbara wasn't unduly concerned. It wasn't unusual for him to stay out at sea especially if he 'got on the fish'. And what with the forecast for the next couple of days, she assumed he'd be getting some extra hours in ahead of being weather-bound.

Chapter Fifty-Four

Maisie had telephoned Helen with news of her 'attachment' to Brian, her job, his house purchase, and news in general. As they hadn't had a chinwag for almost a month Maisie had invited Helen over and she'd accepted. What's more, she had surplus crockery and cutlery and a couple of nice 'hardly used' rugs, if Brian would like them.

Since they had met and spoken of such matters earlier in the week, Colin had taken Brian to see his mate in the motor trade and a deal had been struck; a bright yellow Triumph Dolomite, used but with low mileage, just one previous owner, in excellent condition, taxed and tested for just under £1000. They had also visited the second-hand furniture warehouse, as Colin had recommended. It was indeed quite a vast emporium and Brian was able to identify absolutely everything he would need. A small kitchen table and two chairs, a sofa and an armchair, a bookcase, and a very nice roll-top desk – something he'd always wanted - and of course, a double-bed. Better still, Colin had been as good as his word. He'd given the proprietor the 'heads-up' and Brian got a significant discount and the promise of delivery on Saturday, completion day. Everything was going according to plan and all was well in the life of Brian.

***

All was less than well in the lives of the Three Stooges and their colleagues. The weather forecast had been accurate and at the briefing it was ordered by Chief Superintendent Gibson that whilst Operation Axeman should still go ahead, it should be scaled down.

'Maybe it's something to do with Friday 13th but there's no point in everyone getting soaked and then taking next week off with the flu and making a long Easter break out of it!'

'Simons or Slim Tim would have had us out there, in all weathers and no mistake!' whispered Armstrong. Gibson proceeded with the briefing.

A ten-strong team of volunteers was chosen They would be driven over to Rendlesham in a Ford Transit panel van purporting to be a 'Mothers' Pride' bakery delivery van, disguised especially for such covert operations. There was time, no rush. 'We know these parties don't get going until after schools finish, so let's be in position by say, 1530 hours.' Several in the room looked at their watches.

The bakery van arrived at the airbase at 1500. AFC Schultz, wearing an all-American style waterproof poncho raised the barrier. Lewis who'd volunteered to drive the van had been the only one to notice the Ford Anglia van on the edge of the forest. He'd made a mental note. Schultz gave him instructions and Lewis parked as directed, out of plain sight. The detachment of eight constables with Detective Sergeant Armstrong and Detective Chief Inspector Cartwright were shown the way along the airfield's perimeter fence to the same hole that the American kids used to access the forest. There they were joined by six enlisted American airmen, all with ArmaLite M16s. Only four of the police constables had firearms training and were carrying Heckler & Koch MP5A3 semi-automatics.

Here we go again, thought Cartwright. The bloody wild west show! All for a bunch of kids and one bully with a rifle who won't show up.

Heavy rain continued to fall. To the credit of everyone on the stakeout, they put up with the atrocious conditions. No one complained during the two hours they waited concealed in the trees and the undergrowth, beneath gorse bushes and brambles and anywhere else that might have afforded a little shelter. At 5.30, or 1730 hours as Gibson might have said, Cartwright moved to the centre of the extended circle and blew a whistle. The sight of fifteen dripping wet individuals, who between them were carrying an awesome amount of firepower, emerging from their places of concealment would have been intimidating if not extremely frightening, – if only there had been anyone there to see it. Operation Axeman was abandoned and all police and military personnel were stood down.

From two distinctly separate and remote vantage points, the entire abortive operation had been observed by both a figure in an old army greatcoat and a man in an American ex-army parka carrying a rifle. Neither were aware of the other and they retreated to their respective hiding places.

**

Even when he was at school nobody liked Donald Hetherington. He'd been a spotty kid with National Health Service glasses and questionable personal hygiene habits. He was the snitch, the sneak, the snake-in-the-grass and it was his fawning and boot-licking that had earned him the nickname 'Toady'. In the staffroom even the teachers referred to Hetherington D. as 'Toady'. Since leaving school his acne still hadn't cleared up completely but at least he had a job when so many of his contemporaries were unemployed and happy to be so. He'd worked at Peewit Park, a site for touring and static caravans in Felixstowe and whilst it was hardly what one would call a vocation, keeping the grounds neat and tidy, odd jobs and collecting the refuse bags on a Thursday, he'd held the job down for five years and proved himself to be sufficiently reliable and trustworthy for the site manager to leave him in charge from time to time. Donald didn't mind the work and of his £23 per week wage he'd give his mother £10 for his board. The rest he'd spend on himself although rather too much of it went into the slots in the amusement arcade. But despite having a job, money in his pocket, and a second-hand Lambretta which he was buying on HP, he had no real friends. A few would tolerate him, but no one liked him.

It was the same evening as the aborted stakeout at Rendlesham that Toady Hetherington and Alan Higginson were losing money on the one-armed bandit in the amusement arcade on the pier.

Anxious as ever to win friends and influence people, Toady was bringing Alan up to speed on the welfare of his brother.

'I would 'ave gone again today but it's bin pissing down all day, right? I'll go tomorra, right?'

'Can I come wi' yer?'

'Yeah, course, but you'll be on the back o' me Lambretta, right? And I only got one crash helmet, right?'

***

After a couple of early evening drinks in the Anchor, Maisie and Helen went to the cinema and scared themselves half to death watching Julie Christie and Donald Sutherland in *Don't Look Now*.

***

With 'Axeman' aborted, Cartwright, Armstrong, and Lewis had all gone back to the Red Lion for hot showers, changes of clothes, food and a session of binge-drinking. They felt they deserved it.

Chapter Fifty-Five

Toady pulled up outside the Higginson abode on the Roughs Tower estate and parked the Lambretta. Within a few minutes a crowd of kids had gathered around him and his scooter and although they weren't interested at all in him, his Lambretta was receiving a lot of attention which made him feel popular. Maybe it was something to do with the non-standard extras that the mods adorned their Vespas and Lambrettas with that always attracted a crowd of admirers; the chrome, the wing-mirrors, the handlebar tassels. These 'extras' had certainly been the persuasive force when Toady had been in the market to buy a scooter. On the luggage rack were an old can containing a gallon of petrol and a plastic bag of provisions most of which he'd pinched from his mother's pantry. He'd needed what money he had to buy more cigarettes. He felt sure Ronnie would have smoked all of the previous consignment by now. Alan came out of the front door looking quite ridiculous wearing a girl's black riding hat which he had purloined from somewhere. Hardly suitable for riding pillion even if it had been big enough to fit him. Toady thought his passenger would probably be less conspicuous with nothing on his head but decided to keep his thoughts to himself. They set off for the forest.

***

Mr Potter was most understanding when Maisie had requested the morning off. She met Brian at Crean & Berry's where he picked up the keys to Number 7, Mill Lane, Boyton. With the rugs, bedding and kitchenware donated by Helen in the boot of the Dolomite and the small holdall containing the sum total of Brian's worldly goods on the back seat, they set out for his new abode to arrive ahead of the furniture van.

The previous day's rain had left plenty of puddles on the road but it was altogether a much better day. The sun was shining and it was pleasantly warm for mid-April. By the time the furniture had been installed it was almost midday. At Maisie's suggestion they went for a stroll around Brian's new environs. Leaning on a fence they looked out over Hollesley Marshes. The vista was one of a serene tranquillity. The 'feel-good' factor of the last few days was exactly what Brian had been hoping for when he got on the train at Liverpool Street Station towards the end of February. He could barely believe that it had all happened so quickly. They strolled on, hand in hand simply enjoying each other's company. No words were spoken. None were necessary. As they approached the sign swinging ever so gently in the breeze, neither of them had to convince the other that an inspection of the local hostelry was essential. The Bell dated way back and had a reputation as a favourite haunt of smugglers. 'But then wasn't that true of every village pub in the county?' thought Brian. It certainly had that look and feel of a Suffolk Village pub and Brian instinctively knew that he would fit in as a 'local' before too long.

***

The ride to Rendlesham wasn't without incident. A police panda was parked by the Wilford Bridge and the Lambretta was waved down by the uniformed constable.

'Off for a picnic in the woods then are we lads?' enquired the policeman facetiously. For all his other faults or failings Toady's wits were quick enough when it came to repartee.

'No officer, me mum's sending some stuff for me gran, right?'

'Oh that's nice, he said, peeking in the top of the bag. 'Where's does your gran live then?'

'Ufford.' Alan sat quivering on the pillion. 'I got some petrol for 'er lawnmower an' all, right?'

'Heavy smoker is she?'

'No, they're mine, right?'

'And how about you?' the PC asked, addressing Alan, 'You going to ride his gran's pony or maybe there's a point-to-point meeting at Wickham Market?

'Yo' missed yer calling constable. Yo' should 'ave bin a bloody comedian!'

'Right! That's enough. Come on now, off!'

They were both given a lecture on the new law requiring motorcyclists and their pillion passengers to wear helmets and the constable clearly didn't see Alan's choice of headwear as being compliant.

'Where you from?'

'Felixstowe,' they answered in unison.

'OK, you get off to gran's, and you, get back to Felixstowe. You can catch a train from Melton Station and change at Westerfield. If I catch either of you without a helmet again you'll be nicked! Understand?' Somewhat dejectedly Alan walked back towards the station as Toady sped off on the original mission without giving Alan a second thought.

He had intended to put the petrol straight into Ronnie's car because he'd promised the bloke at the garage that he would take the can back. But strangely the Prefect wasn't there. In its place was a Ford Anglia van. Toady wasn't sure about this.

'P'raps 'e's done a swap. Yeah, tha'll be it, 'e's either done a swap or 'e's pinched it.' He poured the petrol into the van anyway. Then, bearing in mind what Ronnie had told him on his previous visit, Toady left the scooter with the empty petrol can and his crash helmet tied on the rack hidden just inside the tree line, and he set off carrying the bag of provisions into the forest. To begin with it was easy going but as the forest became denser progress through the ground covering of brambles, nettles and ferns became difficult. Remembering that Ronnie had intimated he would be relocating, he couldn't even be sure he was going in the right direction although he felt he'd passed one or two of the landmarks he'd noted the previous week. He wondered whether it would be safe to call out. He didn't want to do anything stupid which might incur the wrath of the very person he admired and wanted to make friends with. Suddenly, not concentrating on where he was walking, he tripped and fell spilling the contents of the bag in the process. As he tried to get up he felt himself being lifted from behind. An assistant? No, an assailant. An arm clutched him tightly around the neck and then there were two hands around his throat, strong thumbs digging into the back of his neck, even stronger fingers pressing on his larynx. He began to gasp for breath, to choke. He tried to yell but to no avail. He squirmed, flailing his arms in an attempt to free himself from the stranglehold. His glasses fell to the ground and he could feel the throbbing of the blood vessels in his temples. His vision was starting to blur, he felt that his lungs were about to burst. He blacked out. The man in the old army greatcoat dragged Toady's lifeless form towards a hollow in the contour of the ground which had previously been covered with branches and undergrowth. He dropped the body into the hollow, knelt beside it and searched for vital signs. There were none. He searched the pockets and removed the small amount of money he found and a set of keys. Then using an army bivouac shovel, he buried Toady's corpse in the hollow and recovered it with the branches. He gathered up the provisions and replaced them in the bag which he took with him and he threaded his way through the dense undergrowth back to his concealed and very orderly campsite. The man removed the greatcoat and put on a blouson-style jacket he'd bought from a charity shop. He followed the now familiar route out of the forest to the road and located Toady's scooter. He put on the crash helmet and started the engine with the key on the ring he'd taken from Toady's pocket and rode into Woodbridge where he parked on Market Hill opposite Potter's Estate Agency. It was closed.

***

The landlord called time. Brian and Maisie sauntered back to Brian's Cottage in Mill Lane. Arriving back, they were both feeling peckish and it was only then that they realised there was neither food nor drink in the place. So, after a quick return trip to Woodbridge, Maisie made a plate of sandwiches which they ate sitting on the new sofa whilst watching the sun move across the sky towards the west.

'Did you know Helen's seeing that nice detective, Chief Inspector Cartwright!' Maisie posed the question in the form of a statement. Suddenly that air of complacent contentment gave way to a certain disquiet. Brian only hoped Maisie hadn't noticed his unease.

'No, I had no idea. Good for her. I don't think I've met him, although I did bump into a Detective Sergeant in the Anchor. Armstrong, I think his name was.'

'My ex-husband you mean.'

'Oh of course, I'd forgotten.' If only Danny McFaddon knew that I am now in a relationship with a policeman's ex-wife, he'd be horrified, Brian thought as he smiled to himself. He was sure that if he played it cool, acted the innocent, forgetting who he had been and remembering who he was now, he would not give himself away. No one would ever be any the wiser.

The rest of their evening was spent enjoying the warmth of each other's company, talking intermittently about nothing in particular and everything in general. They'd witnessed a fabulous sunset and now, although it was still early they were both tired after the exertions of the day.

'I suppose I'd better drive you home,' Brian said as he stood up, yawned and stretched.

'Wouldn't you rather I helped you christen your new bed?'

***

Brian came downstairs to the smell of fresh coffee. Maisie was preparing him scrambled eggs. After breakfast he drove her back to

Woodbridge and the *Ironside*. Back at 7 Mill Lane, Brian discovered that the previous owners or occupiers had left gardening tools in the shed, so he decided to make a start on tidying the garden. Growing vegetables was a pursuit he'd not previously considered and right at that moment it seemed like a worthwhile idea. By midday his back was beginning to complain and on a pretext of not doing it at all once he decided that he would follow the Englishman's tradition of Sunday lunchtime in the pub.

'Morning! What'll be?' The landlord pulled a pint in response to Brian's order. 'That's 13 pence please.'

'Cheers,' said Brian.

'Thought you and your lady friend were just passing through yesterday. Wasn't expecting to see you again quite so soon, but your welcome.'

'Ah well you might see quite a bit of me from now on, I've just moved here into the village to live – Number 7, Mill Lane.'

'In that case you're doubly welcome. I'm Herbert Wilberforce, the landlord. Folks call me Bert.' Brian shook Bert's extended hand.

'Brian O'Connor. Happy to meet you Bert.'

'Judging by that accent you're not from round here then?'

'No, from Northern Ireland.'

'We won't hold that against you,' Bert joked. 'Next one's on the house!'

Brian stood back from the bar as Bert moved on to his next customer.

'Morning Alvin.'

'Morning Bert, how's it goin'?'

'Can't complain.' Bert drew him a glass of lager. 'Have you met Brian from Northern Ireland – he's just moved here?'

'Hi there Brian – Alvin Shultz.'

'Please to meet you Alvin. Sounds like you're a foreigner as well,' observed Brian.

'Yessir. Austin, Texas, US of A – and call me Al by the way.' Brian and Al went and sat with their drinks.

'Smoke?' Al proffered a pack of Lucky Strike.

'No thanks, I don't – well not any more anyway.'

'What, you quit? What's the secret?' The small talk continued and reciprocating rounds were slipping down nicely.

'Been stationed here with the USAF at RAF Woodbridge for almost two years now. I'm living off-base here in the village. Two years but I just can't get used to this Limey money.' Al took a handful of loose change from his pocket and spread it out on the table. Brian couldn't but help notice a cartridge case amongst the coins.   His curiosity got the better of him.

'You go shooting Al? That looks like a .308.'

'Hey man, well spotted, it is. You know your guns,' said Al appreciatively.

'I was military myself until a few months ago. Didn't realise you guys used Winchesters.'

'We don't! Standard US military issue these days is the ArmaLite AR15 or M16 and they're .223. No, I don't reckon this is a Winchester, this baby's from a Remington – I'd say an M21.'

Brian picked up the cartridge case and looked at the base. There was something vaguely familiar about the toolmarks, vaguely familiar and just a little worrying.

'Yes, I think you're right,' confirmed Brian. 'Where'd you get this from?'

'Now, there's the thing. We got teenage kids on the base these days and they've taken to partying with some English kids on the edge of Rendlesham Forest near the airfield perimeter. I was on guardhouse duty week before last and I could hear shooting. When I checked it out later there was a whole heap o' these babies not to mention empty booze bottles and cans and all kinds a crap. We, that's to say the Limey cops and a few of us were going to round 'em up on Friday, but the weather… Jesus man, it's supposed to be spring!'

'Where do kids get this sort of weapon from? Kids with guns – that's just a bit scary.'

'Yeah, I agree. Say Brian, what's your interest?'

'Oh, nothing really. You ready for another one, my turn?'

Back at home, Brian spent most of the rest of the day seriously concerned about the cartridge case he'd seen. Those toolmarks were all too familiar. There was no mistaking that that bullet had been fired from a Remington M21. 'If I didn't know better, I'd say someone has got hold of my gun,' he said to himself. He was becoming paranoid with the notion that someone had found his rifle. 'No, it can't be. Mine's at the bottom of the North Sea,' he kept repeating to himself.

Hoping that it would take his mind off guns and cartridge cases Brian opened the small parcel that had been on his front doormat when he moved in. It was the book that Maisie had ordered for him as a house-warming gift, *Interesting Facts About Suffolk Villages* by Michael Hanson. Reading the card inside gave him a warm glow. He sat in his armchair with a small glass of Bushmills and turned straight to the chapter on Boyton, his new home.

> *Boyton lies to the east of the county, a parish in Woodbridge district close to the River Alde, 4 miles to the south-west of Orford and about 7 miles to the south-east of Melton railway station. The history of the village is largely overshadowed these days by the neighbouring Hollesley Bay Colony which may be seen by looking to the south-west from St Andrews church. The original buildings were used as a training establishment for young men who were going overseas to work in the colonies of the British Empire but they later became a Labour Colony to train unemployed Londoners in farm work.*

Brian's eyelids were growing heavy until a familiar acronym jumped off the page followed closely by the word *Republican*. He was suddenly wide awake again and continued to read.

> *In 1938 the premises were acquired by prison commissioners as an open Borstal Institution. Still referred to as The Colony today it is renowned as the home of the*

Suffolk Punch Stud Farm. One of the institution's most famous inmates who served 14 years for the attempted murder of 2 'garda' detectives was the Irish author, poet and playwright Brendan Behan. Behan was a member of the IRA and a staunch Republican. When he died in 1964 there was a full IRA guard of honour at what was the biggest funeral since that of Michael Collins. Behan described himself as 'a drinker with a writing problem' and in his autobiographical novel 'Borstal Boy' he describes his experiences of Hollesley Bay.

This was fascinating and Brian felt honoured to be a near neighbour of the place where one of his heroes had stayed albeit more than several years ago. He smiled to himself whilst pouring another measure of Bushmills into his glass he recalled the famous Behan quotation, *'I only drink on two occasions: when I'm thirsty, and when I'm not.'* Brian sat savouring his nightcap and hoped that when his time came, his last words would be as sardonic as Behan's. *'Bless you Sister: may all your sons be bishops.'*

It was three o'clock when Brian awoke and he was still in his armchair, the empty glass in his hand, the book in his lap. 'Time for bed' he thought.

Chapter Fifty-Six

Barbara Read was worried. In 22 years of being married to Merv she'd got used to the antisocial hours kept by the local fishermen. Up before dawn, back after dark, sometimes fishing all night and on rare occasions two nights away at sea. But never four. She caught the bus into Felixstowe and went straight to the police station. She attempted to explain her worriedness to the desk sergeant and maintain her dignity and composure at the same time, but it was all too much for her. The anxiety and worry over her daughter was now compounded by her husband, missing for the last four nights. Barbara's stress and distress had increased to the extent that flood gates holding back her tears gave way and with her self-control having deserted her she crumpled into a helpless sobbing state of wretchedness.

'Julia, a cup of hot sweet tea to the front desk quick as you can please.' The sergeant helped Barbara into a chair and held her hand in both of his trying to offer some comfort and relief from the desolation the woman was so clearly experiencing. WPC Julia Robinson appeared with the tea.

'Oh dear, it's Mrs Read isn't it? It's me Julia, we met when Gail…' Being reminded of their meeting did little to ease Barbara's pain and desperation; in fact, it had the opposite effect.

Eventually, having composed herself somewhat she was able to share her worries with the sergeant and the WPC. Barbara was driven down to the boatyard and the harbour at the mouth of the river Deben in PC Clive Randall's panda car. The fleet of fishing boats were all at sea apart from one. Moving with the motion of the tide on its mooring lay *Three Brothers*. Barbara stood stoically staring at Mervyn's trawler whilst clutching and alternately wringing her handkerchief.

'At least we know he's not lost at sea,' she whispered.

***

Brian had driven into Woodbridge. There were some essential items he needed for the cottage and he'd decided to buy some vegetable seeds as well. He parked his car in the Market Square purposely so that he would have to walk past Potter's where he could hopefully catch of glimpse of Maisie at work. He noticed there was a Lambretta parked on the opposite side of the road to the estate agency. With his errands completed Brian had intended to call in on Maisie, maybe get a cup of coffee, but he was distracted not so much by the Lambretta with its garish extra fittings which was parked in exactly the same spot, but by the figure about to mount it. Even wearing a crash helmet the disfiguration of the man's face was unmistakeable.

***

It was proving to be something of a busy day at Felixstowe police station and the duty desk sergeant was ever so slightly peeved when just as he was about to take a break, with a much-needed sit down and cup of coffee, the front door opened yet again.

'Madam? How can we help?'

'I wish to report a missing person.'

'Who exactly is missing?

'My son, Donald.' By comparison to the earlier episode of a missing person being reported, this woman was completely dispassionate and seemingly devoid of any emotion.

The sergeant picked up his pencil and prepared to take down some details thinking to himself 'this is one formidable looking woman, and she doesn't seem to be particularly worried about whoever it is that's missing so why's she bothering to report it?'

'Right madam, let me take down some details. Your name?'

'Doreen Hetherington – Mrs, that is. I'm a widow and Donald lives with me.'

***

Back at home Brian was sorting through the packets of seeds he'd bought and absentmindedly prioritising what needed planting, when and how. He was extremely disturbed by what he had seen; Graham Clarke was obviously stalking Maisie. He made a cup of coffee and sat down with the newspaper he'd bought in town. The article on page 2 captured his rapt attention.

'Mac the Knife' To Be Released

Sean Mac Stiofain, the chief of staff of the Provisional Irish Republican Army is due to be released today having served 6 months imprisonment since being sentenced by a Special Criminal Court in Dublin last November. Responsible for ordering an intensification of the IRA campaign which peaked on 21 July 1972, 'Bloody Friday' as it became known described the operation which saw the detonation of 22 car bombs across Belfast in less than two hours. He was arrested after he described the operation as 'a concerted sabotage offensive' in an interview on the RTE 'This Week' radio programme.

The piece went on to report how Mac Stiofain, nicknamed 'Mac the Knife' was a dedicated physical force in the Republican cause who believed that violence was the only means by which Northern Ireland's status as part of the United Kingdom could be brought to an end.

Brian reflected on his own personal association with Mac in the past. Mac had been the instigator of the 'one-shot-sniper' tactic and the driving force in its development. Brian had become an expert exponent of the tactic; a specialism at which he had excelled and never failed. By the time he came to drink his coffee it was cold. The one-shot-sniper tactic. That was it! Brian's mind was made up. Graham Clarke's days were numbered.

***

When the fishing fleet returned to port the fisherman, as per their normal routine congregated around the big table in the Ferry Boat Inn. The conversation was proceeding along the usual lines when PC Clive Randall came into the pub. The big table became hushed.

'Sorry to interrupt men, relaxing after your long day's work, but we've had a report that one of your number has gone missing.'

'Is it Merv?' asked one. 'We was wond'rin' where Merv was,' said another.

Randall pulled a stool up to the table. Kevin, the licensee, brought him a glass of orange juice and stood by listening. Randall made notes of last sightings and conversations, the generality of their work and socialising, not that much if any of it would lead to finding Barbara's husband. Randall got up to leave.

'If any of you think of anything that might help, please give me call.' He was about to go when Maurice Read took him on one side.

'I din't want to say owt in front o' the others. It's a bit sensitive like.' Maurice related the state of his brother's mind on the day it was discovered that his daughter had been raped, and since; how he'd warned Merv about doing anything stupid especially after the threat he'd made in the White Horse.

'I was going to see 'im later, 'cos I lent 'im me van last Thursd'y and I ain't seen it nor 'im since. I was 'oping me van'd be round 'is 'cos I'm getting too old for coming down 'ere on me bike.'

Perhaps, Maurice thought to himself, now's the time to come clean about that blasted rifle. Perhaps I should mention Ronnie Higginson as well.

Chapter Fifty-Seven

Back at Felixstowe police station PC Clive Randall was with his sergeant discussing the information he'd gleaned from the Ferry fishermen and particularly that supplied by the missing man's brother.

'Call DCI Cartwright at Ipswich immediately. He's heading up this enquiry and it sounds as if this is the breakthrough he'll have been looking for.'

DS Armstrong was the only person in the archive basement which served as the Three Stooges office. Lewis had already taken Cartwright to Pin Mill. When the call came through from Randall, Armstrong was beside himself with excitement and immediately rang his guvnor on Helen Blake's number.

'Fantastic news Doug! OK, here's what we do. Ask Felixstowe to make sure the brother, what was it, Maurice, let's have Maurice Read at the station in the morning. I want to be there when he makes his statement. Probably be as well if we have the lad Matthew there as well. We're closing in Doug, we're closing in! Tell Lewis to pick me up at 7.30 in the morning and we'll go straight to Felixstowe.'

It was 7.20 when Lewis arrived at Helen's cottage. Cartwright was already at the front door waiting for his ride. On the way to Felixstowe Cartwright was giving Armstrong the benefit of his thinking.

'If this bloke Higginson is our man, and if he's still living the life of a rustic fugitive in the forest, what do you think about bringing in Operation Axeman, not to round up a bunch of kids at their party, but to comb the forest for Higginson's hideout.'

'Yeah, why not? Great idea guv. I suppose we'll have to run it past Gibbo first?'

'You see I reckon this is what happened…'

***

'Are we in trouble?' Maurice asked. He and Matt were sat across the table opposite DCI Cartwright and DS Armstrong.

'No, but if you'd have told us about the gun in the golf bag when you first fished it up, when was it…? almost a month ago, we could have had this case solved by now.'

'Sorry sir.'

'Yeah so you bloody well should be. OK, let's go through it. I'll tell you what I think has happened so far, and we'll see if your version tallies with what I think.' With that Cartwright went through a chronology of incidents since the assassination of Jock McClean on Havergate Island through to the report of Mervyn's disappearance.'

'I reckon you got it nailed, Chief inspector. I just knew that blasted gun were goin' to be a problem an' I should a handed it in after we trawled the bloody thing up.'

'Yes you should! Have you got anything to add Matt?' Matthew was on the verge of tears and biting his bottom lip.

'I'm sorry sir. I should a told you about the gun when we was in your Jaguar two weeks ago. I din't 'cos I thought it would get Uncle Maurice in trouble, and then 'e'd 'ave told me dad, and then I'd 'ave bin in trouble.' Matt began to sob. 'I want me dad. Please can you find me dad?' Matt's pleading through the tears that were now cascading down his cheeks was so desperately heartfelt that even the most callous and uncompassionate of individuals would have been moved.

'That's exactly what we're going to do. Your family has suffered a great deal just recently, first with your sister, and now this. Don't worry Matt, one way or another we'll find your dad and bring Higginson in.'

After the Reads had left, the detectives re-evaluated their position in the light of this latest intelligence.

'Time is of the essence Doug. In fact, we might already be too late. I'll wager my pension that Mervyn Read and Ronnie Higginson have had a set-to in that bloody forest.'

'I fear you may be right guv,' responded Armstrong. 'Merv borrowed Maurice's van on the 12th and it's now 17th and neither Merv nor the van have been seen for five days.'

'I saw it guv.' Lewis who had been sitting quietly in the corner during the interview with the Reads spoke for the first time.

'Yeah I saw it, day of Axeman. You obviously didn't notice it, but when we were in the bread van just before we turned into the airbase, it was parked by the edge of the forest, pulled up on the verge.' Cartwright thumped the table.

'Bloody hell, I'm right then. Doug ring Gibbo and Brinkley. We need Operation Axeman mobilised now, and I mean now, not this afternoon, not tomorrow, now! Andy, get over to the forest, see if the van's still there. If it is, give me call and keep it under surveillance. Either way, ring me. Get tooled up before you go. We're going to turn that forest upside down.' Suddenly the sleepy seaside police station was a flurry of activity. Cartwright was barking out further orders.

'Sergeant can you get someone to bring in the other Higginson, what's his name?'

'You mean Alan, sir.'

'Yes, him! Bring him in for questioning pronto! Keep him in a cell until we get around to it. And send someone to that pub, The White Horse was it? I want a statement from the landlord. What did he see or overhear, who else was in the pub – Saturday at the back end of March, when Maurice and Merv were there.

With policemen scurrying hither and thither Cartwright felt for the first time that he was close to nabbing McClean's killer who would then inform on McFaddon who would turn whistleblower on future atrocities planned by the IRA. 'There could be a medal in this,' he was thinking. 'Be one in the eye for bloody Simons.' In the outer office he could hear the telephone ringing.

'Is no one going to answer that?' Cartwright eventually answered it himself.

'This is Gibson, Cartwright. For all that I appreciate and understand the need for urgency, we can't just drop everything and put together the Axeman taskforce at a moment's notice. I've spoken to the Chief Constable and he agrees. We don't want this to go off half-cocked.'

'Well, of course not sir. But a man's life could be at risk.'

'You know as well as I that there is little chance of finding Mervyn Read alive. He is already dead. I'd put money on it.'

'But sir...'

Gibson would hear no argument.

'No, Detective Chief Inspector. There'll be a briefing for Operation Axeman here at 1200 hours tomorrow.' The call was terminated. Within seconds the phone was ringing again.

'Lewis here guv. The van's still here.'

'We're stood down until tomorrow Andy.' The dejection in his voice all too apparent, but Lewis knew better than to ask.

'I'll send a tow-truck for it. Come on in Andy. Doug, Sergeant,' he shouted. 'Stand 'em down. Gibbo's orders.'

Chapter Fifty-Eight

The Bell was fairly crowded. Tuesday was darts night and it was a top-of-the-league tussle between the home team and the visitors from the Anchor in Woodbridge. There was a crowd at the bar amongst which was Alvin, still in uniform. He had spotted Brian when he came in and ordered a pint for him. Someone in the crowd tapped him on the shoulder.

'Evening Brian! I hear you've defected, gone AWOL. Sid's been worryin' after you.' It was Pete, a drinker from the Anchor come to support his team. 'Defected, gone AWOL?' The phrase had a worrying connotation.

'Pete! Hello. Yeah I've moved to live here in Boyton. Can't spend the rest of my life in a hotel. Look I'd love to chat, but I've got a bit of urgent business I need to discuss with a mate.'

'Yeah sure. I'll see you later no doubt?'

'To be sure you will.'

Brian and Alvin managed to find a spot away from the dartboard.

'You look a bit agitated, flustered, man, what's bothering you?'

'I need a favour, but I hardly dare ask,' explained Brian.

'Hey man, name it. We're neighbours, drinking buddies, pals even.' Brian decided that there was no point in beating about the bush so he came straight out with it.

'You mentioned a guy in the forest with a Remington M21. I need that gun for a couple of hours.' Before the inevitable question which Brian was anticipating he said, 'Don't ask!'

'OK, but I hardly think we can just waltz in there and say, 'Hey buddy lend me your rifle for a couple of hours' can we?'

'True, but if you don't mind just helping me find him, that'd be great, terrific even. And perhaps if you had your ArmaLite with you, that might convince him to lend the Remington. I'll even rent it or buy it from him. I desperately need that gun.'

'Mine's no good? You're welcome to that.'

'Thanks, but it has to be the Remington.'

'OK, when do you need it?'

'Like now? I know it'll soon be dark but…'

'No problem my friend. In this light we'll spot his campsite so much more easily. He'll be looking at one his porno magazines by torchlight.'

They downed their pints, eased their way outside and Brian indicated his Dolomite a short distance down the road.

'Hell no, man – too conspicuous! Over here, I've got the firm's car complete with camouflage kit! Plenty of these cruising passed the base at all hours so we ain't going to stick out like a sore thumb like your yellow peril there.'

They got into the M606 Jeep and sped off to the forest. To Brian's surprise, Al drove straight on to the base. He pulled up at the guardhouse, had a word with the duty airman who saluted. The barrier was raised and Al climbed back into the Jeep handing an ArmaLite and a flashlight over to Brian. He turned off the road and on to the actual airfield following the perimeter fence, passed the hole, and way beyond. Given the vast acreage of Rendlesham Forest Brian was beginning to wonder whether this might be something of a needle in a haystack exercise. But Al seemed to know where he was going. The light was fading.

'I got a pretty good idea of where this guy is. When we're on guard duty we have to patrol the airfield from time to time and I've seen stuff going on in the woods. We have a couple of "residents" let's call 'em, in the forest at the moment and we have to keep an eye on 'em. Could be Russian spies, you never know.'

'Who's the other "resident" then?' Brian was curious but suspected who it might be.

'Looks like some old tramp. Creeps about wearing an old army coat. Your guy's just a stretch up here. His little hideaway ain't as hidden away as he might think.'

After driving a half-mile further, Al switched off the Jeep's headlights and engine and coasted to a stop. They walked another 200 yards and into the edge of forest, which on this northern side was much denser than the southern edge by the road. They pulled on their camouflage fatigues and balaclavas. Al put his finger to his lips and both men peered into the gloom. Sure enough, in the distance the diffused light from a torch was just visible through a makeshift shelter of canvas and tarpaulin. Every few seconds, a snippet of pop music drifted on the air. As they crept closer the strains of *Tie a Yellow Ribbon Round the Ole Oak Tree* became ever more audible. Then Slade took over with *Cum on Feel the Noize*. Whatever the programme was, the transistor radio was providing enough of a distraction for the presence of Al and Brian to remain undiscovered. They were right behind the shelter. Suddenly, there was movement within. A burly yet athletic figure of a man emerged and walked off with a purpose into thick undergrowth. He looked neither left nor right but straight ahead. He was on a mission. As Slade's *Noize* began to fade Brian and Al could easily hear what was going on. The man was relieving himself. What better opportunity than to catch a man with his trousers down.

'Just finish off there partner and then stand and put your hands on your head.' The sight of the ArmaLite being aimed directly at his groin was sufficient to guarantee the man's compliance if not accelerate what he was up to.

'Now listen up!' The Texan drawl readily recognisable to all fans of American movies was delivered in intimidating style. 'My friend here is going to borrow your rifle. It'll be returned to you sometime tomorrow.' The man with his hands on his head and his trousers around his ankles was in no position to argue or enter into any debate as he stood there in disbelief with his mouth wide open. With a gesture of his head Al motioned Brian towards the shelter. Lying there amongst the empty crisp packets, bottles and various wrappers was the familiar sight of the golf bag. Brian could hardly believe it. The last time he picked the bag up was to throw it overboard and into the North Sea from the deck of *Samson*. Al walked backwards maintaining the ArmaLite's aim as Gary Glitter launched into *Do you Wanna Touch Me?* 'Not bloody likely!' thought Brian. They retreated the way they came, into the Jeep and into the night. Neither of them spoke. As they were driving back across Sutton Common Al became aware of the single headlight in his rear-view mirror. He slowed right down. Just passed the Red Lodge, the motorcycle or perhaps it was scooter was immediately behind the Jeep until it made an abrupt left turn on to the track leading back into the forest. Brian swung round in his seat just in time to make out a flash of chrome from the Lambretta carrying a pillion passenger. The Jeep accelerated down to Stores Corner and then left and back to Boyton.

'One hundred and eighty!' Al and Brian were back in the Bell. The last leg of the darts match was in progress and the noise and excitement alternating with absolute silence as the thrower took aim indicated a close finish in prospect.

'Alvin, my friend, you were superb, absolutely magnificent. I had visions of us spending hours searching that bloody forest, yet you took us straight there, in and out inside ten minutes, job done. Terrific.' They were both laughing now.

'Yeah, well I knew that guy was there or thereabouts and a pain in the ass with that rifle. It would have been only a matter of time before he killed somebody. Now, I need to know and you're going to tell me what you're going to do with a Remington M21A with a Zeiss telescopic sight.' The tone of Alvin's words left Brian feeling he had no alternative than to tell him.

The post-darts match celebrations were in full swing and when Bert announced a lock-in a huge cheer went up. Brian had almost finished his life story and Al had been a most attentive listener.

'The reason I asked,' Al said, 'was because I didn't want you doing anything stupid. Now I know your background I'm comfortable with what you're going to do and I believe, from what you tell me, that Maisie and your future relationship is worth it. And, speaking of worth, for what it's worth, I have relations back Stateside who are sympathisers and contributors to NORAID. You know, the Northern Irish Aid Committee? I know at first hand that when word came down from NORAID headquarters in Pearl River there was a real sense of outrage that someone was thieving the weapons we were buying for your guys in the IRA. When I tell my folks back home that I have made a good friend of the guy who shot and killed Jock McClean they'll hardly believe it.'

'Don't mention my name for God's sake'.

'You take me for stupid or something?'

When they eventually left the pub, Brian loaded the golf bag into his car and drove the short distance home.

He carefully laid the bag on the sofa and, wearing a pair of thin cotton gloves very slowly took out the rifle and sat with the gun laid across his knees. He ran a hand over the barrel and caressed the walnut stock. It was almost as if he was reacquainting himself with an old friend. He laid the gun on the kitchen table and with a practiced art stripped it down to its component parts. He examined every one carefully, cleaning and lubricating as necessary. When he was satisfied, and the gun reassembled he adjusted the sight, range-finding and bullet-drop features. As far as he could tell without actually firing off a few test rounds, the gun was ready for the very last shot in the hands of its master marksman.

Chapter Fifty-Nine

Since moving back into the area with the intention of finding his erstwhile wife, Graham Clarke's single-minded intention was to demand compensation for the disfiguring injuries sustained ten years ago when she poured the caustic soda solution over him. He hadn't been happy with the advice that his solicitor had offered with regard to the pursuit of a claim through legal channels, so he was left with having to do things the hard way. It had become necessary to make demands with menaces.

He'd been living on the weekly dole money of £7.35 and it didn't go very far. OK, he had been managing so far with a little thievery here and spurious methods of acquisition there. But payback time had come. His life was overdue a change for the better, a life of luxury, the life he deserved. The kidnapping he had carefully planned would be so much more straightforward now, courtesy of Toady's Lambretta.

Graham had been watching Maisie's movements for over a week and whilst there was no pattern as such, she was fairly predictable. Ordinarily, unless she went off with that man she'd been seeing, she'd come home from work and go to the Anchor for an hour or two before going back to her houseboat. On the odd occasion she'd be out for longer. He had it all worked out.

He watched as she walked home. He watched as she left the houseboat and went to the pub. He moved the Lambretta on to the quay and parked it close to the *Ironside's* gangplank. He went to the pub and had hardly crossed the threshold before Sid reacted.

'Out! You're barred!'

'Yeah, I'm going. Just gi' me a minit.'

Sid laid down the ground-rules.

'If you've come in here to make trouble or cause a scene you can leave right now. Understand?' Sid was not inclined to put up with a repetition of the way he behaved on his last visit.

'No, mate, I's come to 'pologise. I jus' wan' a word wi' Mais' tha's all, then I'll be gone, promise.'

'That's all right then, but I'm not your mate. That OK with you Maisie?'

She was sat on a bar stool at the end of the bar and while she didn't appear to be too comfortable or delighted with the prospect of having to listen, or worse, to talk to Graham she nodded.

'OK, five minutes, that's all.'

'Promise!' said Graham.

They went and sat at an empty table.

'I thought yo' might like to know that I bin back to the s'licita and withdrew me claim fer compersation an' I'm sorry Mais. Let me get yo' another an' I'll be gone f'rever.'

Even before Maisie could accept his offer of a drink Graham had gone to the bar.

'G&T please an' one fer yersel. No 'ard feelin's?'

Sid pushed a glass up beneath the Gordon's optic, added a slice of lemon and two ice-cubes. He placed it on the bar and as he turned to reach for a bottle of tonic water, Graham slipped two 200mg tablets of pentobarbital into the gin. The effervescence when the tonic water was added sufficiently disguised the dissolving tablets. Graham placed his last pound note on the bar and collected his change. He took the drink over to Maisie.

'Sorry agen Mais. Night night.' And he was gone.

He didn't have to wait very long. For all the world Maisie appeared to be drunk as she teetered across the road in her high heels, staggering one way and then the other. There was no way she would have made it up the gangplank without mishap. She heard a voice.

'Let me 'elp,' following which Maisie's facility to determine imaginary from reality was fundamentally flawed. Then she was on the back of a scooter clutching on to the person in front for dear life or was it just in her mind?

Rough camping was no hardship for Graham. He had led more than several expeditions with the scouts before he was decommissioned and obliged to turn in his woggle. Although the allegations of interfering with underaged boys was never proven, the stigma would last forever which is probably why he turned to the bottle for solace. Even so his background in scouting now stood him in good stead. His camp in the forest was the complete opposite to Ronnie's. Here there was order. A place for everything and everything in its place. There was even a place he'd prepared for Maisie. The forest was pitch black but undaunting for this backwoodsman. The narrow shaft of light from his small flashlight was more than adequate to enable him to pick out the undefined track to his encampment, even with the comatose form of Maisie draped over his shoulder. He lay her down on a bed of dry pine needles and covered her with a blanket.

When Maisie regained consciousness it was light. She had a chain padlocked to one ankle. The other end of the chain was secured to the scots pine which was serving as one of the supporting uprights for the shelter. Graham was standing looking at her. She didn't speak. He offered her a cup of water which she accepted.

'I 'ave to go inta town. I'll be back in a 'our. When I gets me compersation I'll let yer go.'

There was sufficient scope on the chain to allow a little freedom of movement and her hands weren't tied. She watched as he vanished into the trees and immediately set to attempting to unshackle the chain from the tree. Her attempts were futile. She was a hostage.

Chapter Sixty

The problem with a yellow car, irrespective of the make or marque, is that it is conspicuous. Throughout the whole of his professional career Brian's success had been dependent on his ability to be and to remain inconspicuous. He was up and about very early. He loaded the golf bag into the car and set off towards Woodbridge. He was absolutely certain that the scooter he'd seen last night was the same Lambretta that he'd seen parked outside Potter's Estate Agency. The wing-mirrors and tassels were so distinctive. It had been Graham Clarke for sure. The only doubt in his mind was cast by the pillion passenger. Who might that have been? Whoever it was, was not going to deter Brian from his mission however. Graham Clarke had ridden into the forest to his hideaway last night. At some point today he'd be riding out.

On his numerous trips between Boyton and Woodbridge Brian had noticed the golf club on Bromeswell Heath, and it had been his intention once he was settled and established in his new home to apply for membership. This morning, a fine spring morning, he turned into the club's access road and parked his car in the Club carpark. The location couldn't have been better for two reasons: even though it was yellow, the car wouldn't be out of place in a carpark, and if there was one place where a man could remain inconspicuous carrying a golf bag it was on or near a golf course.

Brian walked a short distance back towards the junction of the B1083 with the road across Sutton Heath. The terrain was flat but there was good cover afforded by gorse, scrub and fern. He found a spot out of sight looking towards Sutton Heath: the road across the heath almost as straight as an arrow. The scooter would be seen coming for miles. Brian settled himself into his cover and loaded a single round. It was now a waiting game although the wait was not long. He heard it before he saw it. Brian rolled over into the prone position and adjusted the focus on the Zeiss ZF42 telescopic sight and with the benefit of the powerful magnification he locked on to his target as it made its approach.

The strident scrape of metal grinding over tarmac was heard a split second before the shot rang out across the heath. The rider, separated from his machine performed several involuntary somersaults and tumbles before coming to a motionless full stop on the verge at the side of the road. The Lambretta, with its structural integrity severely impaired continued along the road, before hitting the base of the signpost at the junction; broken glass, bent chrome and twisted metal lying in the roadway evidence of an insurance write-off, had it been insured. Brian packed away the rifle and walked over to where Graham Clarke lay dead. A single bullet-hole in the bridge of his nose. Brian O'Connor supreme master of the 'one-shot sniper tactic'.

Before returning to his car, Brian called in at the clubhouse and picked up a membership application form. He then drove to Woodbridge hoping to see Maisie before she got to work. He knew she would be delighted by the news that he had persuaded Graham, finally, to desist in pestering her.

It was ten to nine when he parked the Dolomite in the Market Square. The lights were not lit in Potter's offices and it appeared that no one had turned up for work thus far. He waited. The bells in the tower of St Mary the Virgin struck nine. Jeremy Rogers arrived. Seconds later the lights came on. A few minutes later Mr Potter arrived. Where was Maisie?

Brian crossed the road to the office and went in.

'Why, Mr O'Connor! Good morning, I trust you're well?'

'Quite well for sure, thank you. I was hoping to have a quick word with Maisie.'

'Well, I'm not sure where she is. Normally she'd have unlocked and be at her desk with the coffee made before I get here. Most unusual. She's never been late before.'

Brian had a bad feeling. He ran down Church Street and Quay Street and onto the Quayside. He was about to board *Ironside*.

'Morning Brian!' It was Colin.

'Have you seen Maisie?'

'Not since last night. She was in the Anchor but went home feeling unwell after that ex-husband spoke to her.' Brian had heard enough. He ran all the way back to his car and drove as fast as the early morning congestion would allow. Through Melton, over the level-crossing and Wilford Bridge and on to the B1083. As he was approaching the golf club he could see the blue flashing lights. He slowed down, not wishing to arouse suspicion. He was waved down by a policeman. With his heart in his mouth he wound down the window. 'Carefully   as you go sir, there's been an accident and there's still debris in the road.'

'Thanks officer. Is it serious?'

'I should say so. Poor bloke's dead and it ain't the accident that killed him neither.'

'Oh dear!' Brian drove away slowly and gradually accelerated as he came on to the long straight of the Sutton Heath road. Just as the Lambretta had done, Brian turned onto the track a short distance after the Red Lodge and continued until it became impassable. He abandoned the car and continued on foot deeper into the forest. He began to shout.

'Maisie! Maisie! He paused, and listened. Nothing.

'Maisie! Maisie! He stopped again and listened. Nothing. He ventured on further and deeper into the woodland and away from the Upper Hollesley Common.

'Maisie! Maisie where are you for God's sake. Maisie! He yelled with every decibel he could muster. He stopped listened.

Away in the distance he heard her voice. Scrambling over fallen branches, he charged in the direction from whence the voice had come.

'Maisie!'

'Brian, over here.' Then even before he'd spotted the camp he was on top of it, so well it was camouflaged, and there she was.

Chapter Sixty-One

The bread van and following convoy transporting Operation Axeman was just approaching the golf club. There was a police panda and a Cortina at the scene of an accident. An ambulance was just preparing to leave. Lewis brought the van and the following convoy to a stop. A PC walked over to the van and peering in through the open window he saw DCI Cartwright in the passenger seat and ten other PCs in the back.

'Blimey, that was quick.' It didn't take long for the PC to realise that it wasn't the incident he was attending that was of interest to the convoy. That was until he happened to mention the dead scooter rider with the bullet hole in the bridge of his nose.

'Where's the body?' Cartwright was out of the van in a flash and he ran over to the ambulance and just managed to stop it before it drove off. Lewis walked back to the unmarked car immediately behind the van and invited Armstrong to get involved. DI Brinkley was in the next car and clearly getting agitated. He got out of the car and wandered over to the ambulance where Cartwright was examining the corpse.

'Come and take a look Doug. I think you can identify him.'

'By God, it's Graham Clarke… and with all the hallmarks of the Harvey and McClean shootings.'

Cartwright hurriedly explained to Brinkley the interrelationship of what they were about with Axeman to what had happened here by the golf club. At his assertive best Cartwright began issuing the orders.

'Doug, take half of Axeman and if it's our man and he's true to his MO there'll be cartridge case somewhere. Find it! See what else there might be lying about as well. DC Turner, take a few men with you and go and ask questions at the golf club. Did anyone see anything, or hear anything? A shot out here in this blasted wilderness? Carry for miles I should think. Surely someone heard it? Right Andy, as we were. To the woods!'

What remained of the original convoy pulled up to the barrier at RAF Woodbridge. AFC Shultz had been expecting them although he wasn't fully *au fait* with the fact that Merv Read was now the primary objective of the search. Shultz had been hoping Brian would have returned the Remington by now. If Brian's plan was to succeed the police would have to find matey-boy Higginson with the gun.

'We're still obviously anxious to find our killer with the rifle, which we believe may be a Remington, but a very recent development leads us to think neither the killer nor the gun are here at the moment, or even if they'll be here at all ever again. I'm pretty damn sure that will have been Higginson with the rifle that has struck again, just down the road near the golf club.' Schultz was sweating and tried to feign incredulity. The DCI continued, 'So for now we're looking for a missing person.' Cartwright gave Shultz a resume of the Higginson, Gail and Merv Read situation. 'We believe Merv Read may have come here to avenge his daughter and ended up another one of Higginson's victims.'

Schultz was relieved. At least Brian would still have time to return the rifle without being discovered. He would now organise the search in such a way that it was the lair of the tramp with army overcoat that got discovered and not Higginson. Little did he realise that by guiding Axeman to the tramp's hideaway he would be assisting the police with their other missing person search.

With Shultz in the lead, the policemen were driven in US Jeeps. Other military transport including a dog unit proceeded along the runway to its eastern end where the Axeman personnel were dropped off and divided into groups, each one with a dog-handler.

"Why are we coming this way? enquired Cartwright

'Because this part of the forest is at the northern end nearest the road where Merv Read's van was last seen. We have to start somewhere, and this seems the most logical place to me.' It was Lewis who answered, much to Shultz's relief yet again.

'OK Andy, makes sense. Let's go!' and the search was initiated from the northernmost edge and moving to the south-eastern part of the forest. Schultz advised them to form a line abreast and leave the searching to the dogs. He knew Cartwright's men would inevitably come upon the tramp's hideaway unless they were complete Limey morons. For AFC Shultz there was an immediate and urgent other matter to attend to. He rushed back to main entrance on to the base and there in the carpark by the administrative block was a yellow Triumph Dolomite. For the third time in half-an-hour Alvin Schultz felt an enormous sense of relief.

'I was hoping you'd be on the gate. Can you spare ten minutes to run me back up the airfield? I'll never find the camp by myself.' Brian was clearly anxious to get the Remington back to Ronnie Higginson and remove any chance of the police making a connection between himself, the weapon or Clarke. He hadn't wanted to leave Maisie given the state she was in after her ordeal as a hostage, but she was sleeping safely tucked up in his bed at 7 Mill Lane.

'Sure thing buddy! Jump in.'

They followed the route they had taken the previous evening, walking the last few hundred yards. Al led the way into the forest with his ArmaLite at the ready. Brian followed closely behind with the golf bag slung over his shoulder. They found Ronnie Higginbottom's hideaway without any difficulty at all. There was no one there.

'Where the hell is he?'

'Gone walkabout it seems. Judging by the crap in his tent, the empty cans, wrappers, cartons and stuff, I reckon he's getting his supplies, provisions and stuff from American kids who are supplying him from the BX and the base supermarket.'

'Well, it can only be a matter of time before the police find him and the gun and that should put me in the clear and let me get on and make a life with Maisie, if she'll still have me.' Brian replaced the golf bag in Higginson's shelter and the two men left the way they came.

Driving back to the administration block carpark Brian spoke of his worry with regard to his future relationship.

'I'll have to tell her about Graham otherwise we'll be starting out from... well, I wouldn't be happy living with such a secret. I just hope she'll forgive me – maybe even thank me.'

'Listen pal, in your position, I'd have done exactly the same thing. Whether you tell her or not is up to you and your conscience. If it was me, I wouldn't tell her. Could jeopardise everything. Don't rush into anything and don't beat yourself up over it!'

Alvin dropped Brian by his car.

'Cheers Al and thanks for everything. I'll see you in the pub?'

'You certainly will and hey man, no worries right?'

Chapter Sixty-Two

'They're out there now even as we speak,' the desk sergeant was explaining. 'We've had a tip-off and a whole search party has been mobilised.'

Doreen Hetherington was back at Felixstowe Police Station enquiring as to what if any progress had been made in the search for her missing son. The sergeant hadn't had the courage to tell her that search party wasn't actually looking for her son in particular, but he thought the white lie would appease her for the time being. Donald 'Toady' Hetherington was a young man and young men living at home with their disciplinarian mothers all too frequently went missing. Well, not missing exactly, but very often their home environment could be oppressive and they just needed to get away for a few days' freedom, peace and quiet. Having re-evaluated his original character assessment of Doreen Hetherington, the Sergeant had no reason to change his mind and considered this to be the case and therefore the reason for his not having attached any great urgency to a search. Toady would have to wait. The chances were that by the time they came to start looking for young Mr Hetherington, he'd have turned up anyway.

***

In their home in Kirton, Barbara, Matthew and Gail Read were experiencing great difficulty in coming to terms with the fact that Mervyn might be gone forever. The police had returned the Ford Anglia van to Maurice. The vehicle had provided no clues to Merv's disappearance and it was exactly as when Maurice had lent it to his brother apart from the missing gaff. Maurice was offering what help and comfort he could, Matt had assumed the role of man-of-the-house and except when she wasn't cuddling her mother, Gail was studying hard for the exams after Easter.

***

On the eastern side of Rendlesham Forest the search party led by DCI Cartwright was making slow progress. The dogs were covering great tracts of the forest floor with their handlers doing their best to keep up, running with them as far as they could.

'It would be handy if we knew exactly what it was we were looking for,' suggested Lewis.

'We'll know when we find it. C'mon Andy, think positive. Merv's in here, perhaps Higginson as well and we're going to find one or even both of them. Goodness only knows we've been after our man for how long? And now here we are, on the scent…' Cartwright stopped abruptly. Up ahead through the gloom they could see the search groups had also stopped. The dogs were barking and pawing away at a mound of earth which was partially covered with dead branches and fern.

'Sir, here! Over here sir, we've got something. The handlers had their animals back on leashes as airmen and police constables began to remove branches from the heap. It was the shaft of the gaff that they saw first. The shallow grave of Mervyn Read was slowly and carefully revealed. Cartwright moved in closer to inspect the corpse and detected the gunshot wound to the shoulder. The ground beneath the wounded leg was matted with dried blood.

'Hard to establish the cause of death. Hardly the bullet in the shoulder, more likely a combination of the bleeding from that wound and I'd say the femoral artery is pretty well severed by the look of it. Poor old Merv.'

The dogs were straining at their leads and barking at the adjacent mound and as officers were beginning to move the forest debris it didn't take long to uncover a second corpse. Just by the way the body had been covered it was obvious to the DCI that greater care to conceal this body had been taken compared to the first. A pair of spectacles were recovered with one lens broken and the frame twisted.

'Well now, what does anyone make of this?' The question wasn't intended to be rhetorical, but no one offered an answer anyway. Three men volunteered to stay and maintain a watch on the site until the pathologist's team arrived. The remaining members of Operation Axeman were stood down and released for return to their usual bases.

Back at RAF Woodbridge, Cartwright found Shultz and reported what had been discovered.

'We didn't find Higginson's camp so we'll be back tomorrow. There's also probably a cartridge case somewhere not too far from the graves. Ideally we'll find that as well and be able to match it to the Remington as the murder weapon.'

Back at the Ipswich headquarters DS Armstrong and DC Turner were debriefing DCI Cartwright on their findings at the Sutton Common Road shooting.

'We found the cartridge case and Doctor Snotty Pants has already confirmed that it was fired from the same gun as killed Harvey and McClean.'

'Anything from the golf club Turner?'

'No sir. I spoke to the Club Secretary. He said he heard a bang but thought nothing of it. He says there are all sorts of noises from aircraft and the like much of the time. There's also a rifle range on the edge of the forest. Could have been a shot from there he suggested. Oh, he also said there were just a few members there early and they'd all have been out on the course. He saw nobody else, apart from one bloke who called in for a membership application form.'

'Do we know who it was? He might have witnessed something?'

'He didn't give a name. Was driving a yellow Triumph Dolomite though.'

'OK, see if you can trace him. Right, are Gibbo and DI Brinkley up to speed on all of this?'

'Yes guv.'

'We may well have a fourth cartridge case for Hard-Hearted Hannah, another one for comparison if we find it tomorrow. So, not bad for a day's work. Three bloody corpses! Two we know. Any ideas on the third?'

'It maybe a Donald Hetherington. He was reported missing to the Felixstowe Police by his mother last Monday. We'll arrange an ID as soon as we can.'

'Any idea of the motive Doug?'

'It's only guess work but...'

'Well?'

'Donald, Toady they call him, is, sorry, was a mate of Alan Higginson. They were both pulled over on Wilford Bridge on Saturday, on Toady's scooter, off to see his gran in Ufford so he said. Alan Higginson was on the pillion and had no crash helmet, which is why they were stopped. The PC told Alan to catch a train home from Melton.'

'So what?'

'Well, it's a hell of a coincidence and I know how you feel about coincidences, but it was Toady's scooter that Graham Clarke was riding this morning.'

'Oh bloody hell. The plot thickens! Why would Ronnie Higginson shoot Graham Clarke? For nicking his younger brother's mate's scooter? I don't think so. There's more to it than that.'

'Good work today Cartwright.' Chief Superintendent Gibson had breezed into the room. 'Pity we didn't manage to apprehend Higginson though. Still, when we get him he'll have an impressive charge sheet, five murders at least, a rape and driving an unlicensed vehicle whilst uninsured. Righty-ho. Full briefing at 0800 and then we'll mobilise Operation Axeman off to the forest again I think. And this time we'll have him!'

Chapter Sixty-Three

It was Matthew Read who formally identified his father, Mervyn. Uncle Maurice had driven him to the mortuary and was now offering what commiseration he could, but he knew it was hopelessly inadequate and helplessly lacking. Even had he been a man of letters he would have found it extremely difficult to find the words of compassion and sympathy that would have been anything other than that, just words. What does one say when one's brother has been murdered for trying to avenge the rape of his daughter when the rapist and the murderer are one and the same person? As they drove back to the family home in Kirton, Maurice couldn't even begin to imagine the depths of misery, despair and agony that Barbara and Gail would be feeling once they knew for certain that their worst fears were realised.

***

Doreen Hetherington was also a visitor at the mortuary for the purposes of identifying a dead body. She was shown the spectacles first, with their twisted frame and broken lens.

'Yes,' she said, turning to DC Turner, 'they could be Donald's.' The sheet covering the corpse was then pulled down to chest level. She stared at the head and shoulders. The face with the blemished complexion. The face now tinged by the blue-grey tint of asphyxiation and death. The neck with severe bruising and the marks of the fingers that had caused it still prominently visible.

'Yes,' she, said, turning again to DC Turner, this is Donald, my son.'

There was no lamenting, no weeping, no expositions of grief or even the merest hint of sadness. Doreen Hetherington merely pulled the sheet back over her son's head and left the room.

***

The body of Graham Clarke was in the Pathology Department where the cause of death was established as 'intradural haemorrhage and traumatic oedema of the brain tissue.' DS Armstrong had already identified the body as being the husband of his ex-wife, accordingly, the coroner had agreed that there would be no need for Mrs Clarke to confirm the identification.

***

At Ipswich Police headquarters Chief Superintendent Gibson brought the assembled forces to order.

'Good morning, ladies and gentlemen. As you will be aware, this case goes back almost six months to the murder of PC Colin Harvey. In fact, it goes back beyond that as we have very good reason to believe that the killer of PC Harvey has strong connections with the IRA and is implicated in terrorist atrocities. Since the murder of PC Harvey, the killer has assassinated Duncan McClean, also an IRA terrorist sympathiser turned sole-trader.' (This description raised a laugh around the room.) We now believe, and our belief is substantiated by the excellent work of Doctor Hamilton's department in gathering the forensic evidence,' all eyes turned towards Doctor Snotty Pants at this mention as the sycophantic Gibson stood there beaming at her, 'that the perpetrator of these crimes has since shot and killed two others, possibly strangled another and raped a schoolgirl, the daughter of one of the murder victims. Our enquiries and the acquired intelligence so far informs us that our suspect is one Ronald Higginson,

272

known as Ronnie. A twenty-something-year-old thug from the Roughs Tower Estate in Felixstowe. He is thought to be in hiding in Rendlesham Forest where the bodies of two of his latest victims were found buried in shallow graves yesterday. The third was discovered by the side of the road at Bromeswell Golf Club. I'm actually a member there and we can do without this sort of thing on the doorstep!' There were a few sniggers.

'Goodness knows how many police man-hours so far have been spent on bringing this fellow to justice and, at this juncture I would publicly wish to acknowledge the sterling work of DCI Cartwright and DS Armstrong, on secondment to us from the Thames Valley Force.' Gibson paused for an anticipated round of applause. He needn't have bothered. No one applauded.

'So, today, colleagues, with the full force of Operation Axeman plus a detachment of American Serviceman from RAF Woodbridge, which as you know is at the heart of the Forest, we are going to hunt Higginson down, drag him from his hideaway and bring him in. I should remind you that he is armed and extremely dangerous and from what we know so far, an expert marksman. Please be on your guard. Detective Chief Inspector Cartwright, is there anything you would like to add?'

'Thank you sir.' Cartwright stood to address the briefing. 'There are two things which bother me. Firstly, I am far from convinced that the shooting of Graham Clarke, the most recent of the murder victims was carried out by Higginson. I can't think of any possible or plausible motive. Certainly, on the balance of probabilities, the fatal shot was fired from the same gun – a Remington M21 sniper rifle in the hands of an expert marksman. But in Higginson's hands? I don't think so! Secondly, I am far from convinced, and the more I think about it the further from being convinced I become, that a local Felixstowe hooligan was involved in, or even on the periphery of International terrorist crime.' Cartwright was about to continue but noticing the flat of Gibson palm held up in his direction he recognised that as the sign of his allotted time to speak being up. He sat down.

'Notwithstanding the DCI's misgivings, today the focus is on Higginbottom.'

'That's Higginson, sir.' It was Lewis who was brave enough to point out the correction.

'Yes, of course, thank you, Higginson,' acknowledged the somewhat embarrassed Gibson. 'Ok, get to it and bring him in!'

The police convoy duly left Ipswich and made its way through Woodbridge and Melton taking the Sutton Common Road to the airfield. Upon arrival the barrier was already raised, and the bread van and various other vehicles parked in front of the administration building. Two ranks of uniformed airmen were stood at ease. The police forces adopted a similar formation. AFC Shultz was amongst the Americans but no longer the senior officer in charge. He had been gazumped in that role by a Master Sergeant, Garcia, assisted by a Staff Sergeant, Lee. Cartwright and Brinkley liaised with Garcia and both the detectives were more than happy to let him take command.

Garcia addressed the full company of Operation Axeman, some forty men. It was readily apparent to Cartwright that here was a thoroughly proficient and authoritative officer who had earned his stripes. He'd done his homework and although Cartwright didn't mention it to anyone, he was impressed. The company was divided into teams, each one with a German Shepherd and its handler, and they moved off to the north of the airfield since the previous day's search had been to the south. Cartwright and Brinkley were offered the hospitality of the Officer's Mess and this was without hesitation the preferred option. They left Axeman in the capable hands of Garcia and Lee.

Sitting with a cup of strong and bitter coffee which had probably been stewing since breakfast-time, Cartwright tried to explain his doubts with regard to Higginson.

'Despite what Gibbo might think we know that Higginson is not our man. Surely you realise that too? He and Slim Tim, Chief Superintendent Adams at Thames Valley, are two men too alike. Ronnie is certainly no marksman or sniper. How can this be the bloke who takes out Colin Harvey with a 500-yard single shot? No one's going to tell me that Ronnie drove all the way to bloody Foxton in that knackered old Ford Prefect, makes that hit then comes back to sunny Felixstowe. Besides which, we know how he came by the rifle and Harvey and McClean were both dead before Ronnie ever got his hands on it. We've got statements from Sam Reynolds, skipper of the *Samson*. He states that the gun in the golf bag were thrown overboard his boat and Ronnie doesn't fit the description of either of the blokes he picked up off Orford Ness. We have the statements from Maurice and Matthew Read about trawling the gun up from the North Sea, and then how Ronnie subsequently nicked it. We have a statement from Ronnie's brother about the target practice in the forest. No! Absolutely no way!' Brinkley had been listening.

'Yeah, I can see you're right. Do you reckon Gibson just wants to put all of this on Higginson, make him the scapegoat just so he can claim the glory then?'

'Quite possibly. But there again, Higginson is well in the frame for Merv Read and Toady Hetherington. And let's not forget the rape. The bloke is clearly a wrong 'un and should be banged up. Graham Clarke still worries me though.'

An airman stuck his head around the door of the Mess, saluted and announced, 'There on their way back, sirs.'

'Bloody hell! That didn't take long.' The two detectives rushed outside and sure enough the convoy was parking outside the administration building. The Americans formed their two ranks and stood at ease waiting until they were dismissed by Master Sergeant Garcia. The various detectives and uniformed constables stood about chatting and smoking. Then, there was Doug Armstrong and a PC the size of the proverbial brick building and handcuffed between them, and escorted by Master Sergeant Garcia, the man they assumed to be Ronnie Higginson. A short distance behind them was Andy Lewis carrying the golf bag.

Garcia walked over to speak to Cartwright. He saluted. 'There you go sir, as requested one murdering rapist as ordered.'

Cartwright wasn't quite sure how to respond. Brinkley beat him to it.

'That was mighty fine work Sergeant. How'd you find him so quickly? Garcia's answer was delivered in a matter-of-fact style with a shrug of the shoulders. 'Dead easy sir. A few boy scouts could have done it. This here is a military airfield and a USAF base. Security is our top priority. We get guys in the woods all the time and when we check 'em out we let 'em get on with it if we're sure they're not commies. We had a pretty good idea where your man would be and, yessiree, there he was. Dogs sniffed him out and when he saw us he pissed himself and just gave himself up. If you ask me he's small potatoes.'

'Thank you and your men Sergeant Garcia. I'll ensure our Chief Superintendent acknowledges your most excellent leadership of Axeman to your commanding officer.'

'It's been a pleasure sir!'

'C'mon Lewis, there's no time for 18 holes right now!'

Chapter Sixty-Four

'He'll not bother you again Maisie.'

'Yes, you said. How can you be so sure?'

'He's dead!'

'How do you know that?

Brian was wrestling with his conscience and replaying the advice of his friend Alvin over and over in his head, 'Could jeopardise everything'.

'He's been shot. I saw the aftermath of what happened. It seems he'd been riding a scooter and someone shot him. Maybe a kid with an airgun. Anyway, the shot caused him to crash and he's dead. A policeman at the scene told me.'

For all that Maisie was over having been drugged and kidnapped by Graham, this news of his death was not what she had been expecting to hear. In fact, she was just a little miffed by it. Despite everything that had happened between her and her now late husband, had he really deserved to die?

'I think I'd like to go home please Brian. I need a change of clothes and I really must go and see Mr Potter and explain what happened. I don't want to lose my job.'

'Of course. Can I see you later tonight?'

'No, not tonight. I'd like to be by myself tonight.'

***

It was a quiet night in the Bell, just a few of the regulars. Away from the bar counter in the furthest corner of the room Alvin was giving Brian a full and comprehensive report of the day's activities with Operation Axeman; the recovery of two bodies from the forest and the capture of Higginson.

'So, the police have the gun now then?'

'Yep, they found it where you left it after you popped the other guy – Clarke?'

'Yeah, Graham Clarke. I took your advice and I haven't told Maisie, but I think she's a bit upset.'

'Ah, she'll get over it and come round, but what you have to recognise is that falling in love is not the same as being in it!'

'I have a lot to learn.'

***

The following day, Good Friday, in the briefing room at Ipswich HQ, Doctor Hard-Hearted Snotty Pants was reading from her notes.

'I can confirm that the bullet taken from Mervyn Read's shoulder, and the bullet from Graham Clarke's brain matched the cartridge cases which had been found. The cartridge case from Orford Ness and the one recovered from the field at Foxton have exactly identical tooling marks all of which are consistent with having been fired from the Remington M21A which I have also now examined. The fingerprints on the rifle are those of Ronald Higginson.'

'Thank you, Hannah,' the obsequious Gibbo was fawning at her again.

'So, it's a bank holiday so no need to take up any more of your time today gentlemen. There we have it. Case as good as…'

'No sir, we don't!' contradicted Cartwright.

'We have the evidence; we have the murder weapon, and we have our man in custody. Well done everyone!' insisted the Chief Superintendent. He was about to leave when Cartwright's raised voice stopped him in his tracks.

'Sir! What we have is not good enough! There are more holes in this so-called evidence than a slice of that Swiss cheese and any jury will see right through them. Whilst I'm fairly certain we can convict Higginson for the murder of Mervyn Read, as count one, as for counts two to five, well I am convinced that he's innocent and we will never secure a conviction.'

'Explain yourself Cartwright,' the CS ordered.

'Doctor…' he had to stop and think '… Hamilton's forensic evidence as scientifically accurate as it is does not necessarily put the gun in the suspect's hands with his finger squeezing the trigger. This evidence is circumstantial and relies heavily on inference. Therefore, we must accept that there is more than reasonable doubt. Cartwright went on to amplify the bases for his misgivings as he had outlined to DI Brinkley the previous day.

'I see,' said Gibson, although Cartwright doubted that he did, or even wanted to.

'Well, I want him charged!'

'Sir, at least let me interview him first.'

'Oh, very well then, if you must. But I want you to either extract a confession or charge him by the end of the day.' Gibson left in a huff with Doctor Snotty Pants scampering after him.

Cartwright, Brinkley and Armstrong could not believe what they had just heard and it was Brinkley who expressed his concern.

'If we prosecute and go to court merely on what we've got, we'll be a laughingstock. If, and it's an enormous if, he was to be found guilty on all five, counts it would be one of the greatest miscarriages of justice in history.'

'John, you are right,' said Cartwright emphatically. 'OK, let's see what he has to say for himself.

Chapter Sixty-Five

Cartwright, Brinkley and Armstrong were seated on one side of the table in the interview room. On the table were a packet of cigarettes, a lighter, and a glass of water for the suspect. A uniformed PC escorted Ronnie Higginson into the room. He took his place at the table and without being invited helped himself to a cigarette. Cartwright introduced himself and his colleagues and took the lead.

'You ever been to Foxton Ron?'

'Where the fuck's that?'

'You ever been bird-spotting Ronnie?'

'Yeah. Every day when the school chucks out!' He laughed.

'So Ronnie, is that where you were when the school closed on Friday 30th March?'

'Can't say, pig.'

'We're going to get nowhere if that's going to be your attitude and you can't keep a civil tongue.' He removed the cigarettes from the table. Ronnie gave Cartwright an indignant glare.

'I'll try again. Did you pick up a schoolgirl, Gail Read, from school on Friday 30 March?'

'Might a done.'

'Well, we have a witness who saw the girl get into your car, a black Ford Prefect CKY 279A. Is that your car?'

''E's lyin'!'

'I don't think so.'

'OK, 'e needs glasses.'

'Is that your car?'

'Yeah, so what?'

'Where did you go, the two of you?'

'Yo' knows perfec'ly well, so stop buggerin' abaht wi' yer stupid questions.'

'Did you force Gail Read to have sex with you?'

'Nah, she were asking fer it, gaggin' fer it she were.'

'You'd do well to drop the hardman bravado, the great lover act Ronnie. You're in deep trouble. Gail says you had intercourse with her against her will.'

'Well. she's a lyin' little bitch then.'

'Were you aware that she was only fifteen?' Ronnie looked a little taken aback by this question.

'She said she were sixteen – I din't know did I? Still, she let me.'

'Are you aware that sex with a minor constitutes statutory rape?

'I din't rape 'er.'

'In the eyes of the law you did, whether she let you or not. Statutory rape carries a sentence of between eight and ten.' Armstrong took over the questioning.

'Where were you in the early hours of 26th March?'

'In bed wi' your wife, where d'yo' think?'

'We think you were breaking into Maurice Read's shed.'

'Never 'eard of 'im.'

'Isn't it true that you stole a golf bag containing a rifle and ammunition from Maurice Read's shed?'

'Ooever says I did, them's lyin'. I don't know nuffin' about no shed or gun.'

'Your brother Alan has told us that on 1st April you were in Rendlesham Forest doing some target practice with the gun you had stolen. Is this true?'

'Lyin' little toerag. I'll do 'im next. No comment.'

'On 12th April, Mervyn Read, Gail's father, came to look for you in the forest. Did you shoot him?'

'No comment. I need a lawyer. I need another fag.'

'Do you know a man named Donald Hetherington? They call him Toady.'

'Never 'eard of... no comment. I need a fuckin' lawyer!' Ronnie insisted.

'Yes, I think you probably do,' Brinkley admitted.

'Did you strangle Toady Hetherington and bury him in a shallow grave next to the body of Mervyn Read?'

The questions were coming thick and fast now, with the detectives taking turns. Ronnie was becoming flustered and agitated. They were wearing him down.

'No I din't do Toady. 'E were me mate. 'E brought me stuff while I was hidin' out.'

'On a scooter?'

'Yeah poncy thing.'

'Were you expecting Mervyn Read to come after you?

'I thought 'e might, but I was ready fo' 'im. I fired a shot at Gail's dad but only to warn 'im off. 'E fell on the gaff 'e were carryin'. I din't kill 'im. 'Onest, I din't. Can I 'ave another fag? Can I 'ave a lawyer?'

'You fired a shot at Gail's dad? What with?'

'OK I 'ad a rifle.'

'Do you know Graham Clarke?'

'Never 'eared of 'im.'

'C'mon Ronnie, you're going down for a long, long time. You'll be an old man when you get out. Why don't you tell us the truth?'

'I am. I bloody am! Look, all right, I shagged that Gail, I bust into that shed and nicked the gun. I reckon I might 'ave wounded Gail's dad but I never wanted to kill 'im. An' I din't do Toady – 'onest I din't'. Ronnie broke down into tears. It was a pitiful sight.

'Look, I 'ad to give the rifle to some other bloke. I were 'avin' a dump when these two blokes in balaclavas showed up in the woods. A Yank were pointin' 'is machinegun at me... at me bollocks! I was frit shitless. Then the next day the rifle were back in me tent.'

'So, who was this Yank you gave the gun to Ronnie? Who was the other bloke?'

'I don't know. 'Onest. I don't know,' he sobbed.

'You're lying Ronnie, you worthless heap of...!'

'Take him back to his cell please constable.'

The three detectives sat and considered Ronnie's responses to their interrogation.

'Ok, he's confessed to the rape, the weapon and wounding. Never in a million years is he responsible for Harvey or McClean. He didn't shoot Clarke either. He couldn't hit a barn door at twenty paces. Where's the motive for him killing Clarke or Toady? If Gibbo wants to prosecute just on the strength of Snotty Pants' forensic evidence, I want off the case. Ronnie's an arsehole but he's not guilty of anything more than he's admitted.' It would have been a Laphroaig moment back in Kidlington as Cartwright struggled putting metaphorical square pieces into round holes. He made a mental note to buy a bottle.

'Who's this Yank then? Maybe Shultz might give us a pointer. John, can we leave him with you? You happy with that?'

'OK, guv. I'll go and see him.'

'Doug, would you go and talk to Maisie? If she knows anything. She's more likely to open up to you than to anyone else. Now what about this other bloke and the yellow car? I'm interested in this yellow car, the Triumph seen twice near the Clarke incident. And who'd want Toady dead for goodness' sake?

Chapter Sixty-Six

DI John Brinkley drove over to RAF Woodbridge and pulled up at the guardhouse and flashed his warrant card.

'AFC Shultz please.' The airman on duty said nothing but disappeared into the guardhouse where Brinkley could see as he picked up the telephone receiver. A moment later he reappeared.

'He'll be with you in just a couple of minutes sir. Kindly pull your vehicle over to the side of the road there please.' Brinkley complied as directed. Alvin Schultz marched smartly over to the DI's car.

'I know you're familiar with our current investigations… sorry how do I address you?'

'You can call me Al.'

'Pleased to meet you Al, I'm Detective Inspector John Brinkley. Yesterday, as you know, Operation Axeman, lead by your Master Sergeant Garcia arrested Ronnie Higginson, a suspect we've been after for some time. A gun we believe to be a murder weapon was also recovered.'

'Yes sir, a Remington M21A sniper rifle.'

'When we interrogated Higginson, he stated that he was forced at gunpoint by an American wearing a balaclava to give the gun to another man. Do you have any idea who this 'other man' or the American might be?' Schultz swallowed hard.

'Now look John, between this base and our twin base at Bentwaters we form the 81st Tactical Fighter Squadron. We also have an American High School and a community support infrastructure. There must be getting on for 1000 American personnel, military and civilian here or hereabouts. Security is a top priority at this base and set in the middle of a forest we could easily be infiltrated by Russian or Chinese spies, commies and who knows who else. We maintain regular patrols around our perimeter fences and occasionally we're aware of people in the forest, kids, hobos, tramps, boy scouts, I dunno who. We check 'em out and if they ain't a threat we leave 'em alone.' Schultz was hoping that failing to answer the question with a discourse of bullshit would be sufficient to baffle the DI's brain.

'All I can do is make some enquiries here, but I wouldn't hold out much hope. What I can't fathom is why someone would threaten your guy, take his rifle, then bring it back. Beats me!'

'Beats me too! OK, Al, thanks for your assistance anyway. But, if you do pick up any clues or get an idea of who these guys were, please be sure to give us a call.'

'Yeah, sure thing.' As DI Brinkley turned his car around and drove off the base Al heaved a sigh of relief yet again. 'Goddammit Brian!' he thought.

Al walked over to the guardhouse to talk to the airman on duty. As he was doing so Brinkley pulled up at the barrier again.

'Holy shit! What now?' he said to himself through gritted teeth. He smiled and walked over to the barrier.

'John, back so soon? Can't stay away eh?'

'Sorry Al, one thing I forgot. We're anxious to trace the driver of a yellow Triumph Dolomite. You wouldn't have seen one about would you?'

'Yeah sure thing! There was a yellow Triumph here on the first day of Operation Axeman. I thought it belonged to one of your guys.'

'Would you and your colleagues keep an eye out for it please?

'Yeah, sure thing. You got a registration number?'

'No, but there can't be many yellow Triumph Dolomites about! Cheers again!'

***

DS Doug Armstrong had driven to Woodbridge Quay to see Maisie. There were no signs of life aboard *Ironside*.

'Hello again detective!' The cheery greeting came from Colin Smith on his houseboat *Mary Gloster*. 'She'll be at work.'

'Work, but it's Easter Saturday!'

'I know, but it's a busy time for selling houses.'

'Sorry, I don't follow…'

'She works at Potter's, the estate agency.'

With directions provided by Colin, Doug found Potter's.

'Hello Maisie.'

'Doug, gracious me! You're the last person I'd have expected to see today.' Maisie's brain went into overdrive. How much does he know? What'll he ask me? What do I tell him? She was distracted almost to the verge of panic.

'Hey Maisie, come on now it's only me. Can you get off for ten minutes there are some questions I need to ask about Graham.'

They found a table at the Strawberry Café and ordered coffee.

'Did you know Graham rode a scooter, a Lambretta?'

'No, I didn't.'

'When did you see him last?'

'Last Tuesday, I think it was. He loiters outside Potter's, trying to intimidate me.'

'Why?'

'Seems to think I owe him, for his injuries you know? He's threatened to take me to court you know. Well let him try is what I say. I admitted I scarred him for life and I ended up doing ten years for it. I owe him nothing.'

'No, you don't. How long had this intimidation been going on?'

'Since he found out from my probation officer where I'd moved to when I was released from prison. Got to the state earlier this week when I nearly had a nervous breakdown – had to take time off work, ask Mr Potter.'

'I'm sorry to hear this Maisie, but you needn't worry any more. He won't be doing any more intimidating. He's dead.' Maisie tried to feign surprise.

'What do mean, dead?'

'Like dead, you know, deceased!'

'How?'

'Somebody shot him, and he crashed his scooter – except it wasn't his scooter, he'd stolen it. The lad that owned the scooter – he's dead as well.'

'Oh my goodness. Who'd do such a thing?'

'We thought you might know.'

'Me?'

'You don't know anyone with a grudge against him, if he had any enemies, owed anyone money, that sort of thing?'

'Who, Graham or the lad with the scooter?'

'Graham.'

'Not personally, but I bet there are loads.'

'I'm sure you're right. Do you know anyone with a yellow car?' Maisie could feel herself blushing. He didn't notice.

'A yellow car was seen, first at the golf club near where Graham was shot, and then later just before his body was taken to the mortuary.'

'I have seen a yellow car driving round the town now and again, but I don't know who owns it.'

'Ah well, if you think of anything that might help us, please give me ring?'

'Of course.' Maisie looked at her watch. 'I really should get back to work Doug.' Then on an impulse, she leaned across the table and gave him a kiss on the cheek. She left Doug to settle the bill.

***

Unusually, Potter's remained open all day it being Easter Saturday. When five o'clock came, Brian was waiting outside.

'Brian, where's your car?' The fear with which Maisie posed the question sounded alarm bells in Brian's head.

'In the Market Square, why?'

'The police are looking for a yellow car. What've you done Brian?'

From his position behind Shire Hall on Market Square where he sat in his Hillman Avenger, DS Armstrong could see the yellow

Triumph Dolomite. He watched as a man got into it and drove off. The Hillman followed at a discreet distance. The traffic was heavy but the yellow car was conspicuous and although the DS almost lost it in St John's Hill he soon picked it up again in Melton Hill and was right behind it by the time it was in Melton Road. Brian turned right at Wilford Bridge Road and glancing into his rear-view mirror noticed the Hillman follow him. Over the level-crossing and the river the Hillman was sticking to him like glue. Bearing left onto the B1083 Brian accelerated and increased the distance between the Triumph and the Hillman. Without indicating, Brian turned on to the long straight road, passed the golf club and across Sutton Common and he floored the accelerator pedal. The Triumph took off and doing ninety miles-per-hour the Hillman was soon left behind. Brian watched in his mirror as the following car receded into the distance. Just passed the Red Lodge he turned onto the track where he had seen the scooter disappear. He drove as far as the track would allow and stopped. He got out of the car in time to watch the Hillman drive on towards Stores Corner. He waited. And then, as he had anticipated, he watched the Hillman drive back towards Woodbridge at a rather more sedate pace.

'That's was too close. Who'd want a feckin' yellow car?' he said to himself. Allowing time for the Hillman to disappear out of sight, he reversed back down the track and went home to Boyton. He needed a drink.

In the Bell was the welcoming sight of familiar friends, Bert and Alvin. Al immediately took him to one side.

'You've got to get rid of that bloody car!'

'Yeah, tell me about it.'

Two pints later, Alfred Wardle, the tenant at Boyton Hall Farm came in.

'Buy you a pint Alf?' After several more it was agreed that the Triumph Dolomite would be moved to a disused barn on Alf's farm, and subsequently, it was.

***

'I almost had him.' Doug Armstrong was on the phone to Cartwright at Helen Blake's cottage in Pin Mill. 'Whoever owns that yellow car has got something to hide, the way he took off when he clocked that I was following. I lost him somewhere just passed where we found Toady's body. Bloody wilderness this Suffolk countryside.

***

On Easter Sunday, Brian got a lift with Alvin into Woodbridge. He really needed to see Maisie. He'd decided he couldn't live with the lie. He needed to confess, and not just to Maisie. He went directly to St Thomas' Catholic Church, curiously in St John's Street. He hadn't been to confession since Sheringham, and there was this recent killing to get off his chest. Making peace with God would be a start. Making peace with Maisie might not be so easy.

Chapter Sixty-Seven

After Mass and confession at St Thomas' Brian went to the Anchor where he hoped he would find Maisie and sure enough he did.

'You've got some explaining to do,' she said in no uncertain terms.

'Yes I have. There are things I need to tell you Maisie but not here.'

'Be back in a while Sid,' Maisie called to the landlord as she and Brian left to go to the *Ironside*.

'Well, what have you done Brian? I mention the police are looking for a yellow car and you go haring off to Market Square without so much as a "by-your-leave". You must have something to hide. Is there another woman? Why are the police looking for your car? Have you been in an accident? I'm not stupid. There's something you're not telling me. We can't have a relationship unless it is based 100% on trust and honesty.' Brian was beginning to wonder when she would leave a gap so that he could get a word in.

'Maisie, please, just listen. I'm sorry. I would not do anything to jeopardise our relationship. I've only just found you and I don't want to lose you. What I told you after I rescued you from your ordeal in the forest wasn't strictly true. In fact, it wasn't true at all. I lied. This morning I've been to confession and the priest absolved me of my sins…'

'Oh, and that makes it all OK does it?' was the truculent enquiry.

'Please Maisie, just listen, this is hard enough.' Brian's explanation and excuse was rambling and muddled. 'I overheard

Graham in the solicitors' office, and I didn't like what I heard. The lawyers were refusing to take his case and file a claim against you. He was angry and aggressive, and I overheard him say something along the lines of "I'll get compensation from her myself even if I have to beat it out of her." Well, I'm sorry, but I wasn't about to let him get away with threats like that.' Brian continued to bare his soul and confessed to all manner of inhumanity from his past.

'Then I read about the release from prison of an old IRA mate, Sean Mac Stiofain. Sean and me, well we developed the 'one-shot sniper' tactic and it took me back. One shot, that's all it would take. This was all a part of the old Brian O'Connor that I never wanted to tell you about. It was all behind me. But hearing Graham's threats, well I couldn't let it go. Then you disappeared. I was worried sick and dreaded to think what might have happened to you. I eventually put two and two together and realised he'd kidnapped you. I would never have forgiven myself if I hadn't done something about it. I had to do it. One last shot. Get rid of him once and for all but I'd thrown my gun into the sea.' He described how he'd ditched the gun in the golf bag and Maisie was about to accept that perhaps he had changed.

'But my mate Alvin knew where I could get another, and it turns out to be mine, the one I thrown into the sea. Just one shot, that's all it took. I gave the gun back. I did it for you Maisie. I didn't want you to have to put up with his intimidation and threats. I did it for you.'

With Brian's contrition, his humble confession and self-condemnation all but having reduced him to a quivering wreck, Maisie's heart softened almost to melting point.

'Promise me?'

'I promise. Maisie, I love you. Will you marry me?'

'Yes.'

'Welcome back you two. All peace and love is it? Usual?' asked Sid.

'No Sid, Champagne please!

***

'Colin, will your mate the car-dealer be open today?'

'He's always open Brian. Why? Trouble with the Triumph?

'Well yes and no. I haven't got around to registering it yet, and I was wondering if he might do a part exchange deal, swap it.'

'I'm sure he will, but he'll stitch you up for a few quid more I bet.'

***

Maisie was in the telephone box by the railway station bubbling over with excitement. She was giving Helen the entire chapter and verse of recent developments and then wedding fever took hold and became contagious.

'I'm hoping Cartwright might make an honest woman out of me.'

Chapter Sixty-Eight

The three senior detectives were, in a manner of speaking, on the carpet in the Chief Superintendent's office.

'This is wholly unsatisfactory. You are telling me that Higginson is only guilty of one of these murders, and even then he might get away with manslaughter. Wholly unsatisfactory. Wholly unsatisfactory.' Gibson was beginning to sound like DCS Simons back in Kidlington. 'If this is how one gets the further up the greasy pole you go, I'll stay where I am.' Cartwright was thinking to himself.

'So, are you telling me we're no closer to apprehending the murderer of Harvey, McClean, Hetherington and Clarke?'

'I'm afraid so sir. We know Hetherington was strangled, and probably by Clarke. The other three were shot, doubtfully by the same person but definitely with the same rifle. That's the rifle we have recovered.'

'If Higginson is going down for rape and murder, or manslaughter, why can't we pin it all on him? He'll be inside for life anyway and it will do our clear-up statistics a power of good.'

'But that would be a miscarriage of justice sir!'

'Justice? What do these poor dead chaps want with justice?'

'Sir, I must protest...what happens to the integrity of policing if we try and pull a stunt like that? Any public faith or trust would be gone for good...'

Gibson's phone rang.

Cartwright, unhappy with what he was being told, took the opportunity of the interruption to whisper to Armstrong and Brinkley, 'Problem with Gibson is he believes only what he wants to believe and can't see or even think beyond what he believes. Alex Simons is the same, so is Slim Tim Adams. These guys are 'the establishment': the establishment always wins. But they're not going to his time.'

Armstrong was nodding. Brinkley was saying nothing. Gibson replaced the receiver and scratched his head.

'And what is the prognosis then gentlemen? Are we ever likely to bring this assassin to justice?

'Justice sir?

'Yes Cartwright, justice. Divine justice!'

***

'Ronald Higginson. Have you anything to say before I pass sentence?'

'Yeah. I din't do it. The coppers are fittin' me right up. 'It ain't fair. Coppers are bastards!'

'You will go to prison or the maximum duration prescribed for these offences and in your case "life" means for the rest of your natural life. Take him down!'

Chapter Sixty-Nine

Cartwright was at Helen Blake's house.

'I've requested a transfer to Suffolk. I hope you don't mind.'

'Mind? I'd would have minded if you hadn't. You know my friend Maisie is getting married?' Cartwright wondered what was coming next. 'Well, she asked me to be her Matron of Honour... but I'm not married.'

'That's sneaky,' Cartwright thought inwardly smiling. 'Well, we can soon remedy that if that's what you'd like!'

'Oh Cartwright, my Cartwright. Do you mean it?

'I do'.

'Then so do I.'

***

Maisie and Brian's wedding guest list was not a particularly long one and with Alvin Schultz having agreed to be Brian's best man arrangements were well advanced. Ben and Tina Blake had accepted their invitation as had Doug Armstrong and Colin Smith. One or two others from Maisie's past including her probation officer were also invited along with her colleagues from Potter's. For most of the regulars at the Bell and the Anchor, including Sid and Bert, this would be the event of the year. With Brian's past well and truly past, any fear of the law he may have had, once upon a time, was no longer a cause for concern. Two of his wedding guests would be the very policemen who had been the investigating officers in the murders he had committed. The metamorphosis and reformation of Brian O'Connor and his previous existence was complete.

Two weeks before the wedding Brian asked Maisie if she fancied a trip to London.

'I thought you might like to see the sights, perhaps go to a show, a posh restaurant.'

'Oh, Brian that would be lovely.'

'I'm glad you like the idea because I've already bought tickets for *Joseph and his Amazing Technicolour Dreamcoat* at the Albery Theatre.

The day of the excursion came, and Brian drove to the railway station in Woodbridge in his anonymous grey Ford Cortina which he'd duly registered after a part-exchange deal. Having changed trains at Ipswich, the engaged couple arrived at London Liverpool Street and took the underground into the West End. Brian had the presence of mind to book a pre-theatre table at Brown's in St Martin's Lane, handy for the Albery. The day was perfect. Warm early summer sunshine ideal for walking about looking at the sights and doing nothing in particular.

***

To the northwest of London, in the heart of the Capital's Irish community, Danny McFadden was giving last minute instructions to an active service unit of his colleagues in the Alliance in Mill Lane.

***

Brian and Maisie had walked the length of St Martin's Lane to Covent Garden, the fashionista's paradise.

'If you think I'm going to be traipsing around posh ladies frock shops, think again. Here's £20, treat yourself. When you've spent it you'll find me the Coach and Horses.' That was the last time she saw Brian O'Conner.

***

The *London Evening Standard* that evening carried the following 'Stop Press':

IRA Strikes Again!

One man died when a bomb was thrown through the window of the Coach & Horses pub in the heart of London's West End. More than thirty people injured in the blast were taken to St Thomas' Hospital. The IRA has claimed responsibility.

The bombing was reported extensively in national newspapers the following day with a photograph of a bombed-out pub in Wellington Street, almost opposite the Royal Opera House.

Cartwright and Armstrong were sharing the front page of the *Daily Telegraph* together. Helen was doing her best to ease the torment and mental anguish of a totally distraught Maisie but with little success. Suddenly, Armstrong thumped the table.

'I bloody well knew it! I'd had my suspicions since the first time I met him.'

'What was that Gibbo said about divine justice?' enquired Cartwright.

The End

The Author

Born in Leicestershire just after WWII, Bob Bennett trained as a classical musician at the Birmingham School of Music and Birmingham University. After a short time with the City of Birmingham Symphony Orchestra he followed a freelance career as a trombonist, pianist and music teacher. For the last 20 years of his full-time working life, he was an Official of the Musicians' Union in Birmingham and subsequently the London Regional Organiser working mainly in the West End. He is now retired and lives by the sea in Suffolk. This is his third novel.